ADVANCED PRAISE
for
THE HARDSHIP BAZAAR

"Incisive, witty, and generous, Resnick's first novel is a comedic guillotine. Buy it for the laughs, read it for the cultural beheadings."
  —David Andrew Stoler, writer, producer, professor

"A beautiful book! Great characters, and gripping plot. Anyone would be lucky to read this book, and they'd be crazy not to love it!" —Linda Resnick, mother

"Haven't read it yet, but I hear it's very good."
  —Jeffrey Resnick, father

"It's really good. I forgot to finish it for totally unrelated reasons."
  —Karen Callahan, spouse, eventual finisher

"It's not the novel we need, but it's the one we deserve."
  —Adam Friedman, otolaryngologist

"Get back to me when it's a movie."
  —Zev Brown, nephew

"You're weird, but I love you."
  —Avi Brown, niece

"A *literal* page-turner."
  —Elise Choi, copy editor

THE HARDSHIP BAZAAR

JEREMY RESNICK

WEDNESDAY INK

for Karen

"Life is a shipwreck, but we must not forget to sing in the lifeboats."

— VOLTAIRE

"Every book is a quotation; and every house is a quotation out of all forests, and mines, and stone quarries; and every man is a quotation from all his ancestors."

— RALPH WALDO EMERSON

PART I

1

WHEN THE KID came in talking about a missing person, Donald was scouring his cabinets for coffee he'd forgotten to buy. He straightened his bathrobe and received a kiss to his cheek. The kid slouched a little, and there was something furtive about the way her dark bangs fell in front of her eyes, the way she brushed them aside with nail-bitten fingers.

Donald gave up on the coffee, poured himself a whisky.

The kid raised a thin brow. "A little early, isn't it?"

"A little young, aren't you? To act like my mother?"

"You're right," she collapsed onto the couch. "Got another glass?"

Donald liked her better, found another glass. He compensated for the tremors by pouring quick, large slugs. Ignoring the puddle of spilled whisky on the counter, he handed the less full glass to the kid and took his to the easy chair to enjoy in front of his painting. It was his only prized possession, an unframed, abstract-expressionist explosion, always more interesting than TV.

"Now then," he gazed at a speckled middle area that resembled the valley lights at night, "who'd you say was missing?"

"My dad," the kid said. She looked hard at him, seemed to expect some reaction. "Jack? Your son?"

"Right, right. The one who never calls." He raised his glass to her, sipped—and winced at the sudden pain in an upper left molar.

"I'm sure he'll turn up," the kid said. "I only mentioned it because I just got off the phone with Cynthia. Anyway," she glanced at the time on her phone, "you wanna get dressed? We can get breakfast before the dentist."

Donald had no intention of seeing the dentist. He'd already forgotten about the pain in his tooth, or would as soon as he finished his drink. His eyes lingered on the top left quadrant of the painting, where a series of thick globs looked like the Santa Monica Mountains. If he sat here long enough, the sun's movement across the window would wash them into blue-orange ripples that looked like the ocean.

But there was work to do. He tore his eyes from the painting and rummaged through the spine-cracked paperbacks piled on the coffee table. Finding his little notebook and pen, he flipped pages until he found blank space under an illegible note to himself.

"How long has he been missing?"

The kid didn't answer right away. Then, following a sigh, "Since last night."

Donald scribbled. "Police won't be interested until it's been twenty-four hours. Last person to see him?"

"I don't know."

"Enemies?"

The kid snorted. "Just anyone who works for him or with him."

"A bastard," Donald nodded. "Takes one to find one. Now run through it from the beginning."

The "kid"—who was not a kid but a thirty-two-year-old woman named Samantha—noted the titles of the books on the coffee table: *The Murder of Roger Ackroyd*, *The Big Sleep*, *The Long Goodbye*, *Devil in a Blue Dress*. She wondered how far to indulge her grandfather's fantasies. She didn't want him or anyone else to waste time looking for her dad. No doubt he'd turn up with a perfectly logical explanation by mid-morning. Probably just had one of his light-bulb moments, holed himself up somewhere to crank out another volume of *Jack Waxman on Business Ethics* or Version 6.2 of "GRREAT® Communication: A Groundbreaking Character-Education Webinar Led by Jack Waxman."

But Donald could be annoyingly insistent for a guy who seemed to forget on which side of his head he parted his remaining hair. Sam gave in, told him what she knew: Cynthia, Jack's second wife, had called to tell her Jack didn't come home last night. Sam asked her if anything had happened between them, and Cynthia said no. She'd called his cell phone in the middle of the night and again early this morning, but it just went to voicemail.

"And I just tried calling," Sam added. "Mailbox is full."

Donald chewed on the end of the pen. "And what's *your* relationship with the misper been like recently?"

"With the what?"

"Missing person."

Sam sipped from her glass, tried not to cough. "Currently, we're not on speaking terms. It's a long story."

"Tell it."

"I don't want to get into it. Besides, we need to get moving. And I don't think you're supposed to drink before anesthesia."

"Well now, that depends on what and how much you have."

"What?"

"What, and how much, do you have?"

"I'm talking about the dentist."

"Forget the dentist! Why aren't you talking to your father?"

Sam sensed she was losing control of the situation. Part of

inheriting Donald's absurd gas guzzler was that she had to drive him wherever he needed to go, which usually wasn't anywhere. But the man was eighty-three years old. He could decide for himself whether or not he went to the dentist. He could have whisky for breakfast if he wanted. Hell, the rapid clip at which civilization seemed to be collapsing made breakfast whisky seem like a good idea.

And if he wanted to play PI, Sam could roll with it. That was how they'd entertained themselves when he was called in as Babysitter of Last Resort. Back then he wrote detective flicks and TV procedurals under the name Donald West. While her dad negotiated contracts for Lakers, Dodgers, and the odd King, and her mom hosted or attended fundraisers, Sam and Donald solved such whodunits as The Case of the Disappearing Entenmann's Cake (Dad), The Mysterious Dog Shit on the Lawn (neighbor's Australian Shepherd), and, in her middle school years, The Mean Girl Who Spread Lies About Her Friends (plot twist: she wasn't evil, just desperately insecure).

Sam hadn't thought about those imaginary adventures in years, but she had fond memories of them. Now she was sort of curious to see if she had any imagination left. Also, spending an hour or two playing with her grandfather would allow her to put off her job search in this latest, tightest swirl her life made as it circled the toilet.

Also, breakfast whisky. She took too large a sip and coughed several times.

"Quit stalling, kid," Donald said. "Why aren't you talking to your father?"

Sam wondered where to begin. "Remember when I told you he fired me?"

Donald shook his head.

"Remember that I used to work for him?"

"Mm," Donald said without conviction.

"Well, I was his copywriter and editor, and I'm not anymore. He was too cowardly to use his platform, so I used it for him, and he fired me."

"Remind me of the platform?"

"The Waxims? His little radio essays? He hardly ever writes new ones—he's too busy begging for donations—but a few weeks ago, he told me to pitch him some ideas. I thought I could finally get him to speak out against all the fucked-up shit going on."

"What fucked-up shit?"

"Exactly! People aren't paying attention." Sam explained to Donald, as she'd explained to her dad, the sordid details of the latest NSA scandal. A government contractor had blown the whistle on a program of "selective, clandestine web-cam/microphone browsing." Basically, low-level contractors were playing audio/video roulette with any American unfortunate enough to click on a few bad links. One of the links was a porn clip of an absurdly well-endowed man with a beard praising Allah while having his way with a woman dressed as Uncle Sam. The NSA created the video as "terrorist bait." To Sam, and a shockingly slim majority of the country, this was a clear case of right and wrong. The government needed to stop spying—and stop employing total morons who degraded women and couldn't even make a decent porn. And everyone needed to support the courageous whistle-blower who did the right thing at great personal cost.

Her dad had said he liked the topic—it was racy, and racy attracted social media attention. But then he went home, wrote, recorded, and uploaded the new Waxim to the shared drive at 4:08 a.m. without getting anyone's feedback.

Sam arrived at the office that morning to see that the new Waxim, "Public Service or Ego Trip?" had already played three times on the radio. In it her dad parroted the administration's claim that the release of classified information disrupted "Inteliflow," endangered American operatives in foreign countries, and limited the government's ability to stop the next terror attack. He claimed that the FISA Court protected innocent Americans from government overreach, and he wanted the whistleblower charged with treason. Then, her dear old dad, Captain Morality himself, actually said, "If you're doing something you don't want other people to know about, you probably shouldn't be doing it."

"So," Sam explained to Donald, "when I got to work I went into his office and yelled at him. He just said we need to protect ourselves against the terrorists, and he pushed me out and shut the door. I was pissed. I was afraid he was turning his listeners into sheep, normalizing this creep toward authoritarianism. So I wrote an essay."

Donald said nothing for a moment. Then, "Ah. What was the thesis?"

"Basically, 'Jack Waxman is wrong. His centrism is cowardly, and since the country has lurched rightward, he's centrally right wing. He talks about valuing peace and each and every life, but his knee-jerk "Support the troops!" jingoism keeps him from even acknowledging that we're all about endless war, imprisonment without trial, torture, mass surveillance, war on the poor, and murder of civilians all over the world.'"

Donald laughed.

"It was a solid argument. My dad worships at the altar of compromise, you know? He never acknowledges that when you compromise with insane people, you're gonna get *some* insanity."

Donald just nodded. Sam felt guilty for attacking her dad, and that made her angry. "He's never listened to me. He doesn't respect me. I don't even think he read my post. All he could think about was that I tarnished his reputation. And then he told me that my performance was," Sam's fingers made air quotes, "'sub-par.'"

"Then what happened?"

"He fired me, and I fired him from being my dad, and he called security to escort me out of the building."

Sam set her empty whisky glass on top of a crumbling copy of *The Big Midget Murders*. "That was about three weeks ago. I haven't seen or spoken to him since."

"OK, then," Donald's pen hovered over his notebook. "I'll just put down 'strained.' 'Relationship: s-t-r-a-i-n-e-d.'" He picked up his glass, drained it. "Know of anyone who might have a motive to kidnap him or otherwise make him disappear?"

Sam chuckled at the thought. "Lots of people think he's lame, but I can't think of anyone who'd take it that far." She checked the time on her phone again. "A Waxim is starting right now. If it's a new one, we'll know he's OK. If it's old, the station just pulled it from the contingency folder."

While she went over to Donald's antique hi-fi and clicked the knob, Donald hauled himself out of the easy chair and went to the bathroom.

Sam turned the dial until the orange line found the nasal earnestness of Jack Waxman's voice. She turned it up to drown out any bathroom sounds:

...headstrong teen who frequently clashed with her hard-working single mom, June. When Hannah missed her curfew, June grounded her for a month. The next morning, Hannah left early and didn't return until late at night.

"You're grounded for another month!" June proclaimed.

"I hate you, I wish you were dead!" Hannah shouted.

"Old one," Sam said. She went to turn it off, but Donald shouted through the closed door, "Leave it on!"

...slapped Hannah before she could stop herself. Both were shocked, and both retreated to their bedrooms and slammed their doors. June sobbed, berating herself for giving in to her anger, for not being able to control

her daughter. She blamed herself for everything in her life that had gone wrong.

Hannah fell asleep listening to her mother cry in the next room.

In the morning, June was still in bed when Hannah left for school, so Hannah wrote her a note: "I'm sorry, Mom. I didn't mean what I said. I'm grateful to have you for my mother."

When Hannah got home from school, June was sitting at the kitchen table with the note.

"I was going to kill myself today," she said, "until I read your note."

Tell your family members you love them. Let them know you appreciate them. You just might save a life.

This is Jack Waxman from the Waxman Ethics Institute. Be GRREAT today!

The segment was followed by a commercial for the Triple-X Fish Taco with Exxxtreme Ranch. A breathy female voice said, "They're *hot* and *creamy,* to the *exxxtreme.*"

Sam turned off the radio and sat back down. What if her dad was really in trouble? What if something terrible had happened and she never saw him again? Her last image of him would be his angry, wounded face framed by the double bird she'd flipped him.

When Donald shuffled back from the bathroom, she said, "Pop, that didn't sound like a suicide note to you, did it?"

"Fish tacos seems like a slow way to go."

"No, the Waxim. All about a mother who feels unappreciated. Maybe that's how he feels. Maybe he—"

"I don't see it. Listen to how bossy he is, how optimistic. He thinks he's grrr-ate, and you can be grrr-ate too. No, he's no self-harmer."

"I tried to get him to drop that slogan. At least the Kellogg's lawyers put the kibosh on 'Trusty, the Be GRREAT Tiger.'"

"That Jackie," Donald sat back in his chair, smiling. "When he was a kid, he was constantly looking for attention, always showing off. Used to stand in front of the TV and recite all of his Hebrew school prayers. And he was constantly begging me to come outside to witness some athletic feat, which he could never replicate in front of me."

"Sounds like a normal kid. But I don't see you being into the prayers."

Donald shrugged. "Hebrew school, the bar mitzvah, the high holidays—all that was Sylvia's doing." He was silent for a moment. Sam pictured a miniature version of him wading through the foggy swamp of his mind, spotting a memory here and there among the bulrushes.

"You know," he said, "I was just a kid myself when your dad was born. Wasn't ready to be a father. Spent most of my time hanging out with writers, comedians, musicians. Nightclub people. They were wild, which seemed like the right reaction to the world we lived in. Spending a Shabbat at home with your grandmother and your dad was like being stuck in a waiting room."

Sam picked up her phone, "Excuse me for a sec, I just need to text my therapist."

"Nah," Donald mumbled, almost to himself, "Jack would never disappear willingly."

Apparently forgetting that he was wearing a bathrobe and not a trench coat, Donald stood and scooped his Fedora from the hat rack by the door. "Missing since yesterday. Many enemies." He put on the hat and looked at the door as if he could see through it right into the dark, throbbing heart of the city. "Where are you, Jackie?"

Sam watched him from the couch. On her grandfather's face, the large Waxman nose was sublime, curving like a crumbling domed basilica with nostril archways, nose hairs sprouting like ferns from the ruins.

"You might want to put on some pants first," she suggested. "And where do we start?"

"*We?* Sorry, kid. That's not part of the deal. I work alone."

Sam smiled, remembering this bit from when she was a kid. She had to say, "I'm tougher than I look." Then Donald had to think about it for a minute, shrug, and say, "Why not? You can help dig the graves," or, "Why not? If there's trouble I can use you as a human shield."

This time he squinted at her flannel shirt and said, "Why not? If he's been kidnapped by militant lesbians, you can infiltrate the gang, report back."

2

FIRST STEP in your typical misper: scope the spouse.

Somehow the kid knew where to find Donald's silver '67 Mustang on the street. She also had the keys, and she approached the driver's side with the clear intention of driving. Had he loaned it to her and forgotten?

Donald said nothing as he got into the passenger seat, breathing the sweet perfume of old leather, gas, and tobacco. He said nothing because he was beginning to accept these jarring events as a normal part of leaving the house.

One day, a week or a month ago, he'd walked halfway to the college in a state of panic, wondering what he was going to teach, why he hadn't prepared, why he hadn't brought any of his students' screenplays home with him. He passed the former site of his usual diner. Now it was a sleek-lined café, all white and chrome, and he remembered that the change had happened before he retired. *He was retired.* Felt like he needed to sit down, so why not try the new café? When he ordered a coffee though, the girl with the ball bearing embedded in her dimple asked him which kind and then gave him a menu. Baffled, Donald picked an Ethiopian bean that promised "flavors of lemon and caramel with a silky mouthfeel." The girl took way too much of his money, ground some coffee, filled a cone with it, set the cone on top of a mug, grabbed a tea kettle with a long spout, filled that with hot water, and dripped that water agonizingly slowly into the cone. That's when Donald remembered that the world had gone totally ridiculous and/or he'd outlived his ability to understand it. Whichever, he figured he owed it nothing.

"Great car," he finally said as Sam accelerated out of a curve on Bundy. "I used to have one just like it." He had to get in at least one shot.

"Yeah, DUIs are a bitch."

Ah, yes. The rotten memory surfaced like a corpse: motorcycle cop pulling him over for failing to signal a lane change. Donald said he didn't signal because there'd been no cars behind him or in the adjacent lane. The cop smelled the whisky on his breath, or maybe he noticed the flask on the passenger seat, and Donald failed the sobriety test despite his repeated insistence that he wasn't drunk so much as he was old. They booked him, and some internet rag picked the incident up off of the police blotter and ran a story about how Jack Waxman ought to extend some of his vaunted character education to his washed-up screenwriter father. Since then, Jack had refused to speak to him.

Donald shook off these depressing thoughts, considered instead all of the possible whereabouts of the missing man. In very few of them was that man still alive.

While she steered the oversized go-kart into Brentwood, Sam was thinking that Donald, always strange in the best ways, seemed newly, differently strange. Last year, after the DUI, after forgetting to show up to teach a few times, he'd quit altogether. He abandoned the screenplays he'd been tinkering with for years, said he was retired. He stayed home and read his entire library over again. Recently, Sam noticed, he'd begun to complain that business was slow. He talked about putting an ad in "the classifieds" to "drum up some trade." He suspected random waiters, pedestrians, baristas, and Dodger Stadium peanut vendors of "lookin' hinky."

"Here we are! Saruman's castle!" Sam said grandly as she pulled to the curb across from her dad's house. It was a huge, poorly insulated Tudor, filled with the Waxman Family 2.0.

Of all her father's hypocrisies, his second family bugged Sam the most. The alleged ethicist was responsible for a total of four first-world, upper-middle-class children, a slow-motion explosion of the Waxman carbon footprint. Barring a catastrophe, the explosion would continue for generations, consuming products, pumping greenhouse gases into the air, launching tons of plastic toward the Great Pacific Garbage Patch. When she thought of it, Sam pictured her fallopian tubes tying themselves into knots, or just constricting until there was no possible passage. The only thing that made her OK with driving a car that got ten miles per gallon was that no new carbon junkies were coming out of her.

The Waxman lawn had recently been fertilized, and the fishy-shitty-ammoniac stench was so bad it almost made visible waves in the air. The house next door had recently been fertilized too. This was a rite of autumn in rich L.A., replenishing nutrients the soil didn't have and the climate didn't support to grow plants that didn't belong.

Sam knocked. After a minute, the oversized door heaved open, revealing a new, middle-aged Central American housekeeper in jeans and a t-shirt. The Waxmans went through Central American housekeepers like normal people went through kitchen sponges, and this new housekeeper didn't know Sam or Donald.

"Is Cynthia home?" Sam said.

"She is not home. I have a green card," the woman said, and shut the door in their faces.

Sam and Donald traded a look, and Sam knocked again. After a moment, the housekeeper opened.

Sam said, "I'm Samantha, Mr. Waxman's oldest daughter. Aren't there pictures of me around the house?"

The housekeeper peered at her. "*¡Si, si! Tu eres la diabla.*"

Sam was insulted until she remembered the framed Halloween photo on one of the shelves in her father's home office. She was twelve and dressed as a she-devil.

"*¿Como se llama? ¿Podemos entrar?*" Sam asked, pretty much exhausting her supply of Spanish.

The housekeeper looked them up and down before she fully opened the door and let them in.

Immediately Donald peppered her with questions. "When was the last time you saw Mr. Waxman? How long have you worked here? Notice anything strange lately? Mind if we look around?"

"Slow down," Sam said. "I don't think she speaks—"

But the housekeeper said quickly in fluent, slightly accented English, "My name is Luz. I last see Mr. Watzman yesterday morning. I work here six months. Everything is strange here. Yes, I mind you look. I don't know you. Maybe you are addicts, here to steal for drug money."

"That's absurd," Donald said. "I've never paid for drugs in my life. No, ma'am, we're here representing a man called," elbowing Sam, "Andrew Jackson."

"Dude," Sam said, "what?"

"Give her a twenty."

"*You* give her a twenty."

Donald put his hand in his pocket. Left it there. He breathed deeply and noisily, the wind rustling through the tiny forests of his nose hairs.

"Fine!" Sam pulled her money wad out of her pocket, handed the housekeeper a twenty.

Luz straightened the bill and held it up. "You sure you don't work for Ben Franklin?" She laughed at Sam's confusion. "Go, look. I don't care. I need to launder." She stuffed the bill into the pocket of her jeans and walked down the hall.

Sam and Donald wandered through the dark living room, which was ripped right from the pages of *Landed Gentry* magazine. Over the mantel, past the paisley couch and chairs, Sam recognized an Old Master knockoff of some dead birds and vegetables on a table. It had hung on the wall in the pre-divorce house, had probably started her on the road to vegetarianism. Below it, among several framed photos, was one of Cynthia on horseback, expertly jumping a gate at a competition. Sam couldn't help but chuckle whenever she saw it because of course high-maintenance Cynthia loved a sport that required a thousand-pound animal and silly dress clothes.

In the next room—Jack's office, though he insisted everyone call it "the library"—there were leather wingback chairs facing a big desk, bookshelves lining every wall. On one shelf, a bust of Abe Lincoln gazed at a bust of Socrates rolling his eyes. It was one of the few objects Sam wanted to inherit, as it seemed to scoff at you no matter where you were standing or what you were thinking.

Several stacks of paper covered the desk, each topped by a *GRREAT Quotations* Lucite paperweight. One said, *Character is much easier kept than recovered. —Thomas Paine.* Sam recognized the top sheet, part of the grade-school curriculum she'd created as part of her job as the Ethics Institute's writer. This particular assignment was for "Ambition," one of the Six Keys to GRREAT-ness. (The other Keys were Generosity, Respect, Responsibility, Empathy, and Trustworthiness.) The instructions said to read a parable and answer questions about it. Ambition wasn't something Sam knew much about anymore, having concluded that nothing most people cared about was worth doing. So here she toed the party line, writing a parable about two brothers who grew up on a farm. One dreamed of becoming a management consultant and spent all his time studying in the library. The other preferred the joys of fishing on the river and wandering through the woods. The boy who studied made partner at a top firm and enjoyed a long, full life of wealth, family happiness, and the respect of his community, while the fisherman died young of a treatable cancer because he had no money or health insurance. First reflection question: "Who would you rather be in this story and why?"

How had she not been fired sooner? And what would she do now? That job had been her last resort.

While Sam tried to distract herself from her shame by checking the closets for a scarf she'd lost, Donald strolled through the other rooms to see what had changed since Jack disowned him. The TVs seemed to have grown bigger, and they'd multiplied. And the bar in the den was pathetically stocked. The few dusty bottles he found had about an inch of booze left in them. Donald's tooth was beginning to wake up again, so he downed what was left in a Jack Daniel's bottle. He swished it around, hoping the alcohol would seep into the nerve, but the liquor had been severely watered down, probably by one of the kids. Jack and Cynthia never touched the stuff.

Donald climbed up the stairs and looked into Immanuel's room, where the posters of football and basketball heroes had been replaced by blown-up comic-book and video-game heroes. When did that happen? He was missing out on his only grandson's formative years. It was probably too late, and the kid was already one of those video-game-addicted zombies.

The girls' rooms had changed too. Sophia had a Frida Kahlo self-portrait, a "Rosie the Riveter" poster, and not a doll in sight. Harper had discovered '60s counterculture, and she had a dreamcatcher over her bed and a trippy tapestry tenting the ceiling. Maybe now she'd be more interesting to talk to.

Sam caught up to him in Jack and Cynthia's room. The sage

carpet was spotless, the bed made, e-readers perfectly aligned on both bedside tables. Donald casually sauntered over and opened the drawers.

"Whoa—respect their privacy!" Sam said, thinking of the battery-powered tool and lubricant in her own bedside drawer.

"Grow a pair, kid. This business ain't for the squeamish."

But Donald found no kinky sex toys in either drawer, which made Sam a little sad for her dad and Cynthia. Some hand cream and spare glasses in Cynthia's, and anti-snoring tape, pencils, and scribbled-on notebooks in Jack's.

Donald flipped through the notebooks, but his son's handwriting was no better than his own. He deciphered a few fragments:

Revisit Mother Teresa Waxim?

Practice: in communication, pretend you aren't
smarter

From ballfield to boardroom (to bedroom?): Your
kids are watching!

Donald put the notebooks back and shut the drawer. "Call the wife."

"Cynthia? Really?"

"Dammit, kid, we need leads. Get her on the horn!"

"OK, OK." Trying not to show that she was laughing at him, Sam dialed, turned on the speaker, and held the phone between them.

To her great surprise, Cynthia picked up right away and said, "Any news?"

"No. I was hoping you might have some."

"Nothing. And I have meetings all day and a million things to do for tomorrow."

"Tomorrow?"

"The bar mitzvah? Remember, you have to be there at four o'clock for the pictures."

"Dad still wants me in the pictures?"

"You're still his daughter."

"And Manny's my bro!"

"Hold on," Cynthia said, and her phone went silent.

The truth was that Sam had completely forgotten about Immanuel's bar mitzvah. She now recalled seeing the invitation a couple months ago before it got buried under other pieces of mail she couldn't throw out but for which she had never devised a system. Also, Immanuel was only half her bro and not too interested in being that.

Cynthia came back, "That was Bonnie. She just got into the office. Your dad's not there, and she hasn't heard from him. I've already called every hospital in the city. I called the police too, but they could care less. They said to call back if he didn't show up by this evening."

"Could*n't* care less," Sam said. "'Could care less' suggests they care somewhat."

"Gotta run!"

"Sorry," Sam said. "Pet peeve."

"Wait," Donald pulled Sam's phone hand toward him. "It's Donald West, ma'am. When was the last time you heard from your husband?"

"Oh—hi, Donald. Around nine o'clock last night. He just said he'd be home soon."

"Where was he?"

"Didn't say. I assumed he was still at work."

"Everything OK between you two?" Sam said.

"Of course! I mean, you know how difficult your dad can be. I just . . ." she paused, started over: "He went from working day and night raising money to working day and night for this charter-school contract. And he's been totally nuts about the bar mitzvah. Two hundred and fifty people he's making us squeeze into that room. And he's insisted on controlling the DJ's playlist—no offensive or sexually suggestive songs allowed—"

"What?" Sam said. "Those are the best ones!"

"—but he hasn't even given the DJ his list. And then there was the thing with you. I still can't believe you wrote those things, Samantha. And published them!"

"I stand by my argument!" Sam said. "Don't you think he's been acting weird lately? Maybe he has a brain tumor."

"Shut your mouth!"

"Hey, I know I'm just the daughter from the starter marriage, but I'm still his daughter."

"And you live to break his heart."

"No, I'm just the only one who calls him on his bullshit."

"Ladies, please!" Donald drew a dirty look from Sam, and probably from Cynthia too. He leaned toward the phone, "Did you notice anything funny in the days leading up to this? Odd telephone calls? Visitors? Talk about anything unusual?"

"He was preoccupied with work, but he always is. Also, we had some trouble with Sophia. I don't want to talk about it, but she and Harper—actually and Immanuel too—have been giving Jack the silent treatment for a few days."

"Why?" Sam asked.

"I said I don't want to talk about it! God, sometimes you are just like him. He'd better show up soon. We have temple tonight."

"Tonight?"

"Friday night services? Immanuel does the *Kiddush*, and we have to open and close the ark. Didn't you do that?"

"I have no memory of my bat mitzvah. I think it was too traumatic."

Cynthia didn't reply, and they heard the tapping of her keyboard.

"Ma'am," Donald said, "did your husband owe anyone money or have any professional enemies?" He waited a moment before adding, "We're assuming, of course, that you didn't pay someone to bump him off."

Cynthia's gasp came clearly through the speaker. "Donald! How could you say that to me?"

"I said we're assuming you *didn't* do that."

Sam said, "He didn't mean anything—he's just eliminating possibilities. We don't think you'd do that."

"I'm starting to think maybe she would."

"Goodbye!" Cynthia hung up.

"Hello?" Donald said, but the line was clearly dead.

"She's sensitive," Sam said. "You can't talk to her like that. What should we do now?"

"Look for him, of course." Donald pulled a butterscotch candy from his jacket pocket, unwrapped it, popped it in his mouth, winced, moved the candy over to his right side. "What if he were being blackmailed for something?"

Sam couldn't picture it. "My dad is a freaking boy scout. He spends all his time trying to figure out the best way to make people be nicer to each other so the world will be better, or so he'll be remembered as The Man Who Made the World Better. Sure, he does it by being an asshole, but it's like, minor-league, well-intentioned assholery, you know?"

"Hey, show some respect," candy clicking against Donald's teeth. "That's my son you're talking about—and I just had a memory. When he was a kid, he stole a pack of bubblegum from the store. Got away with it, too. But then, he was so guilt-ridden after he chewed all the gum that he came to me and confessed, leaving me no choice but to punish him."

"With like, a spanking?"

Donald shook his head. "Your father is a third-generation non-spanker. I made him do chores until he earned enough money to go back to that store and pay the manager for the gum, plus interest."

"Ouch."

"I think that's what he wanted. He felt so guilty, he wanted to suffer, and he *loved* the attention. He enjoyed giving his solemn little speech to the manager so much, I felt like I'd accidentally rewarded him."

"OK, *Diabla, Señor Viejo*," Luz stood in the doorway, "vacuuming time for me, leaving time for you."

"Just one more thing, sweetheart," Donald smiled his most charming smile. "Can you point me toward the *baño*?"

A few minutes later, after the front door slammed rather loudly behind them, Sam and Donald stood for a moment on the manure-scented front walk. The sky was that deep, wintry blue that always made Sam feel like she should be lying on a picnic blanket just looking up at it. Which she never did. A squirrel chased another squirrel along the branch of the sycamore in the yard, driving panicked little birds into the air. It was that special brand of California idyllic until a leaf blower revved up down the street.

"Let's go to the kids' school," Donald pulled open the car door as Sam went around and hopped into the driver's seat. "Maybe they know something."

"Can we even do that?"

"Why not?"

"Schools are locked down like prisons now, Pop."

Donald fell the last few inches into the passenger seat and pulled his door shut with a groan. "Felt pretty prison-like in my day."

Sam blinked at him. "I didn't know schools were invented way back then."

"They were, and so was that joke. Now," he tapped the dashboard as if it were a horse's rump, "to the school!"

Sam knew she was supposed to gun the engine and peel out into the street, but instead she asked, "Do we have to?"

"Yeah, kid, we do. Good investigators go wherever the case leads them."

"You don't know what it was like. At my worst moments, when I'm too depressed to even get out of bed, I can always soothe myself with the thought that I'm not still at that school."

"Well, when we leave it again in an hour, you can have all sorts of fresh memories to console yourself with."

Sam tried breathing deeply, taking in the good, dread-free air and expelling the bad, dread-full air. She pointed the car toward West Brentwood and the Hancock School.

3

THE SECURITY GUARD checked Sam's driver's license against her face and the senior yearbook photo he pulled up on his tablet. The gate went up, and Sam drove along the sprinkler-bedewed lawns toward the stucco halls of the Hancock School

"Here we are!" She announced. "Mordor!"

Donald didn't know what she was talking about. The place was ancient in L.A. terms, with a bell tower nestled among old oaks and eucalyptus, and he was trying to remember when it had gone from military academy to elite prep school, and when it had become necessary to block the driveway with a gate and guard shack. They drove along the soccer field, which reminded him of watching the kid's games. He'd always sat next to Susan, Jack's ex-wife and the kid's mother. Susan was a kind person, and she didn't judge Donald for reading the paper instead of watching the game, and she was good about telling him to look up whenever the kid got near the ball. Then he saw how this usually nervous, gangly girl became fierce and relentless on the field. Though not the fastest or the strongest, Sam was always assigned to shadow the other team's best scorer. And she plagued those girls, stuck with them up and down the field, poking and prodding the whole way.

Whenever they managed to score, Sam would fight away tears and play with renewed ferocity. And then, after the game, she'd go right back to her uneasy, non-confrontational self. Donald loved and pitied her, felt like he understood her. She was a sensitive, angry misfit, like him. In his high school days in Boyle Heights, he'd been a pretty scrappy middleweight, and he'd made the alta-cockers proud.

While she drove past the field, Sam recalled her greatest sports triumph: during a game toward the end of her junior season, she broke for the far edge of the visitor's box, timed her leap perfectly as the ball curved to meet her. She headed it just over the goal-keeper's outstretched hands into the back of the net. Sam was so surprised that she raised her arms triumphantly above her head. Which ended the beautiful moment, as it just made her feel like an arrogant ass. Her goal didn't even matter—they'd already been ahead by two.

Sam eased over one speed bump after another as they made their way to the parking lot. She'd spent so many years actively not thinking about high school that now, even confronted with the reality of the place, she could only muster a handful of other memories, all minor traumas. On that same soccer field, for exam-ple, eighth-grade Stephanie Guthrie had called seventh-grade Samantha "Samsquatch" because she hadn't begun to shave the dark hairs beginning to grow on her shins. There, in the first building with the red-tiled roof, was the chemistry classroom where tenth-grade Sam had told her friend Olivia Leibowitz she liked Mark Newman. Olivia was smart and pretty, and her dad was a movie executive, so they got DVDs before the movies were even released. A day later, the whole school knew about Sam's crush, including Mark Newman, whose reaction was, reportedly, "Samantha who? . . . Oh, you mean 'The Nose'?" A week later, Olivia was with Mark.

Sam begged her parents for a nose job. She enlisted help from two friends who'd already had their noses done, and who reported heightened self-esteem, overall mood improvement, better grades, and boyfriends. Jack was receptive to these arguments, probably because he and Cynthia had just begun their own family, and he was guilt-ridden about his lack of participation in Sam's life. Sam's mother absolutely refused, telling her that her strong nose gave her character and added a depth to her beauty. But then she had her eyes done, and she couldn't stand Sam's cries of "Hypocrite!"

Sam had the surgery in the summer before her senior year. The moment the bandage was removed, she knew she'd made a huge mistake. She looked fine, pretty even, but she didn't look like herself. Maybe it was just her nature to do something irreversible and immediately regret it, but now she felt alienated from her own face.

Finally, Sam pulled the Mustang into the massive parking lot. Where she remembered a little meadow next to the old lot, now there was just more blacktop, filled with the dusty economy cars of the teachers and the shiny luxury sedans and SUVs of the students.

Once they'd parked and Donald had extracted himself from the car, Sam led him down a wide path lined with lavender. The Dean of Students greeted them on their way to the main office. A petite woman with short silver hair, she'd taught "Human Development" to Sam back when she was the guidance counselor and her hair was brown. What was her name? Sam had no idea.

"Samantha 'Spade' Waxman," the dean said, walking toward her with arms spread like she was going to hug her, and then actually hugging her, with genuine warmth.

Sam was surprised to be remembered at all, but especially to have the pen name from her senior project remembered. She'd written a heavily researched, dreadfully ponderous "novella" based on a dream she had after watching the Julia Roberts film *Flatliners* on cable. A fictional version of Sam solves the mystery of consciousness by attempting suicide with an over-the-counter sleep aid. She wanders like a gumshoe Orpheus through hell, heaven, purgatory, limbo, the bardos, and, briefly (because there was nothing to do there), absolute nothingness. Midway through the story, her mother discovers "Sam" and screams for her father. They both work to resuscitate her, and in the end, "Sam" wakes up from her dream, having dutifully cited the six required sources. (Hers were Hawking, Sagan, Popper, Dante, Homer, and *The Tibetan Book of the Dead*). She concludes that all those realms and versions of the afterlife are just dreams, fairytales human beings tell themselves because they can't handle the truth, which is that we're blips of electrical impulses that flicker on for no reason and then, because nothing lasts forever, flicker off. Conclusion: Why bother killing yourself when it's all going to end soon enough and forever anyway? Might as well stick around, see what there is to see.

"I can't believe you remember my senior thesis," Sam said to the dean, whose name was still a blank.

The dean said, "Of course I remember. That story got *all* of our attention."

"Hey, it was only fiction," she tried to return the dean's smile but could tell she was grimacing.

"Are you still writing?"

Sam slouched involuntarily. "Nah."

"Well, you should be." The dean continued to gaze warmly at her, causing Sam to fidget. One thing her family members had going for them was that they knew her so well they hardly looked at her.

The dean told them that Sophia had Mandarin during second period, which had just started, Immanuel was in the gym for P.E., and Harper had a free period and was probably in the library studying. "She's usually right in the middle of things, holding court. You remember where the library is?"

"Of course," Sam said. "I spent all my lunches there."

The dean handed Sam a pass and stuck one on Donald's lapel before she fast-walked back down the hallway to her office.

Sam and Donald took a jasmine-lined walkway toward another large stucco-and-tile building. "Nice lady," he said.

"She pities me."

"You're nuts."

"Or she wants the alumni fund donations I've been shirking for the last fourteen years."

"This place doesn't need your piss-ant check."

Sam led the way up the steps and into the library, which had tablet computers where the magazine rack used to be, and no computers where the desktops used to be. They found Harper playing with the drawstring to her hoodie while she chatted with her friends at a long table. Golden curly hair whipped around at the sound of the door opening, and she said in a stage whisper, "*Whathefuh?* Sami? Grandpa?" Not rising to greet them, "What are *you* doing here?"

The librarian, a woman younger but way more authoritative than Sam, said, "Take it outside, please, Harper."

Rolling her eyes, Harper got up and led the way to the courtyard. The trees had been smaller in Sam's day. Now there was a lovely canopy shifting in the wind. She used to eat a quick lunch out here with her friends Lisa and Stephanie before they all went inside and did their homework. All three of them were unhappy, diligent girls whose intelligence was inversely proportional to their ability to deal with the "cool kids." Sam had semi-intentionally lost touch with them years ago because she didn't like having to look at her life in relation to theirs. Also, she couldn't bear to be around anyone who knew the naïve, melodramatic high school version of herself. They'd witnessed her huge, debilitating crushes on boys who looked right through her. They'd dealt with her constant worry that nobody liked her and she'd never be loved by anyone, and that life was going to consist mostly of coping with general joylessness and fear. (Years later, the FDA determined that suicidal ideation was a common side effect of the acne medication she began taking in tenth grade. Somehow this comforted her.)

Donald asked Harper if she knew anything about her dad's whereabouts.

"I didn't even know he was missing! Last night Mom said he was working late. This morning she said he went to work super early. God, Mom is *such* a pathological liar. Why wouldn't she just tell me the truth?"

"She probably didn't want you to worry."

"Like I would? I'm not even talking to him. Neither is Sophia."

"Yeah," Sam said, "what happened?"

Harper's eyes went big and round. "Sami, you are totally out of the loop. You didn't hear the Waxim last week?" Before Sam could reply, she slapped her forehead, "Duh! You got fired!"

"It was a mutual parting of ways."

"Dad said he fired you. Aww—are you OK?" She didn't wait for Sam to answer. "Well, he screwed up *big time.* Sophia thought she was pregnant for like, five minutes, and she broke down crying in front of Dad and told him all about it. He went right into his office and wrote a Waxim about it. I mean, first he went to the drugstore and bought like ten different pregnancy tests. They all came back negative. *Then* he wrote a Waxim about it."

Guilt clawed at Sam's stomach. She was a totally absent half-sister, abandoner of her own blood. As a survivor of this low-grade hell, she had a duty to shepherd Sophia and Harper through it. It wouldn't have killed her to call them every now and then and check in, take them out to dinner. She should have been the one Sophia came to, but she'd never put any effort into their relationship. As always, Sam was too wrapped up in herself.

"What'd he say in the Waxim?"

"He called her 'a young woman I'll call "Sarah,"' but like,

toward the very end of the audio, he slipped and called her Sophia. Not like it wasn't already obvious who he was talking about, since he knows exactly two young women."

"Hey, I'm still a young woman," Sam said.

"Of course you are," Harper patted Sam's shoulder while rolling her eyes at Donald. "Anyway, he said thinking 'Sarah' was pregnant really made him reexamine his beliefs about abortion and about the, like, efficacy? Of the lesson plans for the 'Responsibility' Key?"

"Don't tell me he's anti-choice now."

"No, he's all, 'Abortion is awful, but people have to be able to do it. The, like, wellbeing of a woman is more important than the embryo inside her.' But the totally screwed-up thing is that Madison Platt's mom heard the Waxim and sent her the link, and once Madison knows something, the whole school knows. Some douche called Soph 'Plan B Sophia' the other day. That's a nickname that could have legs."

"Ouch."

"And in French this total dork threw a condom at me. Still in the wrapper. He said I needed it because we Waxmans are so fertile. I got him back though. I said, *en Français*, that I would keep it because *he* certainly wouldn't need it before *la date d'expiration!*"

"Nice one," Sam said.

"Thanks. Madame Huerta almost fell off her chair laughing. Anyway, that's why we're not talking to Dad. He and Mom are probably fighting too. He's probably just, like, chilling out in a hotel."

"That ever happen before?" Donald asked.

She shrugged. "They don't tell us anything. But I wouldn't be surprised. Do you know, none of the three of us has ever walked in on them doing it? Isn't that weird? All of my friends with married parents have." She looked down at her phone. "Totally loving this family reunion, but I have to go. I have a million math problems to finish before next period."

She hugged them, kissed the air near their ears, and stomped back through the library's doors.

"Well?" Sam said.

"Well," Donald said, "we should talk to Sophia."

"We can't interrupt her language class. She's had to deal with too much embarrassment already."

"Fine," Donald said. "Let's talk to the boy."

Sam didn't think he'd have anything to tell them, but she led the way to the ivy-walled athletic center. Inside there were two full-court basketball games in progress, with about five mopey boys scattered on the periphery. Some dribbled ineptly, others shot baskets on the side hoops.

Immanuel was off in the corner, occasionally bouncing a ball. He was like a mini Jack Waxman with a jolly Jewfro on top. Sam watched as he bounced the ball off his foot, looked around to see if anyone had seen, and casually walked over to the folded-up bleachers to retrieve it. When Sam called his name, he looked over and blanched. "Oh, no. Who died?"

"No one," Sam said.

"As far as we know," Donald clarified.

"Isn't anyone supervising you guys?"

Immanuel pointed to one of the games. A mature, albeit short, young man moved among the players. He seemed totally absorbed in the game, stealing the ball from a hapless seventh-grader and leading a fast break, barking, "Fill the lane!" to his teammates.

"When did you last speak to Dad?" Sam asked.

Immanuel shrugged and looked at his shoes.

"Not on good terms with your dad, kid?"

"Not really, Pop-pop. He's been super pissed at me since school started. My grades are bad, and he pulled a lot of strings to get me in here. I told him I didn't even want to go to this school, I wasn't smart enough, but he never listens to me."

Sam couldn't suppress her urge to hug the little guy.

He pushed her away, "What the hell, Sami?"

"Sorry."

Immanuel went on, "I was going to tank my finals so I could get kicked out, but my friend told me I'd be eaten alive in public school. He said I'd end up as some sixteen-year-old eighth-grader's bitch. Maybe get traded to some other big kid for a pack of smokes."

"Easy there," Sam said. "It's not that bad."

"How do you know? Didn't you go to private school your whole life?"

"Yeah, but I have friends who went to public schools. They survived."

"I went to public school," Donald said. "Got a decent education."

"Back in, like, the Depression," Immanuel said. "Before they had to begin every semester with psyche evals. Now I bet all the brown and black kids see every white kid as a jerk who wants to shoot up the school or just build walls and be a dick to everybody who isn't white."

"Forget all that," Donald said. "What do you *want* to do?"

Immanuel scratched nervously deep into his hair. "Get a private tutor. Get my GED, go to USC's game design program, and just make video games for the rest of my life."

"OK," Sam tried to be supportive. "That sounds like a plan."

A whistle blew, and the little coach shouted, "Hit the showers!"

Immanuel shook his head. "I have to go. Oral report on *O Brother, Where Art Thou* in ten minutes."

"Good flick," Donald said.

"I fell asleep during it. But I know F. A. O. Scott says it's a tribute to the venality of the American imagination.'"

"A. O.," Sam corrected. "And maybe you mean *vitality*?"

"Hey-ho to you too, freak. See ya, Pop-pop." Immanuel didn't bother hugging or in any way touching either of them before walking away.

"OK, you were right," Donald said, "waste of time. How do we get out of here?"

Sam led Donald back up the steps, past the library, down the path to the huge parking lot.

As she was unlocking the car, someone behind them called out, "Sami?"

Sam took an SSRI for her depression and anxiety, but it never did anything to reduce the distress she felt upon hearing her name called out in public. Maybe it was residual paranoia from all the pot she'd smoked in high school and college, but more likely it had to do with her self-identification as a failure. A second ago she'd been coping with the world—minding her own business, recovering nicely from having to talk to the dean—but suddenly she had to talk to someone else, to account for herself again.

Always best to take a deep breath and face whoever it was. She turned and found, walking around a Honda in the next row, her old high school lunch buddy Lisa Kline.

"I heard a rumor you were still alive!" Lisa pulled Sam to her for a warm hug.

"Rumors of my life have been greatly exaggerated." Just the sight of Lisa made Sam smile. "Didn't you have another baby?"

"Yes, Tara! She's eleven months already. Just dropped her off at daycare. Zach is at preschool, thank God. I'm only here half-time right now, which is still too much. What are you doing here?"

Sam introduced Donald and lied, saying they'd just stopped by to say hi to the kids.

"I had Harper for English last year," Lisa said. "What a pill!"

Sam looked around and shivered. "I can't believe you come here every day."

"I know! But it feels totally different now. In a year, I'll have been here longer as a teacher than I was as a student. And I'm too busy cramming *Grapes of Wrath* and *Their Eyes Were Watching God* down their throats to think about what it was like for us."

"You're doing important work," Donald said.

"Alienating them from their parents and the plutocrats? Thanks."

Sam was jealous. Lisa had a job, a sense of purpose, a family, *and* she'd just gotten a compliment from Donald Waxman. Sam suspected that her purpose in life was to die in an accident in the home and not be discovered until the smell of her decomposing corpse attracted her neighbors' attention. We can't *all* be the protagonist, she thought. She, or her corpse, would provide the stench for someone else's lurid second-bottle-of-wine story.

"So," Lisa said, "I heard you were working for your dad?"

Who could she have heard that from? Sam's mother, of course. She leaked like an FBI agent. "I quit a couple of weeks ago. Needed a change."

Lisa laughed. "Oh, you always need change. I miss you. Stephanie misses you too. Next time we make plans, you're coming. I'll email you some dates!"

"Sounds good!" Sam said. What else could she say? They hugged goodbye, and Sam collapsed into the car and waited while Donald reassembled his bones into a sitting position inches above the seat before falling into it. Sam tried to identify her feelings: Jealousy? Loss? Self-pity? Loneliness? Mid-morning hangover? She needed to get a grip.

Donald and the door groaned together as he slammed it. "Let's go to the misper's office. Maybe someone there can tell us something."

Sam frowned. "I'm sort of banned for life." But she knew Donald wouldn't budge, so she said, "Fuck it," and headed to her most recent place of misemployment.

4

THE WAXMAN ETHICS Institute occupied the fourth floor of a brick fortress on the low-rent edge of Culver City. The ground floor had sat vacant since the closure of the bespoke underwear store, which had replaced a failed monocle-and-mustache-wax shop. The entire second floor was occupied by *bomBard*, a guerrilla telemarketing firm scornful of capitalization rules and the Do Not Call list. A casting agency and law firm divided the third floor.

In the lobby, Sam and Donald avoided the security guard by hiding behind three muscular, model-handsome, brown-skinned men who happened to be entering the building at the same time. In the elevator, their combined cologne was dizzying. Sam had a toe in the waters of a filthy sexual fantasy starring herself as a pirate queen and the men as Queequeg, Daggoo, and Tashtego from *Moby-Dick*, when all three men abruptly exited for the casting agency.

As the elevator doors closed behind them, Donald turned to Sam. "There a jazz club on that floor?"

"Be less racist," Sam said, projecting her disgust with her own racism. She wondered how one became a casting director and why she'd never considered it. Oh, right: the bullshit. And the essence of the job was meeting people and talking to people. She was lucky to have dodged that bullet. Life, when looked at in the right way, was a series of dodged bullets, so many worse than the one that actually hit you.

They got out on the fourth floor, which was all Jack Waxman, all the time. Immediately inside the suite doors, busts of Martin Luther King Jr., JFK, and Sandy Koufax sat on mismatched bookshelves. Above the empty reception desk, a portrait of Justice Oliver Wendell Holmes Jr. suggested that true virtue was measured by the span of one's mustache.

Donald scanned the portrait of his ex-wife mounted on the opposite wall. Beneath it, a golden plaque proclaimed,

This Institute would not exist without the example, encouragement, and love of Sylvia B. Waxman, selfless and compassionate mother, friend, and teacher.

Donald hadn't looked at a photograph of Sylvia in years. But there she was, with her '60s bob, strong Katharine Hepburn cheekbones, big Audrey Hepburn eyes, those full Gezundheit lips. And she was smiling, showing the lovely little gap between her front teeth. That was when she was still a young mother, before everything went to hell and the smile retired permanently. The eyes though, the nervous brown eyes, just reminded Donald of how they looked wet, red-rimmed, alternating between rage and despair. He could actually see her, maybe ten years after she posed for this photograph: hair disarrayed, grief lines arcing from above nostril to below lips, she stood in the middle of their bedroom, confronting him with the latest evidence of his infidelity. He didn't remember what it was—something trite like a cocktail napkin with a phone number, lipstick stain or strange perfume on a shirt —it hadn't mattered. This was the last straw, she said. He wasn't the man she thought she'd married. He'd abandoned their God, abandoned any kind of decent morality, and basically abandoned his family to hang out with degenerates and make shlock entertainment. She told him she wanted a divorce, but she would keep his name so she'd always remember who was to blame for ruining her life.

"*And* you won't have to go back to being a Gezundheit," he pointed out. Then, feeling low, thinking how unflattering crying was for her face, then berating himself for thinking that, he put forth a half-hearted argument. "You don't want a divorce."

"I do. And so do you."

Donald didn't reply to that, and she pounced. "Go on, admit it."

"Admit what?"

"That you don't love me. That you never loved me."

"You're crazy." He tried to head for the bathroom, but she grabbed him by the shoulders, forced him to look at her.

"Say it to my face! You don't love me and you never did!"

Turning his eyes from the portrait, Donald shuddered. This was exactly why it was best to avoid remembering things.

He said to Sam, "How is your grandmother anyway?"

"Dead, for like, ten years?"

"Right." Cancer. Not lung, thank God. Then she could've blamed him for ending her life in addition to ruining it. Time to think about something else. He nodded toward the empty receptionist's desk. "Where's the girl?"

"You just assume she's female?"

"She isn't?"

"They let her go. Tough year." Sam squared her shoulders. "Let's get this over with."

She led the way past the desk and through the hallway door. Donald scanned the walls, filled with pictures of Jack shaking hands with famous athletes, actors, and politicians.

As they approached the first office, they heard Jack's trusty assistant Bonnie talking on the phone, ". . . sends emails to me every three hours, twenty-four hours a day, and suddenly silence?" There was a pause, and then, "Yes. Yes, I did. I know it's technically illegal, but I just asked myself, 'What would Jack want me to do?' And I knew. Jack would say, 'Be *GRREAT*, Bonnie. Check my email.'"

Sam prided herself on not being an eavesdropper, so she knocked on the open door and poked her head in before Donald could stop her.

Bonnie nearly jumped out of her chair. She glared at Sam and said into the phone, "I'll call you back. The daughter is here—I know!" She clicked the button with her hand but kept the receiver to her ear. "You're not supposed to be here. You don't appreciate your father's greatness."

"Granted," Sam said, "but can we talk for a minute?"

"No, I'm calling security." She began dialing.

Donald muttered, "Jeez, kid. Must have been some hatchet job you did."

"It wasn't that bad. I just thought he needed a wake-up call."

Donald leaned over the desk and hung up the call. "Please, honey, we're here to help. Can we just talk for a minute?"

Bonnie put the phone down. "My name is Bonnie.'"

"Bonnie, right. I know you're worried about Jack, but we're looking for him, and we could really use the help of a pretty lady like you."

"You're so gross," Sam blurted.

"I'm not sure he'd be any happier that *you're* here," Bonnie said to Donald. "You know, Jack has a reputation to uphold. What if he comes back?"

"If *my son* comes back," Donald said, pinning Bonnie's eyes with his, "the case will be closed, and we'll be on our way."

"Please, Bonnie," Sam said, "just tell me what was in Dad's calendar yesterday and what you found in his email. We're worried about him." As she said it, Sam realized she was actually starting to worry a little. No matter how late he'd stayed up working, her dad should be awake by now.

Bonnie seemed to consider Sam's words, but then she reached for the phone again.

Sam lunged over the desk, grabbed hold of the cord, yanked it from the wall.

It didn't go as smoothly as it does in the movies. The line had been tangled with about ten other cords, including one connected to the bulky hard drive that sat on the desk next to the monitor. The drive tilted in slow motion, tipped onto Bonnie's knock-off Tiffany desk lamp. The lamp fell. Its glass shade smashed the fish bowl that sat on the edge of the desk, sending a small tide of water and one blue betta fish over the desk and onto the floor.

"Blue!" Bonnie screamed. She scurried after the fish, which was too stunned even to flop.

Donald hadn't moved, and now he just stared at Bonnie's substantial ass. Sam pushed him aside and ran to the kitchen. In the hallway she ran straight through a familiar perfume cloud and barely veered around the large bosom of Vivian, the *Be GRREAT!* Program Director while shouting, "Fish out of water! Fish out of water!" In the kitchen, she found an empty plastic soup container and filled it from the tap.

Cradling the fish in her hands, Bonnie met Sam in the hallway. She dropped it into the container. They watched. The fish drifted for a moment, looked around, did the fish equivalent of a shrug, and resumed the slow circle it had been swimming around its bowl.

"It's going to live," Sam said, with feeling. "Your fish is going to live!"

"You're evil, Samantha. I'm sure you're the reason he went away! It's all your fault."

The high forehead and wet-looking eyes of Elliott, the assistant bookkeeper, peered skeptically over the top of the nearby cubicle wall. "Hey, Samantha."

"Hey, Elliott," Sam said, still catching her breath. "How are you? How's the wife and child?"

"Good, thanks. Everyone's good. How's the . . . how are you?"

"Dandy," Sam said. "Sorry for the disturbance. Come on, Bonnie, tell me about my dad. I don't think he 'went away.'"

"Is that my phone ringing?" Bonnie hurried back to her office, clutching the plastic bowl. Sam followed, noting that she couldn't even rip a phone line out of a wall right. They found Donald ignoring the ringing phone and staring at the cluster of photos pinned to Bonnie's bulletin board.

The phone stopped ringing just before Bonnie picked it up and said, with terrifying enthusiasm, "Waxman Ethics Institute! How can we help you be *GRREAT* today?" But there was no one on the other end.

"Shoot!" she replaced the receiver. "What if that was Jack? What if that was Jack, and you made me miss him?"

"Then he'll call back. Now, can you tell me what he was up to yesterday? Please? I'm trying to help. I . . . love my dad and I want to find him."

Bonnie had the grace not to call attention to the way Sam had hesitated and sort of mumbled the word "love." And, probably because Sam had said please, Bonnie nodded.

While Sam helped her right her lamp and computer, pick up pieces of glass, and soak up the water on her desk with paper towels, Bonnie told her, "Your dad spent yesterday morning sending personal fundraising notes to donors. He drafted and sent an email to the Assistant Secretary of the Education Department in Equatorial Guinea. They're considering testing *Be GRREAT* in a few pilot schools. In the afternoon, he had his weekly meeting with the department heads, and after that he met with Nick Vigor of SBT regarding the Venture Charter School project."

"SBT? Where do I know that from?" Donald asked.

"Strych, Batracht, and Tetra," Bonnie said. "They started as a development firm, but now they do all kinds of things. Vigor's the CEO. They're the ones who built that beautiful shopping center in Studio City."

"The one with the zip line and the climbing wall?" Sam asked.

"No, the one with the trapeze school and the trolley. That other one's in Toluca Lake. But they did that too."

Sam said, "Didn't they also build that deathtrap shopping mall on that base in Iraq? The one that burned or fell down or electrocuted people?"

"Samantha, SBT is saving this company. We were about to have another round of layoffs when, like an angel from heaven, Vigor swooped down and gave us the contract for Venture Schools."

Sam preempted Donald's question, "They're these charter schools SBT is suddenly building. I still can't believe private, for-profit corporations are allowed to run schools."

"Samantha," Bonnie said, "if you'd watched that video of him on FOX Business like your dad asked, you'd know the move makes sense because SBT values education and believes in the charter-school movement. And SBT is positioned perfectly to start schools because they already do similar things, like commercial construction, industrial food production—"

"Nonlethal weaponry, private incarceration," Sam continued for her.

"Can you give us this guy's number?" Donald said.

Bonnie shook her head. "I already called his office. His assistant said their meeting ended around 6:30 last night. Now, if you'll excuse me, I'm going to hire the investigators we use for background checks. I need a board member to approve the expenditure first."

"Doesn't everyone on the board hate my dad since he blew that Iowa charter-school contract?"

Bonnie's face reddened. "They complained that the Respect Key implied 'acceptance of aberrant behavior forbidden in the Bible.' They wanted to change it from 'Respect' to 'Rejoice!' Your dad *had* to push back. Now, I have work to do. Please leave."

"Just one more thing," Donald said. "Can you look up Vigor's address for us?"

Bonnie peered at her screen as her hand guided her mouse around a small puddle of water she'd missed in her wipe-down. She typed, peered some more, jotted the address on a notepad, and tore off the page. She paused before handing it to Sam. "Do not antagonize him. This is the account that saved us."

"I would never!" Sam pulled the paper out of her hand. "And I'm really sorry about the mess."

"Just go." Bonnie gave her full attention to her screen. "And shut the door behind you—please."

In the hallway, Sam started toward the elevators, but Donald said, "What's your hurry?" and pulled her the other way.

"This place is really bumming me out."

"Five more minutes," Donald said. "Let's just get the lay of the land."

Sam noticed herself slouching. She pulled her shoulders back and led the way. They started in Accounting at Elliot's cubicle.

"You like your job?" Donald asked him.

Elliott looked at Sam before answering. "Sure? I mean, the pay is . . . pathetic, but I work with nice people for a good cause."

"Company hit a rough patch recently?"

Elliott shook his head. "Thanks to SBT, we're back in the black."

"Any large sums of money moving around mysteriously?"

"Nope."

"Know of anyone who might want to make Jack Waxman disappear?"

Elliott laughed. Then he looked at Sam, "Sorry. Has he really?"

Donald reached into his inside pocket, pulled out a pack of cigarettes.

Sam took a step back. "Whoa, you're smoking again?"

"You can't do that in here," Elliott slid back in his chair, looked around.

But Donald West played by his own rules. He shook out a coffin nail, torched the end with his thumb-polished Zippo.

"Tell me, Elliott," exhaling, snapping lighter shut, flicking ash into the mug on Elliott's desk, "did *you* want to make Jack disappear?"

Elliott cut off his laugh when he realized Donald was serious. "Of course not. Jack's OK. He pays almost no attention to me. That's my kind of boss!"

"I'm going to need names of everyone who's been laid off," Donald said.

From down the hall, someone said, "You smell smoke? I smell smoke!"

There were clacking high-heeled footsteps, and then Vivian rounded the cubicle wall, her rose-jasmine perfume billowing up right behind her, fighting Donald's smoke for odoriferous supremacy.

"What the hell is going on here?" She got right in Donald's face. "You cannot smoke inside this office, or inside this building, or within fifteen feet of any entrance to this building. The designated smoking area is around the corner between the loading dock and the dumpster!"

"So sorry." Smiling coolly, Donald dropped his cigarette in Elliott's mug and held out his hand. He said to her cleavage, "I'm sure I'd remember if I'd met you before. I'm Donald West."

She shook his hand as briefly as possible. "Vivian Cruz, Director of *Be GRREAT!* And we *have* met before."

"Of course. I'm a big fan. Grr-ate-ness! It's . . ." he snapped his fingers, searching for the right word and somehow only finding:

"*good*." Then, "Miss Cruz—is it Miss?—do you know of anyone who might want to make Jack Waxman disappear?"

"Ha!"

"Why's everyone get such a kick out of that question?"

"Because my dad pisses everyone off," Sam said.

"He's the boss," Vivian explained, "and bosses are pains in the ass. They change their minds suddenly, make everyone throw out stuff they've been working on for weeks to begin whimsical new projects . . . or they host truly sad holiday parties, like, on a Wednesday, at lunch, with no alcohol, at a Mexican restaurant one Yelper charitably described as 'middling.' I'm sure more than one person in this office has imagined chaining him to a garage door opener like Dolly did to Dabney in *Nine to Five.* But most people don't act on those impulses. Most people know he's a good person, deep down."

"Way deep," Elliott added.

"Any idea who might act on those impulses?" Sam said.

Vivian thought about it. "I'd try reading through the blog comments. Half of those people are totally bonkers."

Sam cursed herself for not thinking of that. In the thirteen years that her dad had been doing these radio pieces, he'd addressed the ethics of everything: how to be a good husband, father, son, friend, citizen; how to make money without losing your soul; yes or no to panhandlers; full-service or self-; paper or plastic; hybrid or electric or ethanol or hydrogen; preemption or prevention; rehab or incarceration; how to cope with the death of a beloved parent; what to do when a surviving parent is a toxic bully, etc.

The Waxims were featured on AM news stations, so many of Jack's listeners and blog readers were insane. Maybe one of the super-religious commenters couldn't handle Jack's pro-choice Waxim and decided to do something drastic. Those people were always pro-gun.

Sam thanked Vivian and led Donald toward Creative and her former cubicle.

"You're back!" Cathy Wong, the graphic designer, jumped up and hugged Sam.

"It's good to see you," Sam said. She introduced Donald and gave Cathy the short version: "My dad's missing. We're looking for him."

"Oh no!" Cathy's hand went to her mouth. "Did anyone look behind his desk? He might just be lying there ..."

Sam started to laugh, but then she realized she didn't know for sure. She left Donald staring at the action-figure menagerie that sat on top of Cathy's screen and ran down the hall just to make sure. Her dad's office was cluttered, but there was no body in it. She looked behind his desk to make sure, and found that she was shaking. She took a few deep breaths, avoiding looking at any of the family photos, and walked back to Cathy's desk.

Donald hadn't moved, but now he held a Pikachu in his hand, studying it like it was a message from the future.

"Cath," Sam said, "can we borrow your computer for a few minutes to check the recent comments? Maybe one of those weirdos kidnapped him."

"No problem." Cathy got up to let Sam take over her computer.

One of Sam's jobs had been to approve Waxim comments. Spam bots commented on everything: "yes, BIGger IS better, see my photos!!" or "So insightful piece!" or "I agree. I saw some similar but ever better thing just yesternight. Check out!"

Then there were the rage commenters. Sam's job was to delete anything containing foul language or attacking the character of Jack Waxman or a fellow commenter. People could quote scripture, argue about abortion and gay marriage, could even suggest moderate Muslims were just fundamentalists biding their time until "mainstream Americans" lowered their guard. But people could not call other people names. "Commie" and "fascist" were case-by-case, but "Hitler," "Nazi," and "Stalin" were forbidden. Creative insults like "turd gurgler," "douche residue," and "Republicunt" were appreciated and then deleted. Sam was supposed to maintain a document recording every deleted comment, but that was one of the first duties to slide once she began spending her drive to work fantasizing about checking herself into a sanatorium.

It only took seconds to realize that no one had been monitoring the blog since Sam quit. There were more than two hundred comments awaiting approval. She tried to scan for those submitted since the controversial pro-choice Waxim, but even if she weeded out SPAM and anti-Semitic, white-supremacist garbage, it would take hours to go through all of them.

"Here's one from 'John316': 'You preach tolerance, but tolerance of immorality, of sin, is wrong. I refuse to tolerate it, and so should every righteous man and woman.'"

"Eh." Donald wasn't impressed.

"How about this one from 'Otto'?" In her most surf-bro voice, Sam read, "'In your Fourth of July Waxim you celebrated our freedoms, but who will free us from ourselves? For we are all imprisoned by our fear, our prejudice, our greed.'

"Or this reply from 'blotto': 'otto, we aren't the problem the problem is that our government serves the illuminati spies on us extorts unreasonable taxes takes our guns limits our speed wastes our money on programs that don't work . . .' yadda yadda yadda, '. . . in the new world order we're all slaves and our masters the rothchilds and their servants like jack waxman are anything but great we must rise up.' Jeez, this guy knows about the Rothschilds, but not periods or commas."

"You're wasting your time," Cathy said. "People who talk, they don't really do. And people who do, tend not to talk so much."

Donald said, "Where's a gong when you need one?"

Sam punched him in his bony shoulder.

5

ON THEIR WAY to SBT's downtown office, Sam and Donald sat in traffic on a high-walled section of the 10 freeway. The world had simplified, consisted now of nothing but cars and concrete and relentless late-morning sun. There were too many people, and they all had cars and drove them everywhere. Sam wondered how this city had ever made sense.

Then she remembered *Who Framed Roger Rabbit*, which had taught her about the conspiracy among auto, tire, and oil companies. They'd bought all of the major cities' streetcar lines, ruined them with high prices and shitty service, and then replaced them with more profitable, less efficient, less convenient buses. *That* old story: the rich and powerful doing terrible things to increase their riches and power, and being rich and powerful enough to get away with it. And what did it portend for the future of civilization that, even now, knowing what we did about the environmental effects of fossil fuels, not to mention the psychological and physical effects of car-commuting, we still hadn't changed course?

And why did the citizens of this drought-stricken city wash their cars so often, making them extra reflective, so not one sun, but thousands flashed blindingly from every shining surface?

Not an equivalent problem, she realized, but where in the fuck had she put her sunglasses?

She had to think about something else. She switched on the radio, but the jazz station was way too bebop, so she switched it off.

Donald didn't seem to care one way or the other. He just kept looking out his window at the drivers of the other cars.

When he turned finally, he seemed surprised to see her. He blinked a few times, peered closely at her face.

"What?" she glanced at her nostrils in the rearview mirror. "Do I have a boog?"

"Your nose . . . if it had a little more curve, and a tiny bump toward the top, you'd be the spitting image of your grandmother."

"So you've told me."

"I don't think I've ever seen another one quite like yours, so perfect."

"Drop it, please."

By now Sam had talked about her nose to three different therapists. They helped her accept it as hers and accept that her parents had only allowed her to have the surgery because their judgment was clouded by their love for her and their guilt over the divorce.

That was the tragedy of it: their love for her had fucked her up. It made them tell her she could be whatever she wanted, and she'd believed them. And thanks to Donald, she wanted to be a crime novelist. He'd thought she should write screenplays, of course, but by age sixteen, she'd met enough people in the entertainment industry to want to stay far away from it. But she'd been a smart and hardworking student, and she made it all the way into her thirties with the vague expectation that any moment now, the switch would flip and she'd start churning out books. Other people did it. But now it seemed those other people were smarter and more talented. They worked harder, saw their ideas through to completion. Since the failure of her first novel, Sam wrote outlines and chapters but never got more than fifty pages into a book before she lost faith and gave up. Her writing professors had never been overly enthusiastic about her work, but at the time, she took their coldness as a natural defense against clingy, entitled students. Lately she suspected she'd misunderstood them.

The cars on the freeway were not moving, and the cars in her lane were not moving the most. Just the thought of trying to switch lanes filled her with anxiety, so she leaned back, sought acceptance. But like the dull headache from morning whisky, Sam's uneasiness seemed here to stay. Was it guilt for distressing Bonnie and nearly killing her fish? That was an accident. No, what gnawed at her was the visit to the old school and the resurfacing of the old *Where'd My Life Go Wrong?* question.

Obviously, it was when she decided to get an MFA. Her dad had paid her tuition, happy she was doing *something*, though he'd have preferred law school. For years, any time she complained or expressed doubt about writing, she heard from both parents, "It's not too late to go to law school!" It was the only thing Jack and Susan had agreed on since their decision to get divorced. Its short-term effect was always to end the conversation. Its long-term effect was to keep Sam on the East Coast.

During her two years in New York at a school that clung to the bottom of the top tier of creative writing programs, Sam's generalized anxiety spiked. Her Carroll Gardens studio was too small to be awake in. Everywhere she went, she found herself having to rub shoulders with strangers. On the rush-hour subway, she breathed in their exhalations, grabbed a pole, or sat in a seat still warm from their heat. It was all uncomfortably intimate for a Californian.

She ended up spending a lot of time in dive bars on off-nights, drinking with her classmates, but that brought its own share of social anxiety as she was an introvert who dreamed of being a hybrid Lorrie Moore/Raymond Chandler or Mary Gaitskill/Elmore Leonard or, at least, a female Kinky Friedman. She often felt she had no idea what to say to the cis white guy hell-bent on becoming the next David Foster Wallace or Brooklyn Jonathan, or the girl who wrote story after story about sleeping with awful men who made her feel bad about herself, or the poor guy trying to write about being molested by his older cousin, but he couldn't bring himself to write it so he just wrote around it and around it for two-hundred pages. Sam treated her imposter syndrome with alcohol and nicotine, a line of cocaine here, a bump of ketamine there.

Relationship-wise, she did what she'd done in college, which was cling to the first attractive, sensitive guy who pursued her. In this case his name was Aaron, and he was the delicately featured second-best poet of the program. One of his best poems was a meditation on jealousy that intricately plotted the murder of someone who resembled the best poet in the program. Sam helped him with the ideal murder weapon: icicle (obvs, because it nearly rhymes with *thigh pickle*).

One night, seven or eight months into their relationship, Aaron stood on two of the four linoleum tiles that comprised Sam's kitchen, watching her do their dishes. He suggested they move to Queens and have a baby. Sam was shocked, first, that he was serious, second, that she was old enough for it not to be an obvious joke, and third, that he'd mistaken her for someone who wanted to bear and raise a child, especially with someone like him, who really was more self-destructive than she was. In fact, she argued, his desire to be a father was just the latest and most extreme manifestation of his desire to destroy himself. With a baby to take care of and worry about, he could completely forget about his art. This, to Sam's melodramatic mind, seemed like a huge cop-out. The only children she was interested in mothering were those of her imagination.

Aaron took this in, stroking his smooth chin. "Maybe you're right. My friend Mira says all our relationships are doomed because everyone moves here to *be* someone, not to *be with* someone."

Before she could stop herself, Sam turned to him, sponge in one hand, large knife in the other. "Who's Mira?"

Mira was the woman he left her for, of course. Last Sam heard, they were raising two children in Port Washington. Aaron was a development associate at a small college. If he still wrote poems, he didn't publish them.

But New York wasn't a complete waste. Sam got into the habit of running around Prospect Park a few times a week as both confession to her body and penance for her sins against it. And in those two years, she managed to finish a draft of her novel, a hard-boiled thriller about a feminist FBI agent named Morningstar Jones. Daughter of a Buddhist flower child and militant Black Panther, a beloved disappointment to them both, Morningstar uses the homespun wisdom of her parents to achieve justice and stand up to The Man. In her first big case, while investigating the murder of a liberal female congresswoman, Morningstar unearths a far-reaching conspiracy between high-ranking military officials and two members of the Appropriations Committee.

RIP, sweet alter ego.

The car in front of Sam and Donald finally rolled forward, so Sam eased off the brake. Thinking about New York always made her want to smoke. She woke Donald with a tap on his shoulder. "Still have those cigarettes?"

"They're mine!"

"Can you at least give me one? And light it for me?"

"Filthy habit," Donald said, but he did as she asked. Sam took a drag, winced. Took another drag, smiled. The nicotine receptors in her brain awoke from their long slumber and had a dance party.

Inching the car forward in space but looking back in her mind, she thought each step had seemed logical, or at least acceptable, at the time. As soon as she finished school, she pitched her book to every agent she could find. Meanwhile, she worried obsessively about turning into an old hag, waiting tables with a bad cough and flat feet. When the worry became outright panic—as her inbox filled with rejection emails—she applied to be a writing lecturer at every college and community college that advertised an opening. More rejections filled her inbox. No one even wanted to interview her. She studied her resume and cover letters, looking for red flags like syntax or spelling errors, a sentence that subtextually advertised her tenuousness. Her friends told her it wasn't her—the job market was tough, a thousand MFAs flooded it every year, and there were only so many positions. But she began to wonder if she might be going crazy, blind to warning signs that were obvious to others.

Every Wednesday her dad called her from the car on his way home from work, gently demanding a progress report. These calls were an unspoken condition of the monthly checks that paid half of her expenses. In one of these conversations, she mentioned applying to Cal State, Murcia, in the San Joaquin Valley, a half hour north of Fresno. She hadn't even heard of it until she saw the job listing, but Jack was elated to hear she might come back to California, and he happened to know the faculty dean, who'd once taught at UCLA. Sam's phone interview lasted five minutes and ended with a job offer. Nepotism to the rescue!

But Murcia was a parched farm town that smelled like manure or garlic, depending on the direction of the wind. Addiction, homelessness, soaring unemployment, failing public schools, all combined with a dwindling tax base and proudly regressive population to ensure that nothing would improve. Sam moved there and became a hermit-teacher. Four times a week, she rode her bicycle to the university along a windy highway with corn on one side and a recently abandoned, half-constructed housing development on the other. She did her best to teach her students how to write logical, grammatically correct essays. Mostly, she failed. The rest of the time she read or watched the TV shows she'd missed while living an actual life in New York.

She tried using social media but quickly realized it wasn't for her. She clung to the old definition of the word "friend," and she could never believe anyone was as happy as they seemed online. On Wednesday nights, she joined her fellow lecturers for karaoke at the one bar in town where no one ever got stabbed. No one—not even her mother—came to visit her.

Sam lasted three years at CSUM, her longest-held job by two years. She decided to quit when she realized that she was the most negative person she knew. One karaoke night, during a lull between songs, she drunkenly asked her colleagues, "What are we doing? I mean, seriously, *what are we doing?* We're lovers of language, believers in its power and beauty! Why do we spend all our time reading the ugliest, most impenetrable sentences ever constructed?"

Everyone laughed at her. Brenda, the one Latina in the group, played a tiny, invisible violin. Derek, who supported a wife and two children on the same low salary as Sam, told her she needed to get laid. Then he shot his hand over his mouth and begged her forgiveness, begged her not to report him for harassment.

As if Sam would beggar his wife and children because of something he said drunk in a bar. But he was right: she hadn't had sex in over a year. She had only the faintest memory of what it felt like to be hugged.

At the end of the semester, she quit her job and moved back to Los Angeles. She found a tiny studio apartment in Santa Monica, on the wrong side of Lincoln, and began looking for work. Stopped even thinking about writing. She felt like she had nothing to offer, began to wish nothing was a viable thing to do. Her psychiatrist gently suggested she increase her sertraline dosage.

Four months after moving back to L.A., with savings depleted, Sam again asked her dad for help. Jack was morally opposed to giving her more money, but the Ethics Institute's editor had recently quit due to "personality conflict," so Jack gave her the job. Nepotism, again, to the rescue.

But only temporarily, because here she was, stuck on the goddamned freeway, broke, unemployed, and out of ideas. Already pretty close to maximum sertraline dosage. And she hadn't written in probably a year because she'd spent her days badly doing her stupid job and her nights reading or watching TV. Maybe she had to revise her idea of herself: it wasn't literature she loved, but escape. She'd take it in whatever form she could find it.

Finally, the traffic jam culminated in the denouement of an action flick: emergency workers standing around fire engines, ambulances, and police cruisers that partially blocked the view of an SUV on its side, chassis exposed like the belly of a dead roach. Black smoke puffed from the engine. The drivers of the cars in front of her, beside her, and behind her all stared at the scene as they slowly rolled past. Too many stuck their phones out the window to record it.

Sam judged them. She judged them all.

SBT's West Coast headquarters were located on the upper floors of a Brutalist office tower in the high-rise section of downtown. In the lobby, the sight of armed security personnel and electronic gates guarding the bank of elevators gave Sam serious doubts about the mission.

She pulled Donald aside. "What are we doing here?"

"Gee, kid, I thought you knew."

"I mean, what's the point? I'm sure he'll turn up."

"Who?"

"Focus, Pop! We're looking for Dad, remember?"

"Of course," Donald said. His tooth had begun to hurt, and he'd thought for a moment they were going to the dentist. But of course they weren't. They were here on business—personal business. "We need to see if this Vinegar guy knows anything."

"Vigor," Sam said.

"I can handle it if you wanna wait in the car."

Sam seriously doubted he could handle it. She followed him up to the front desk, where a young woman wearing a blue uniform shirt asked them who they were here to see.

"Whom," Sam said, to herself, she hoped.

Donald leaned over the desk and said in a low voice, "We're here for Mr. Vega."

"Vigor," Sam corrected.

"Do you have an appointment?"

"No," Donald said. "We just need to ask him a question or two, about a missing person."

"Are you police?" she said doubtfully.

Donald nodded while Sam shook her head. He shot Sam a dirty look, said, "We're *private* investigators." As if that were superior to the police.

"I'm the missing person's daughter," Sam said quickly.

The guard surprised Sam by smiling compassionately and nodding. "I'll see what I can do." She took their names and called Vigor's receptionist.

Sam and Donald listened while she repeated their names and their story and then waited. They waited for at least two minutes. Sam found the awkwardness of standing there unbearable. She took a step back, scanned the cavernous lobby with the weird monumental corporate painting on the wall. It was a light-blue, billboard-sized field with an off-center, hunter-green suggestion of a tree, but nothing so edgy as an actual tree. Finally, the guard said, "Got it," and hung up the phone. "Mr. Vigor's receptionist says he's very busy, but he can squeeze you in for a minute. IDs please."

Donald's driver's license was hole-punched and expired, but the guard didn't mind. She pressed a button and the Plexiglas gates slid open. Sam and Donald walked through and took the elevator up to the fourteenth floor. The eight-foot-high, blood-red SBT logo greeted them with its severe top horizontal line and the arms and legs of the letters dangling like dead things below it. Behind a glass door, an Amazonian blonde sat at a reception desk that seemed modeled on a World War II machine-gun nest.

Sam followed Donald into a lobby lined with several empty

chrome and black leather chairs. The receptionist refused to turn her silver-shadowed eyes toward them for an aggressively long time, and then she smiled with her mouth only.

"Please sit down. It shouldn't be too long."

They sat on the cold, stiff chairs. Without consciously deciding to do it, Sam took out her phone and checked her email. She'd never been so popular: a request from NARAL to sign a petition against the right-wing attack on reproductive freedom; another from CREDO to fight another pipeline through Native American land; SumOfUs wanted thirteen dollars, a pittance considering the dire need for action on climate change.

There was also an email from Lisa Kline. She said seeing Sam at school made her realize how much she missed her, and she asked her to pick a date in the next few weeks for dinner. Sam had enjoyed seeing Lisa too, remembered how much she enjoyed her company, but just thinking about making plans filled her with dread.

Her stomach growled. In her new unemployed life, she usually had lunch at the stroke of eleven, and now it was already past noon. Without conscious intent, she put her phone back in her pocket. She'd sign those petitions and reply to Lisa later.

The inner-office door opened, and Sam and Donald both looked up. A tall, broad-shouldered, blue-eyed bro walked out wearing a dark suit.

Sam felt the blush spread over her cheeks. She'd had sex with this very bro two weeks ago, her first sex in two years.

"Samantha?" Chris Camfer stopped short, fired both dimples at her. "What's the haps?"

"Hey!" Sam attempted a smile. "What are you doing here?"

"I work here. Marketing department, remember?" He mimed shooting himself in the head. "What are you doing here?"

"My dad's missing. He had a meeting here yesterday," Sam found herself standing up for some reason. She didn't remember ever talking about where he worked. "We're just seeing if Mr. Vigor knows anything. This is Donald, my grandpa."

"Missing? That's crazy. But it's nice to meet you, sir." Chris stuck out his hand. Sam caught the scent of his cologne, which was all burnt cedar and cinnamon-flavored tobacco. It made her think of a fairytale wolf, and it went distractingly straight from her nose to her nethers.

Donald shook the hand, but he took his time about it.

"We met in a bar a couple of weeks ago," Sam explained to Donald. Then, to change the subject, "Totally weird that you work here."

"I know! 'Of all the bars in all the world,' right?"

"Nope!" Donald said.

"What?"

"Come on, Pop."

"It's 'of all the gin joints in all the towns in all the world, she walks into mine.' There's a rhythm to it."

"Right. Sorry." Chris stood a second more in awkward silence. Finally, "Well, it was good to run into you. I'll give you a call. I meant to earlier, but things have been ..."

"Oh yeah, same. Super busy," eyes glued to the magazines on the coffee table.

"Don't forget to read my screenplay!" Chris said as he went through the glass doors.

Sam just smiled and half-nodded. She would never read that screenplay.

While Chris waited for the elevator in the hallway, Sam and Donald and the receptionist sat in silence. It took a thousand years for the elevator to come. Chris stepped inside, and it took a hundred more years for the doors to close.

"Tell me the truth, kid. Are you turning tricks? Was that your pimp?"

"Jeez! What's with you?" Sam slapped Donald's arm even

though she'd vowed not to hit him again after she'd socked him back at the office. He'd totally rubbed his shoulder when she wasn't looking. "Your mind is filthier than ever."

"You haven't answered my question."

"No, he's not my pimp. We just . . . hooked up."

"What's that again?"

"It's none of your business. What I'm wondering is what you thought you were doing there. What's with the tough-guy routine?"

"*Routine*? Kid, I don't do routines. That cub looked hinky. Smelled hinky too. Never trust a man who wears cologne," Donald rubbed his nose. "He's hiding something."

Sam didn't think so. In fact, she suspected Chris of being extremely dumb. She'd met him on the night of her quitting/firing from the Institute. She'd gone to Tal Vez, her local organic, vegetarian Cal-Mex restaurant. She liked to sit in the dark bar under strings of multicolored Christmas lights, eat a couple of nopales tacos, drink a couple of beers, watch whatever random soccer game was on. She was doing just that, recalling her own sweet memories of successful tackles and completed passes, that one glorious header, when this Adonis sat down next to her and ordered a beer. Sam noticed how the stubble on his strong jaw caught the light like tiny slivers of gold. She looked back at the screen, but it was halftime. She looked at her beer. Empty. The whole time he was there in the corner of her eye, possibly checking her out? Her peripheral vision was shit. He finished his beer in four big gulps, then ordered another and said, "And one for the lady."

Sam assumed he was talking about someone else—and so did the bartender, because he looked over Samantha's shoulders before placing the bottle in front of her.

Sam looked at it, turned with a questioning look to the Adonis.

He pinned her to the wall with those Paul Newman blues and said, "Hey, this Modelo's for you."

"Thanks." Sam was too stunned to refuse. Sometimes she chatted with the middle-aged regulars, but no one just went and bought her a drink. Especially not someone with such a strong jaw or, for that matter, thick traps, bulging delts and pecs, and what she had to assume were washboard abs. Not to mention the thick forearms, one of which boasted a globe and anchor tattoo. The men she'd dated were always thin and neurotic English and philosophy majors, writers of overwrought love letters, sufferers of panic attacks and eczema.

"Losers, you mean," Chris said after she'd explained to him why he wasn't her type.

"Sensitive guys," she corrected, finishing the beer he'd bought her. "Guys who don't have Marine tattoos on their arms. Guys who definitely don't kill brown people in service of their corporate overlords."

"Whoa, I didn't do that. I killed brown people to make them free."

Sam slammed her forehead onto the bar, harder than she'd intended.

"You OK? I was kidding. Any people I killed were terrorists, or people standing really close to terrorists . . ."

"Thanks for the beer!" Sam signaled the bartender for her check.

"Don't go," Chris said. "I'm sorry. I'm totally fucking with you."

Sam met his laughing eyes. At least he had a sense of humor. "There's nothing funny about killing innocent people."

"Totally. And I didn't. I swear. Can I buy you some tequila?"

"You can," Sam conceded.

Since it was extremely rare for Sam to be sitting next to a Marine, she asked him about it. He said he fought in Afghanistan and Iraq. He'd disagreed with the decision to invade and occupy

Iraq, but he had to do his job. Now though, he was just "an ad guy." He asked her what she did.

Sam laughed bitterly at that. She couldn't say she was a writer. Writers wrote (always!). She shrugged and picked up the shot of tequila that had appeared in front of her. She toasted him, noticed his long, scarred fingers and the veins on the back of his hand. She followed the line of his arm up to his broad shoulders. The voice in her head, quieter and more confident than of old, asked what she hoped to gain from sex with this man. Simple skin-to-skin contact, she'd answered. An orgasm if she was lucky.

A few more tequila shots later, in her bedroom, she wrapped her legs around his narrow hips and felt her mind going blank. For the first time in way too long, she was an animal ecstatically embracing another animal. He moved rapidly over her, a grunting blur of eyes and teeth, and she closed her eyes and tried only to feel the pleasure, the fullness building inside her until it exploded —but his exploded first.

That was fine. She was proud of herself for going out and getting some, for saying yes instead of no. Maybe this was a sign that her luck was changing. She'd find another job. She'd start going on dates, maybe even go online. Even from a physical perspective, this encounter wasn't a total loss. She'd liked feeling him clutch her desperately as he came. It reminded her that she liked feeling needed, though she could've done without the accompanying cry of "Fire in the hole!"

Post-explosion, Chris neatly knotted the condom, dropped it on the floor, patted her thigh gratefully, and slept. Sam rolled her eyes, got out of bed, went to the bathroom, finished the job. Then she got close to the mirror, looked at the deepening lines of her face. Near her left temple, two coarse gray hairs stood out among the softer dark brown. She zeroed in on a tiny zit she'd been monitoring just in front of her ear. Its time had come. She angled her head so she could see it in the mirror, and she pinched it to a crater. It was so satisfying that she hunted for more.

No! the pores on her nose cried in unison, *Why are you doing this to us?*

"Shut up—I'm helping you," she whispered to them.

Bullshit! the porous chorus replied. *This is just a pretext for attacking your own face!*

She answered by applying more pressure.

By the time Sam made her blotchy way back into bed, Chris was awake, face aglow, eyes on his phone. He asked her for her email address. Since she was an English professor, she'd be a great person to read his screenplay.

Sam shot out of bed. "You didn't say anything about writing screenplays."

"Don't be a snob," he said. "I write, I direct, I'm even learning how to edit. Come back."

Sam obeyed. "What have you directed?"

He looked away, "Oh, nothing special. Just like, marketing videos. Some, uh, sports."

"Cool," Sam said flatly. "Seriously though, you don't want me to read it. I don't know anything about movies, and I'm not an English professor. I *was*, past tense, a 'composition lecturer.'"

"Bah—what's your email?"

"Maybe later. I have to sleep now."

Chris leaned away from her. She heard him set his phone down on her dusty floor and then felt him turn toward her, scoot over in bed, and press his warm front against her back. She scooted back into his warmth despite herself.

The next day Sam squinted through her hangover at the first few pages of his screenplay. She just wanted to make sure it was awful, and it *was*, beginning with the machine-gun murder of a bunch of Iraqi women and children, then cut to PFC Ramirez on top of a tank, sitting behind the smoking gun.

"Oops," he says, and the other guys just stare at him, like, *WTF?*

Lieutenant Barnes comes running from around the corner, pulling up his pants, holding a roll of toilet paper. "What in tarnation? Ramirez! You sick son of a bitch!" But Ramirez turns the machine gun on Lt. Barnes.

Sam stopped there. What had she been thinking when she took this guy home? Maybe her primate brain had been attracted to his extreme confidence, the way he seemed to stroll through the world, taking what he wanted. There had to be some kind of evolutionary advantage to that. Or maybe she'd just hoped he'd fuck some of that extreme confidence into her. With each of his thrusts she'd gain some of his strength. When they were finished, he'd be a limp, depleted thing, and she'd be a great red-scaled demoness with a thrashing tail and sharp talons.

That certainly hadn't happened. Sam could add "succubus" to her list of unsuitable occupations. Still sitting in that waiting room next to her snoring grandfather, she ignored the wet spot she felt in her underwear and thought instead about what she wanted for lunch.

The receptionist finally turned her silver-shadowed eyes on them. "Mr. Vigor will see you now."

7

Nick Vigor resembled a giant toad with its own personal trainer, nutritionist, and tailor. The sunlight streaming through the wall of windows bounced off his bald head, which skipped a neck altogether and flowed straight into broad shoulders that strained against a tight white dress shirt. He strode forward on short legs and offered firm, abrupt handshakes to Sam and Donald.

"So glad to finally meet you!" His large, dark eyes scanned Sam from head to toe and back to head. He noticed that she'd noticed. "I'm sorry—I was expecting someone younger."

"Oh? Why's that?"

"Because Cynthia looks so young," he said, holding his wide smile. "Oh—but she's your stepmother! That makes sense."

Sam had no response. It was hard to concentrate on anything but the panoramic view of the city and the mountains. Then she noticed many pointy weapons on the wall behind Vigor's enormous desk, and it was hard to concentrate on anything but those. There were crossed daggers, cutlasses (or were they sabers?), and maybe rapiers, framed by a horizontally mounted spear above and longsword below.

Vigor walked back to his desk, gesturing to two pop art chairs in the shape of cartoon lightning bolts, chairs that didn't look like they could support the weight of a pair of pants, let alone a human ass.

The CEO himself had no chair. A whirring began behind the desk, and he started walking slowly in place. "It's a walking desk. Just ignore it."

Donald pointed to the spear, which was tipped with a sharp-looking gray blade. "What is that, African?"

"Maori," Vigor said, walking. "It was pulled out of an English soldier's back in Wairau Valley, 1845. I just love underdogs. That dagger on the far left allegedly lived under a mattress in a Flemish brothel, just in case any of the customers got unruly." He showed his perfect, extremely white teeth and glanced at his watch. "So! What can I do for you?"

Sam said, "Do you have any idea where my dad might be?"

"No," Vigor said, eyebrows furrowing. "As I told your father's assistant, he was in fine fettle when he left me yesterday. But there's always a logical explanation for these kinds of things." He steepled his fingers in front of his thin lips, a gesture that didn't quite work on a walking man. "Maybe he went out to celebrate our deepening partnership, and he's sleeping it off."

"My dad doesn't know how to celebrate."

Vigor studied Sam, and Sam caught herself waiting for him to walk through the desk and past her. "You remind me a little of my daughter. I don't think she'd simultaneously try to take down my company and tell the world I'm a coward, but we have our issues."

Hot blood rushed to Sam's cheeks. "That's not what I—"

"As long as you're here, can you tell me why you did something so destructive?"

Sam sighed. She was starting to regret writing that essay, especially since it hadn't done anyone any good. "I thought there were some things that needed to be said. Corporate control of government is fascism. Our rights are being taken away from us.

Climate change is happening, and we're not doing anything to stop it."

"So you wrote an essay," he said with a big smile. "That's so cute! And I bet people said you'd never use that English degree!"

Donald laughed at that, and earned a glare from Sam.

"Look," Vigor continued, "I don't know much about your father as a father, but he's my business partner, so when you speak ill of him, you're speaking ill of me. When you threaten his business, you threaten mine. And you shouldn't do that."

"Um, OK." Sam looked at Donald, waiting for him to say something aggressive, like, "You should stick your Maori spear where the sun don't shine." But Donald said nothing. He just groaned. Then his eyes bugged, and he fell out of the chair. Clutching his left bicep with his right hand, he gasped and twitched on the office carpet.

Sam rushed to help him. Vigor jumped off of his treadmill, staggering and nearly falling on the unmoving floor.

"Pop!" Sam shouted. "Pop!"

Donald's eyes rolled back in his head, his left arm spasmed. Then he went still.

"Heart attack!" Vigor said. "I'll get the defibrillator from the kitchen! You call 911!" He ran out of the office while Sam fumbled with her phone.

Donald sat up. "Hurry! Check out that computer!"

"What? The fuck!" Sam scrambled to her feet. "I thought you were dying!"

"Sha! Get the file!"

"What file?" But Sam rushed over to the computer. She clicked the mouse. The screen came alive. "Gross! He plays fantasy football!" Next to the window full of names and numbers and the NFL logo, another window was open, showing an artist's rendering of a multi-storied, faux-Spanish building fronted by palm trees. The header read "La Bohème, 801-899 Ocean Front Walk."

Sam heard the hard heels of Vigor's dress shoes coming quickly down the hall. She darted around the desk but cut the corner too short. She tripped, fell practically on top of Donald, so that she was very much at his side when the door opened and Vigor came through with defibrillator pads in hand.

"Oh," Donald said. "Oh."

"I'm so glad you're OK!" Sam knew she was a terrible actor.

Vigor hung his head a few degrees. He seemed disappointed to see that Donald was conscious, like he'd been looking forward to shocking life back into the man, or at least making his body jump. "What happened?"

"He just woke up." Sam's hands were still shaking, which helped her sell it.

"I just need to raise my blood sugar." Donald slowly sat up, and the three of them looked at each other in awkward silence.

Vigor was unconvinced. "What about the pain in your arm?"

"Cramp? I play a lot of racquetball."

"Well," Sam struggled to pull Donald to his feet. "I better get him some food."

Vigor frowned. "Aren't you being a little casual about this? Shouldn't you wait for the ambulance?"

"Nah! I mean, the phone rang and rang, so I hung up. I think he's OK. Just needs rest and liquids, some protein."

Donald gave Vigor a goofy smile. "Maybe all your walking made me dizzy."

Sam grinned insanely, "And we can't afford to pay for any unnecessary ambulance trips since I'm unemployed—ha-ha-ha." Sam straightened her shirt, brushed her hair out of her eyes. "I'll drive him home and make sure he's OK. Thanks!"

Sam didn't look back.

"Bye-bye!" Vigor said. Before they were through the doors, the treadmill resumed its quiet whirring.

8

Back in the car, Donald snapped his fingers at Sam. "OK, kid, hand me that file."

"What file? There is no file!" Sam was still pissed about having to pay for parking because Donald had suddenly and conveniently needed to find a restroom right as they'd approached the attendant.

"Why no file?"

"Well, Pop, I don't know what file you're talking about, and even if I did, I wouldn't have had time to find it. And I definitely wouldn't have had time to copy it onto a drive, which I don't even have."

"There's usually a file," Donald muttered.

They exited the garage a different way than they'd entered. No pedestrians in sight, but dense car traffic lined the canyon formed by the skyscrapers. Sam managed to squeeze in ahead of a texting idiot before he looked up and shot forward. They were on 6th Street, which was one-way in the wrong direction, but Sam just went with the flow. Donald seemed lost, so she'd figure it out by herself.

Not remotely lost, Donald was concentrating, reviewing every detail of the meeting while opening himself up to anything he might have missed the first time around. His brain used to be a sponge. He could capture every line of dialogue, every sound effect, every stage direction. These days, though, there were blank spaces, unconscious edits he just had to trust kept whatever was essential. Now what stood out most in his mind was their initial encounter with Vigor, who'd appraised the kid like she was a sturgeon of dubious freshness and then compared her to Cynthia.

"Hey," he said to Sam, "how does Vigor know what your step-mother looks like?"

"She's not my stepmother!" Sam squeezed the wheel with both hands. "Maybe the Vigors and Waxmans hang out together as, like, couples." The glass skyscrapers had given way to older, gentler buildings of brick and stone. Here, people walked the side-walks. "Where am I going? Can we get some food?"

"Maybe Cindy and Vigor are having an affair and decided to ice your father, get him out of the way. Let's find her, observe her for a bit."

"That's completely insane. She's at work. And her name is Cynthia."

"OK. Maybe Jack's been kidnapped, and she got a ransom note, but she's not telling anyone about it."

"Really? That's what you think? That she stole her plan from Danny DeVito in *Ruthless People*?"

"Good flick—big box office." Donald rubbed his chin. "But you heard her on the phone; they were having problems. She'd do a lot better as his widow than his ex. And you can't get a ransom for a husband whose wife doesn't want him back."

"Completely insane," Sam repeated. But she saw Donald deflate a little, so she added, "but sure, it's a motive."

"Pershing Square?" Donald pointed at the park Sam drove past. "Where you going, kid?"

"I have no idea."

"Well, make a left."

Sam signaled, but the cars crowded into the left lane weren't moving, and the cars in her lane were. She wasn't good at L.A. driving. She never forgot that she wasn't the center of the world, that she had no business stopping all of the traffic in her lane just so she could wait for an opening in the next one. Often, like now, she drove for a while in the wrong direction. They crossed Maple, passed stores that sold piñatas, quinceañera dresses, bags, rugs.

"What the hell are you doing?"

"It's called 'being considerate.' Just chill out!"

"No, it's called 'being a wimp.' Start moving over. They'll let you in."

Donald reached for the wheel, but Sam shrieked and slapped his hand away. "Never, *ever*, touch the wheel!"

"Sorry," Donald said. He looked out the window, "Oy, the humanity."

Pieces of cardboard and torn newspaper pages littered the sidewalk. The block was lined by long, short, windowless buildings with huge metal doors, some open, most shut. People Sam didn't want to look at too closely stood or sat or sprawled around tents, tarps, and carts. People limped, wheeled, crutched, and crawled.

Sam finally managed to change lanes, and at the next intersection she turned left. She saw signs for the freeway, found the 10 West ramp. She accelerated up it and away from the carnival of suffering, eager to be back in a more familiar, less desperate neighborhood, particularly the one that housed her bed.

She took a deep breath. "I probably haven't been down there since we fed the homeless in high school. It's so much worse now."

Donald just looked out his window.

"Anyway," Sam said, to change the subject in her mind, "I don't like Cynthia, but I don't think she had my dad kidnapped. And there's no way she'll agree to see us while she's at work. She's a power player. Why don't we get lunch, and then I'll take you home? Unless you want to call the dentist? See if they can squeeze you in?"

"Don't change the subject. You can't just give up."

"But I can. I *so* can."

"No. You can give up on romances, friendships, even family, but you can't give up on the job."

"Uh, what job?"

"Uh, finding a missing person?" he said, mocking her. "Bringing him back to the bosom of his loving family?"

Sam took a deep breath. "We're not exactly closing in on him, are we? And I think I've earned a little staycation. Especially after your fake heart attack back there."

"This is your father we're talking about! If you or Tina, or Harpo, or Samuel was missing, you know he'd keep looking."

There was so much wrong with that statement, but Sam could only focus on the grammar. "'*Were* missing.' But yeah, I'm sure he would."

Donald said nothing for a while, and Sam kept driving in the direction of his apartment. As they passed the Fairfax exit, Donald smiled and patted her shoulder. "Get off at National."

"No."

"Yes. It'll be good practice for you to see something through to the end."

Sam looked doubtful. "Will it? The end is usually the worst part. And I'm hungry."

"Here." He handed her a butterscotch candy.

Sam unwrapped it and put it in her mouth. It was kind of delicious. And the lot *was* on the way to Donald's, and they'd probably just get turned away at the gate.

9

THE SIGHT of the studio's ornately arched main gate brought Donald right back to his first successful screenplay, *Mortgage for Murder*. He was twenty-seven, suffering at the *Examiner* because the paper had moved decidedly rightward. The editors wanted Hollywood scandal, not deep investigation of bad policing and systemic corruption. Donald had no choice but to allegorize it. He did his pointless job during the day, came home, ate quickly with his wife and child, and stayed up half the night writing his screenplay, living the cliché.

The whole film was a neat little metaphor: Beautiful Angela is married to banker Lawrence Folsom, a thinly disguised Mayor Poulson, the red baiter who killed public housing and seized Hispanic-owned land to build Dodger Stadium. In Donald's film, the banker never loses his smug grin, even as he belittles Angela in public, beats her in private, and withholds money just because he can. But Angela has some fight in her. At The King Eddy Saloon, she finds a down-on-his-heels sap named Art who makes the mistake of falling in love with her. She hires Art to kill her husband, but she has no money of her own, so they agree she'll pay him in installments. In Donald's original existentialist draft,

Art proves that he isn't a sap, and Angela falls for him. She murders her husband herself and gets the gas chamber. All Art's left with is a pair of diamond earrings she gave him to remember her by. He pawns them to pay his rent.

The studio bought the film and produced it—with some changes. Art, they decided, *is* a sap, and he gets shot in the back by the cops, and the wife still dies, insane and unrepentant, in the gas chamber. Kind of twisted up the whole point of the film, in Donald's opinion, but they put him on contract, so he kept his mouth shut.

When the kid rolled down the window to talk to their third security guard of the day, Donald leaned over her and told him they were here to see Leo Bronson. They couldn't use Cynthia's name if they wanted to maintain the element of surprise.

The guard typed on his computer, looked back through the window. "No one here by that name."

"Right—prostate. How about Larry Federman? No—pancreas. How about—"

"Sir, drop-ins are highly discouraged. You're supposed to have an appointment."

"I know, kid, I know. Just one more: Bruce Evans? He's still on the lot, isn't he?"

The security guard sighed, but he looked up the name. "Big Cheese Pictures?"

"That's the one." Donald sat back in his seat, said to Sam, "Bruce is an old poker buddy. And I mean old. Born Baruch Eisenstein. This guy was like, the second Jew in Hollywood. The first Jew sent for him because he had no one to argue with. Smart guy, too. When he was on top, he negotiated an office on the lot and an allowance at the commissary, *for life*. Nuclear winter could happen, the Russians could take over all of Hollywood, and they'd still have to give him his little office. Aliens could land—"

"I get it. When was that?"

"'62, I think. Before the Kennedy thing. He hasn't made a movie in thirty years, but they can't get rid of him."

Sam picked up her phone, told it to search for "Big Cheese Pictures." All that came up were high-resolution wheels of parmesan and blocks of cheddar, literally *big pictures of cheese*.

Holding the receiver to his ear, the guard said, "Mr. Evans? There's a Donald West here to see you?"

"Donald West? Donald *West*?" They heard a hoarse shout through the phone. "Is he a slouchy, big-nosed, shifty-eyed bastard?"

The guard peered through the car window. "Yes, sir."

"Oh, send him in! Send him the fuck in!"

"He sounds nice." Sam drove them around the lot at the prescribed five miles per hour, coasting past a couple of office buildings and a series of soundstages, the edge of a New Yorkish city street, the edge of a small town. Donald had forgotten about this landscape and how it had provided the settings for his dreaming life for decades. These few acres had been the world to him when he was young and hopeful, when life was at its most exciting.

He'd also forgotten, until he saw Bruce—poor, shrinking, wrinkling Bruce—rolling up his sleeves and shifting his weight from one foot to the other in the doorway of his little beige bungalow, that Bruce was no longer his friend.

"Come here, you, shtick drek, you fercockte kholerye, you momzer! Let me give you the ass-kicking I owe you!"

"Um," Sam said, slowing to a stop, "should I turn around?"

But Donald opened the door and climbed out. "Bruce! Bubbe! What are you angry about? We're mishpocha!"

"What the fuck are you talking about?" Bruce's huge white eyebrows jumped up and down as he spoke. "I told you if I ever saw you again, I'd do to your face what you did to my movie."

"That was ... many years ago, Bruce, and I apologized."

"You did not," Bruce's fists were clenched still, but he'd obviously grown tired of the boxer's stance, so he dropped his hands. "You never apologized."

"Well, I'm sorry."

Sam got between them and asked her grandfather, "What'd you do to his movie?"

Bruce gave Sam a once-over. "Who's this beautiful girl you've obviously abducted and brought here against her will?"

"Samantha," Sam held out her hand. "Granddaughter. Here semi-voluntarily."

Bruce shook it, used his other hand to scratch his unevenly shaved cheek. "I'm sorry, honey, but you've got some defective genes. Your grandfather jinxed my whole career."

"As I remember it, I took a moral stand."

"That happens *in* the movies, not in the *making* of movies, you schmuck." He turned to Sam, "He broke our leading man's nose, blackened his eye. Fucked up the schedule, cost me a fortune. Jinxed me, permanently."

"That guy insulted the script supervisor."

"Who you were trying to make."

"That had nothing to do with it. I stood up for decency."

"Bullshit. You wanted to make her, and you wanted to punch that shaygetz in the face for weeks because he was on the upswing and you were on the down. You knew you were washed up. You committed career suicide to avoid getting executed."

"I'm telling you, I was being chivalrous."

"Anyway," Sam said, before Bruce could reveal any more detail about her grandfather's sex life, "thank you, Mr. Evans, for letting us in. Can you point us to the legal department? We need to spy on my dad's wife."

Bruce Evans furrowed his bushy brows. "What's this? Here, come inside and tell me what the hell you're talking about."

As Donald approached the door, Bruce tried to sucker-punch

him. Some buried muscle memory from Donald's boxing days kicked in, and Donald's torso tilted just out of reach and then bounced back with a body blow. Bruce crumpled and gasped for breath.

"Pop!" Sam screamed. "What the fuck?"

"I'm sorry," Donald said. "So sorry. Muscle memory." They helped Bruce to his feet and supported him through the doorway and into a chair.

"You—meshuga—bastard," Bruce wheezed. "Only you would hit a ninety-year-old man!"

"Are you OK? Should we call an ambulance?"

"I'm fine! Sit!"

They sat on a couch and chairs facing a TV that took up most of one wall. Bruce took another minute to regain his breath. Then he said, "Spill it."

"We're trying to track down her father," Donald said. "Either he took a bunk or it's a snatch job. We wanna get a peek at the second wife."

"I'm not bored," Bruce's eyebrow antennae went high and slowly descended as he spoke, "and this kid is cute, kind of a *Dragon Tattoo* meets *Fifty Shades* meets Liz Lemon. Who's the dick?"

"I am," Donald said.

"What? Like, *you* you? Don, you're way off demo on this. You want anything greened these days, you need hot people, young people, in 3-D. With," eyes scanning Sam, "full frontal."

"Gross."

"This isn't a movie, Bruce. Cindy—Cynthia—works in legal."

"Cynthia? Waxman? She deposed me once. Little sexual misunderstanding . . . I thought the intern was a hooker."

"Honest mistake," Donald said. "Anyway, we're going to sneak in there, observe her behavior, then ambush her with a few pointed questions."

"We are?" Sam felt that line form between her eyebrows, the one her mother said needed Botox.

"Well, I'm not busy," Bruce put on a golf cap, picked up his cane. "I'll walk you."

He led the way down a tree-lined sidewalk, past a small-town square of the New England variety. A couple of inches of "snow" dusted the mailboxes and rooftops. Sam dimly recognized the set from a made-for-TV movie about a figure skater who teaches the local bad boy how to love before she gets cancer and dies bravely.

"See how the tree branches are bare almost all the way to the top?" Bruce said to Sam. "They get up on ladders and snip each one by hand so it looks like winter in Massachusetts. Commissary's just up there if you want a nosh."

"Please!"

Bruce pointed to a beige layer cake of a building with golf carts parked along the sidewalk. One was an eight-seater, with a tour guide shouting into a headset microphone the history of the commissary and its notable patrons. Though it was November, the day had grown sunny and warm. Attractive, well-dressed people sat at picnic tables scattered here and there.

One of those people, Sam noticed, only about thirty feet beyond the tour group in the cart, was Cynthia. She wore a slim gray business suit that said she'd break your balls herself but could afford to pay someone else to do it. Her blonde highlighted hair was pulled back, and large sunglasses hid her eyes. She looked too glamorous for a woman with three teenage children, a stressful job, and a missing husband. She sat across from a man in a suit. His face was turned away from Sam, but he had full, dark hair. Cynthia was leaning over the table toward him, smiling, and even reaching across to briefly touch his hand.

Sam pulled Donald and Bruce behind the golf cart. "Look!" she whispered and pointed.

"What am I looking at?" Donald said.

An elderly woman sitting in the last row of the tour cart leaned back and scowled at them. "Shush! I can't hear!"

Sam whispered, "Straight ahead. Gray suit, sunglasses."

"Oooh!" Bruce said at top volume. "Is that one of the Hemsworths?"

"No, the woman—it's Cynthia!" Sam answered, too loudly. Cynthia looked in their direction just as the golf cart suddenly lurched away. Exposed, Sam tried to salvage some dignity by stepping forward and saying a cheerful hello. Donald and Bruce followed, the world's oldest entourage.

Cynthia stood up. "Samantha! What are you doing here?"

"Just hanging out with Pop and his buddy Bruce," Sam said. "What are you up to?"

"Having lunch!" Cynthia said. "With a colleague. Tim, this is my . . . husband's daughter, Samantha. And my . . . husband's father. And Bruce Evans—nice to see you again, Bruce."

"You look lovely as ever," Bruce replied. "And that's all I'm going to say."

Tim was young, probably not yet thirty, with dreamy green eyes and a perfectly symmetrical smile. He seemed to blush a little as he stood up and shook Sam's hand.

While he shook Donald's hand, Donald shot Cynthia a hard look, "Are you sleeping with Nick Vigor?"

Sam said, "Come on!"

Cynthia slapped Donald.

Tim's face went completely red and he jerked his hand away. "Just remembered, I have a meeting!"

Sam noticed Cynthia's phone still on the picnic table next to the remains of her salad. She didn't think past *Grab!*, which she did, and *Run!*, which she also did.

"Samantha!" Cynthia yelled. "Stop!" When that didn't work, she added, "Thief!"

But Sam was at full speed, running along the side of a soundstage, already feeling the cigarette and wishing these buildings weren't so freaking long. She finally got to a corner and turned. As she did, she glanced over her shoulder. One security guard pursued her in a golf cart. Behind him another jogged and panted into his walkie-talkie.

What was she doing? She had no idea, but she saw the familiar fire escapes and stoops of the New York City set. She sprinted toward it, spotted a bodega on the far corner. Flung open the door, found fake food on the shelves and fake meats behind the counter and a fake door that might lead to a fake closet if it opened. And that fake closet might have a fake secret passage, and that—

Focus! She saw another door to the right and went through that, into an empty space of plywood and two-by-fours. She found a plank door to her left, burst through that back outside, across an alley and around the corner of a small office building, nearly colliding with a young man holding a walkie-talkie, who cried, "Stop! Fifty-one-fifty! Fifty-one-fifty!" while Sam disappeared into a crowd of people in late '70s clothing silently protesting something.

Someone shouted, "Cut! Security!" through a megaphone.

Sam broke through the crowd, coming up quickly on two improbably attractive EMTs pulling a stretcher out of an ambulance. She swerved to avoid them and darted through the hospital doors. Inside there were about fifteen feet of entrance and furnished waiting room that ran abruptly into more plywood and two-by-fours. Gasping and seeing spots, she ran down a dark hallway and out another door, and it was like she'd just burst through a door of the White House, just like the staffer who gets vaporized by aliens in *Mars Attacks*. She glanced back—two new blue-shirted security guards gave chase, walkie-talkies squawking, and she heard a high-pitched whine in the air that may have been a drone—"Scramble the drones!" someone must have said—so she pulled a Crazy Ivan, going quickly left toward a line of bungalows, then right, and ending up in the wintry, eerily silent small town set. She ran into the park but tripped on the blanket of snow that was actually a huge sheet of cotton. With no breath or strength left, she scrambled behind the gazebo at the center of the plaza and collapsed.

Phone—unlock code. Her first and only idea was the date of Cynthia's wedding to Jack. She remembered because she had gotten drunk and kissed a boy (a cousin of Cynthia's) at the party. It was her first time doing either, and the resulting diary entry was her most hilarious and embarrassing.

She was breathing so hard she typed the code wrong. But on her second try, the wedding date worked. What did that mean? Think about it later. Sam scrolled, found no evidence of any contact with Nick Vigor, and no emails conveniently titled "Ransom Request" or "We have your husband" or "You Have 24 Hours to Respond." She was an idiot for entertaining Pop's absurd theory for even a minute. Then she noticed several recent texts from Tim.

She read them from the bottom up, most recent first:

Tim: *Be right there!*

Cynthia: *Lunch? Now? Please???*

Tim: *OK.*

Cynthia: *In 10.*

Tim: *In 15?*

Cynthia: *Coffee?*

Before Sam could read any more, two beefy security guards threw themselves on top of her.

10

SAM KICKED one guard in the shin before the other pinned her arms at her side. He flipped her onto her stomach so the other guard, now very angry, could handcuff her. They hauled her to her feet, completely violated her with a pat-down, and carted her to some sort of studio police station where Donald and Cynthia were waiting.

The guards sat Donald and Sam down in the back of a room filled with surveillance monitors. The lot commander, who might also have been Steve Martin's stunt double, sauntered in wiping his mouth with a napkin.

"Well, your little dash through my lot cost the studio roughly a hundred grand. And that number could go way up if Sergeant Marino files a PTSD claim."

"You guys have sergeants?" Donald said at the same time Sam asked who Sergeant Marino was.

"The officer you attacked."

"Let's not overdo it, Rick," Cynthia said. She'd been standing there shaking her head, refusing even to look at Sam or Donald, but she seemed to have come to a decision. "The man has a bruised shin. The shoot was delayed for five minutes. Donald here is easily confused, and Samantha is heavily medicated and sick with worry over her missing father. Also, they're broke. The studio would be lucky to get a hundred out of them, let alone a hundred thousand."

Sam wanted to argue a couple of points, but she had enough sense to keep her mouth shut. In the end, she and Donald were let off with a lifetime ban. Commander Rick directed an underling to photograph them for the Unwelcome list.

While that was happening, Sam kept an eye on Cynthia, who was scrolling through something on her phone. Cynthia looked up at her, their eyes met, and Sam thought she saw something distinctly guilty in that glance.

"Cynthia," Sam said, "is there anything you want to tell us? Anything we should know about who might or might not have a motive to kidnap Dad or hurt him?"

"No," Cynthia said. But then she said to Commander Rick, "I'll walk them to their car."

"I'm sorry to hear about your husband," Rick said to her. "I know some great private investigators who can find him."

"No need," Donald said. "We'll have him home by dinner time. By the way, I loved you in *Cheaper by the Dozen 2*. One of those rare sequels—"

"Get off my lot. And no detours!" Commander Rick nodded to the video screens, "We'll be watching."

Cynthia led the way through a maze of little buildings. They passed a foursome of cowboys squeezed into a golf cart and a bunch of medieval peasants playing half-court basketball on a rusty hoop.

While they walked, Donald time-traveled again, to 1963 or '64. He was in the middle of his divorce, working day and night punching up some dreck Western version of *Hamlet*. Instead of the Prince of Denmark, they had "Hamilton Lester," son of Malachi Lester, miner turned mining magnate. Malachi's jealous younger brother, who happens to be the Sheriff, murders him, and it's up to young Hammy to avenge his death. Rewrite after rewrite by various hacks of varying intelligence had muddied the themes of alienation and guilt and oversimplified the psychology of the indecisive son.

Donald had been in his little office trying to shoehorn some nuance into Hamilton's final decision to take revenge on the Sheriff and his cronies when Sylvia stormed into his office with young Jackie and dumped him on Donald's couch.

"I've got things to do today," she said, taking out her compact and touching up her powder. "Give him dinner and drop him by the house after seven."

"Excuse me?"

"You heard me. He hasn't seen you in weeks."

Donald's slightly chubby, pre-adolescent progeny slouched shyly on the couch. His belly strained the zipper of his pants, and his bare shins showed between socks and the too-short pants. She'd probably made him wear those on purpose so Donald would have to acknowledge what a poor provider he was. Couldn't even buy his son a pair of new pants!

But Donald and Jack ended up having a lovely day together. First stop was the massive costume department, where Donald slipped a double sawbuck to his friend Loraine in exchange for a nice pair of trousers.

"Know what movie they're from?" Jack asked, while she hemmed the cuffs.

"*Hud*, I think? Yeah, that kid who played Lonnie wore 'em."

"Gee whiz!" (Donald's memories of Jack's childhood often became confused with memories of *Leave It to Beaver* episodes watched half-drunk, so much of Young Jack's dialogue had a Beaverish flavor.)

Jack hadn't been to the lot in at least a year, and he'd become a real movie buff. Kicking out his legs in his new, roomier pants, he asked if he could see the soundstage where they made *Robinson Crusoe on Mars*.

"You *liked* that film?" Donald asked.

"Oh yeah, Pop! Think of how neat it would be to explore Mars!"

"But what's on Mars?" Donald said. "Nothing! You can't go to the movies on Mars. You can't sit at the drug store and watch the girls walk by. There are no girls! There's nothing but rocks!"

Jack thought about this for a moment. "Yeah, Pop, but there aren't any Russians either. Nobody's gonna nuke the Red Planet. It's completely safe—like a giant fall-out shelter!"

"Oy," Donald said, because it didn't take a shrink to see that the kid was terrified of things far beyond his control, things Donald barely allowed himself to contemplate, and only with help from his good friends J & B. Wrenched by the heartache of fatherhood, Donald took a deep breath and tried to straighten the kid out.

"You been studying this in school?"

Jack nodded. "We do drills."

"Of course. Well, let me tell you, kid, I don't think you have to worry."

"But the Cuban Missile Crisis—"

"That *was* a close one," Donald conceded, "but you gotta understand Mutually Assured Destruction. Everyone knows that if they press the button, the other guy's gonna press the button, and no one's crazy enough to risk that."

Jack nodded again, but he didn't seem all that comforted.

"Hey, what say we walk to the commissary? I'll buy you an ice cream."

"Gee whiz, Pop!"

If Donald remembered correctly (which, he probably didn't), it was only a few weeks later that Jack and his friends sneaked into a showing of *Dr. Strangelove*, and Jack had nightmares for months.

Donald was so lost in his 1964 reverie that he missed all of Sam and Cynthia's first real conversation, ever.

It began with Cynthia's confession: "The answer is yes, OK? I'm sleeping with Tim. But it's purely physical. Your dad just doesn't want me anymore."

"I'm not totally comfortable—"

"For about the last year or two, I've had to be the initiator, and at least half the time he said he was too tired. Six months ago, I finally stopped trying, and since then, nothing!"

"This is a lot of personal info—"

"But I'm still at—or near—my sexual peak! And I figured, if I need to find my own intimacy, why not go with a young man? When Jack was my age, he got to have me as a young woman."

"This feels inappropriate?"

"Please, Samantha. Can't you just try to be an adult for five minutes?"

Sam nodded and took a deep, adultifying breath. "Are you going to keep seeing him?"

Cynthia cried, "No! I'm his boss. I'll get fired, shunned, if anyone finds out. Your dad would leave me in a second. And I don't want that. Tim's not as smart or as thoughtful as your father. He's kind of a big, dumb animal, really. Watches a lot of sports, plays fantasy football."

"Gross."

"Right? But he thinks I'm the smartest, sexiest woman in the world." She looked down at the sidewalk cracks. "I sound so pathetic."

"No, you don't." For the first time in nineteen years, Sam considered the possibility that a human soul inhabited this blonde android. "I don't blame you. I never understood why you wanted to marry my dad in the first place."

"Are you kidding? I was totally in love with him! I mean, I still love him. He has a brilliant mind, a huge heart."

"I think you mean 'enlarged heart.'"

"He's a patient, generous teacher and loving father, the kind of person who wakes up every morning and tries to make the world a little better. And he used to be funny. He used to take himself more lightly. Something's changed—I don't know what."

"Yeah, I know what you mean," Sam conceded, though "funny" had never been a word she'd used to describe her father.

They found the car where they'd left it outside Bruce's bungalow. Cynthia said, "Call me if you hear anything, and I'll do the same. Follow the road straight to the front gate. No stopping, Donald. Or Sam. I don't even know which one of you to treat like the grown-up." She gave them quick, strong hugs, and walked away.

"Can we please get some lunch now?" Sam asked Donald.

"I could eat."

THE INDOLENT LILLY'S main charms were that it was never crowded and no one in a hurry went anywhere near the place. Sam and Donald sat at the rickety table by the window for about ten minutes before a server in board shorts finally wandered over to them and took their order.

As the server drifted toward the kitchen, Sam rubbed her temples. "I still can't believe you got me banned for life. Like, I never *wanted* to write for film, but now I actually can't, at least not at that studio."

"Hey, I'm not the one who ran through the shot. You never, *never,* run through the shot."

She'd just acted instinctively, both in the running and the shin-kicking. For the next few minutes, she silently interrogated herself. When exactly had she decided to stop thinking? To just forget about the consequences of her actions? Instinct had never been her strong suit. She thought of the *Seinfeld* episode in which

George realizes that his instincts are terrible, and he needs to do the opposite of whatever he thinks he should do. By the end of the episode, he's dating a beautiful woman and working for the Yankees. It just might be a strategy worth trying.

The server finally reappeared and set down a plate that contained a few slices of lox and a big scoop of cream cheese. A few minutes later, he came back with a slightly burned bagel. Sam's veggie burger arrived five minutes after that, followed surprisingly quickly by a small plate of avocado slices the sandwich maker had forgotten. Lastly came the water.

Donald, grimacing from tooth pain, chewed slowly. He squinted at the lentil-carrot-mushroom mess oozing out between the bread in Sam's hand. "You can't just order a hamburger? You look like you could use the iron."

"I don't eat meat, Pop. Too much suffering. Also, animal agriculture is a major contributor to global warming."

"Fine, fine. Gey gezunterheyt," Donald said.

They ate in silence until Sam's butt vibrated. She pulled out her phone, saw "Mom." This was unusual since they hardly spoke in between their regular Wednesday phone calls and Sunday brunches. She went to answer it, but her thumb was so in the habit of rejecting calls that it automatically swiped "Ignore." She cursed and called back.

"Hello? Mom?"

"Hi, how are you?"

"Fine, is everything all right?"

"Sure, fine," Sam's mom coughed. "Well, Matthew's got diarrhea again, but that's what happens when you eat every piece of shit you can sniff out." Sam's mom was obsessed with her Great Danes, Matthew and Lady Mary Crawley.

"That's rough," Sam said, trying to be patient.

"Yeah. The vet says it could be parasites, or anxiety, or just some evolutionary thing. If it lasts another day, I'll have to take in a fecal sample."

"Uh-huh. Listen, Mom, I'm kind of in the middle of something, and I bet you didn't call to tell me about Matthew's coprophagia, right?"

"Such a vocabulary! You would have been a great doctor."

"Mom," Sam said. She wasn't that annoyed. She'd been wanting to use that word in a sentence for nine years.

"Well, I was just calling to see if you've spoken to your father. He left me a very strange message."

"He did? When? He's been missing since last night."

"Missing? Where?"

Sam didn't feel the need to reply to this. "Mom, *when* did he leave the message?"

"This morning, but I didn't see it until just now. Nobody calls the landline or leaves a message on it. We haven't talked since his annual Yom Kippur apology, but he said my number was the only one he remembered. Said he was stuck in Venice, and he'd been beaten and robbed."

"He's been beaten!" Sam said to Donald. "And robbed!"

"Oh, honey," her mother said. "I'm sure he's fine. You know how dramatic he is, and he didn't sound too bad—a little distracted, but OK."

"He said he was in Venice? Do you have the number he called from?"

Susan told her to hang on a second, accidentally hung up on her, called her back and gave her the number.

Sam dialed it and filled Donald in while the phone rang and rang. Her dad obviously had no money and no phone. How would he get home? They had to go look for him.

Finally, a man picked up: "So you should come on down here, lend me some money."

"Excuse me?"

"Yeah, come down. Help me get my Ferrari out of the shop."

"Um, OK," Sam tried. "Where are you?"

There was a pause, and the man said, "Didn't you call me?"

"And who are you?"

"This is a public telephone, baby. What are you wearing?"

"Are you in Venice?"

"Go Gondoliers! You're wearing sexy *panties*, aren't you? What color are your *panties*? What cut? Thong? Briefs? Hip hugger? *High* cut?"

Sam hung up and explained to Donald, "Pervert. On a payphone. I didn't know there were any left. Should we go to Venice then?"

Donald nodded, "To Venice!" Then he shouted in the direction of the kitchen, "Sweetheart? Chinese almond cookie! To go!"

11

IN THE EARLY 1900s, real estate developer Abbot Kinney tried to build a "Venice of America," a magnificent city of important buildings and shimmering waterways. The people wanted something else, so instead of a new center for high art and culture, Venice became a West Coast Coney Island. By the time Donald was hanging out here in the early 1970s as a divorced man, it wasn't even that. Just stinking canals full of trash, the abandoned half-burnt pier at Ocean Park, and a hippie chick named Rosa. Venice was the ruins of Abbot Kinney's dream, and so the perfect setting for the ruin of Donald's own dreams.

Professionally, Donald had been well on his way to becoming a punch-up hack. Personally, he'd found himself cast in a divorce melodrama with maudlin ex-wife and clinging son, and this too-young Venice beauty. Now Donald could recall only Rosa's long black hair and bright smile, and her use of the word "ball" as a verb, in such sweet phrases as *"Amorcito*, let's ball." She'd taken him to the unofficial nude beach near Windward, the first place he'd ever been hit on by a man. See? He could remember things . . . like the absolute paleness of his own dick, almost blue in the blazing, suddenly menacing sunlight, or the dust motes floating through Rosa's tiny room while she put her hot mouth on his neck, and he concluded that a hot hippie mouth on his neck was the greatest feeling in the world.

While Donald moaned softly to himself, Sam found a once-in-a-lifetime spot on Rose between Main and Pacific. She pointed out her sweet parallel-parking work, since he hadn't seemed to notice.

He looked front and back, whistled. "I'm surprised people aren't taking pictures of it."

"Totally."

"If only I had my easel and paints."

"OK." Sam got out, waited as he placed his legs onto the ground one by one and then simultaneously pulled down on the roof and pushed up from the seat to propel the rest of him out the door.

They walked straight into the afternoon sun to the boardwalk. It was a paved street, so "boardwalk" wasn't the right term for it, but that's what everyone called it. This was almost Sam's neighborhood—she lived only a mile northeast in Santa Monica—and she loved the narrow, salt-weathered houses that still held on here and there between the big modern boxes. She'd always liked the vibe here, the mix of rich and poor, housed and homeless, locals and tourists, hippies, hipsters, stoners, drunks, tweakers, gangsters, posers. Things were changing quickly though, with the tech companies and the super-rich buying all the land and building little walled fortresses. It was hard to imagine, but one day Venice could end up as bland as the rest of L.A., the city of Sam's childhood, where you got in your car bubble and went to your job bubble, or your shopping center bubble, or your friends' house bubbles, and everyone looked the same, said the same things, wore the same brands, passed the same judgments on any outliers, and it was all so empty you wanted to scream loud enough to pop all the bubbles.

Finding no such scream inside of her, Sam always just left

town. And something always pulled her back. Her mother thought it was daughterly love, but Sam knew it was at least partly failure. She'd failed to make rent in New York, failed to make a decent life in Murcia, failed to find a job somewhere else. Los Angeles was the dark cave where she holed up to lick her wounds.

But also, yes, it was daughterly love. She needed to see both of her parents at least once every couple of weeks lest seeing them become too jarring and sad. While she lived in Murcia, she once went six months without seeing them. When she finally came down for a visit, she noticed their deepening wrinkles, graying hair, increasingly eccentric minds. They were both pretty healthy, and they could both live another twenty years, but Sam half-expected sudden family cataclysm every time her phone rang. Their luck had been too good for too long, so they were due for disaster. Maybe now it had finally arrived.

Sam and Donald walked past small cottages tilting this way and that next to charmingly dilapidated apartment buildings. Palm trees swayed over jungly gardens, and people cruised by on bikes and skateboards. The boardwalk opened up before them: parking lot, public restrooms, tall palms adding vertical stripes to sand, ocean, and the distant flash of white spray from breaking waves. Though it was November, the weather was sunny and mild, and there were people everywhere. They bought and sold t-shirts, jewelry, pipes, sunglasses, paintings of widely varying style and quality, photocopied comic books, furniture, bicycle parts nailed or glued to pieces of plywood in interesting patterns.

Gusts of wind shook the palms, fluttering the vendors' t-shirts like prayer flags, propelling nonsensical messages to the gods of pop culture. There were Jedis, Storm Troopers, Captains America, Deadpools, cartoon animals, representations of Yahweh, Jesus, Buddha, Mohammed in a bear suit, Satan, both *The* Man and *Da* Man. Bacon, gluten, beer, and cannabis were praised. War, zombies, and vegetarians were denounced.

There were also new shirts celebrating the famous Venice Beach Coyote, a wily, possibly mythical creature that had been spotted slinkily roaming the boardwalk in the wee hours. Local biologists surmised that housing development in the Santa Monica Mountains had so shrunk its habitat that the coyote crossed Pacific Coast Highway in search of food. Now it lived on the rats, opossums, cats, pigeons, and discarded pizza crusts of Venice. People blamed it for every lost pet, theft, and act of senseless vandalism. One shirt showed a large-eared coyote wearing a turban and standing on its hind legs, which wore inline skates. The forepaws held an electric guitar, and beneath it, in Comic Sans, *Don't blame me, blame Hairy Perry!*

Sam and Donald walked south, scanning the crowds and the storefronts for Jack or some sign of him. In one stall, chimes made of silverware dangling from colanders clinked and clanked in the wind like a resentful dishwasher. Sam and Donald passed a huge plywood sign propped against a light pole. Uneven hand-painted letters spelled out: *It is your civic duty to start a rebellion against tyranny.*

For a block, they got trapped behind three slow-moving, androgynous young people in tight pants and bright sneakers. All their haircuts were asymmetrical. Were they Googlers? Snapchatters? Dollar Shavers? Whisperers? Maybe they worked for a new startup Sam hadn't heard of yet, creating an app that reminds people to take daily pictures of their own belly buttons so they can track the subtle changes over time. Or they were a team of geniuses hard at work on scent-replication technology so porn could finally become truly immersive.

As if picking up on Sam's thought waves, one of the techies said, "Smells like ass around here."

"I thought it smelled like urine," another one said.

"The VR version is so much better."

"Especially with the No Panhandler filter."

"Anyone want a coffee?" the third asked.

"There's free coffee at work."

"What about a slice?"

"What's your deal, man?"

"I just don't want to go back yet."

"Dude, I haven't spent a dollar on weekday food since the day I started."

"Way to contribute to the economy."

"Fuck the economy. I got student loans."

The group veered left on Market Street.

Sam picked up the pace, but she had to backtrack when Donald paused in front of a blackened shell of a two-story brick house. The windows and doors were covered in plywood, and a sign offered a reward for information leading to arrest and conviction.

"Don't see much arson these days," Donald said in what might have been a wistful tone. His gaze drifted toward the bike path, and he got lost in the rhythmic reorganization of the young flesh of two jogging women. His eyes moved from bouncing breasts to shivering buttocks.

"Hey, Dirty Old Man," Sam snapped her fingers, "should we start asking people if they've seen my dad?"

"Who? Oh, right. You have a picture?"

Sam pulled out her phone and went to the institute's website. Her father's addiction to self-promotion meant there were several professional head shots she could use.

For the next couple of hours, with time-outs for ice cream and coffee and the emptying of Donald's hyperactive bladder, they showed Jack's picture to all the street vendors they passed. They showed it to the artisanal ice cream scoopers, the baristas, the pizza and t-shirt sellers. They showed it to the tall guys at the basketball courts, the swollen guys at Muscle Beach, and the skinny guys at the skate park. No one had seen him. The only person who had more than two words for them was the bearded lady on a smoke break outside the Dungeon of Monstrosities. She said to send Jack her way when they found him. Then she twisted the end of her waxed mustache and purred.

When at last they reached the end of the shops beyond the paddle-tennis courts, and the sun had sunk nearly to the horizon, Sam conceded defeat. "So much for this plan."

Donald said nothing for a moment, and then he slapped his forehead. "We've been so stupid! We've failed to talk to a whole segment of the population."

It took Sam a few seconds to understand what he meant. "The homeless? A lot of those people are mentally ill. I'm not sure it's safe to engage them."

"What, you're afraid to talk to someone? To ask a question? You're never going to make it as a PI."

"I'm not afraid," she lied. She *was* afraid—not that they'd attack her—but that the conversation would be awkward, and she'd be judged for her awkwardness, for her ineptitude at life, for her privilege, which, after all, was the only thing that separated her from homelessness. And what if whatever quality that landed these people on the street was contagious, and Sam could catch it from slight contact? It seemed too easy to go from having a job, friends, and family to having nothing. All you had to do was give up. Before you knew it, you'd be right here.

Sam almost said she didn't want to be a PI either, but she couldn't hurt Donald's feelings like that. Also, doing this, whatever it was, with her crazy pop, was at least doing something. Maybe they'd find her dad. Even if they didn't, this was better than just worrying about him. And yes, fine, it would probably be good for her to face her fears and actually speak with some strangers.

"All right, let's dance!" she definitely did not say aloud.

She kept close to Donald as they neared two guys sitting on a bench across from a café. A pit bull leaped out at them from behind the bench, snapping its jaws and snarling. One of the men yanked the dog's chain and shouted, "Heinrich! *Nein!*"

Sam and Donald kept walking.

They saw a faded flower child sitting on another bench, sipping from a water bottle. Her silver hair fell thickly past her shoulders, and she wore a long, wine-dark sweater. Her face was weathered, and the bottom of her long floral-print dress was dirty. Sam said hi, showed her the picture of Jack on her phone, told her that he was her father.

The woman gasped. "This is your father?"

"Yes, have you seen him?" Sam's heart sped up. She had to remember to breathe.

The woman wiped away a tear. "He's a dear, dear man. Made me feel like I was sixteen again. Oh, how I enjoyed him."

"Um, OK," Sam said, trading a look with Donald.

"Did you say he was missing?" the woman asked.

"Yes. Since last night."

"I saw him last night. I thought he was just a drifter who crossed the wrong people."

"What do you mean?"

"He flew out of a moving car right in front of me, like a special delivery. I tended to his scrapes, made him a bed." She winked at Sam, "This morning he was sleeping so soundly, I just let him be. He needed to rest, after all that."

"All what?"

The woman laughed, "Oh, who knows what buccaneers like him get up to!" She reached out, squeezed Sam's hand with hers. "I have a daughter. We don't talk though. She told me to go to hell. But look at you—you could totally be my daughter..."

"That's very sweet of you," Sam said, gently pulling her hand free, "but I've got all the mothers I can handle."

"Well, don't worry. He'll turn up. Fathers always turn up, once they've had their fun."

Sam thanked her, and she and Donald walked on. Once they were out of earshot, Sam said, "What do you think?"

"Nuts."

"Maybe. But, supposing she did see him, how could he not have made it to a phone by now?"

Donald had no answer. He was looking to the west, where the sun had gone down without their noticing. They kept walking in the pink light, showing the picture to backpackers, shopping-cart people, suitcase people, plastic-bag people. Most of them were friendly. Some said they'd seen him but didn't recall when or where. Many asked for money. They needed it, they said, for: "a bite to eat"; "beer, to be completely honest with you"; "kind buds"; "tasty nugs"; "the bus to Cucamonga"; "to call my mother"; and, Sam's favorite, "an ounce of yohimbe extract to complete my love potion."

Evening settled over the beach. Sam and Donald passed the burned-out brick house again. Sam realized she knew this building. "Dr. Hoff's," she told Donald. "Pot doctor. You could get a prescription there for anything, from insomnia to menstrual cramps to overactive salivary glands . . ."

Donald said something then, but Sam didn't hear it. Her gaze had fallen on the adjacent building north of the one that had burned. It had only recently been fenced off for construction, and a sign still hung out front advertising in huge capital letters: *TOE RINGS*. Below that, the building's address: 853 Ocean Front Walk.

Something occurred to Sam. Or it almost occurred to her.

"Be right back." She jogged up the block, scanning the front of the next building, a big brick box. On the ground floor, Vine, a new wine bar, served small plates to an upscale crowd packed around tiny tables. Sam had never been inside, because small plates were bullshit. Give her a big plate or give her death. In the window, there was a sign with large, bold, underlined, and italicized letters:

<u>*Preserve Venice History!*</u>
<u>*Save 847 Ocean Front*</u>
<u>*Home of Caffe Carnevale*</u>
<u>*(Sign petition inside.)*</u>

Sam speed-walked back toward Donald, who'd taken the opportunity to light another cigarette.

"Check it out," she pointed at each building in the row from south to north. "Arson at 869. Construction already underway on 853. New owner wanting to tear down 847. I bet it's Vigor, and I bet he's also trying to buy the dispensary at 839."

"Who's Vigor?"

Sam looked hard at him. "Really?"

"I mean, why Vigor?"

"Well," now Sam looked at her shoes, "it didn't seem relevant at the time, but his computer had an architectural drawing of this whole stretch. It was kind of Spanish-looking but for some reason called La Bohème."

"Ah-ha!" Donald raised a finger in triumph. "I *knew* there was a file!" He cut his celebration short, "But what's it got to do with the misper?"

Sam's phone vibrated in her pocket. Cynthia. Again, her thumb automatically rejected the call. She cursed and called back.

"Samantha?"

"Cynthia! Is he back? Do you have him?"

"No." Cynthia's breathing was hitched.

"Where are you?" Sam asked.

"Temple. The service is about to start, but Harper just showed me . . . one of her friends sent her . . ."

The phone was silent, and then Sam heard a sob.

"What? What is it?"

"She's sending it to you now," Cynthia's voice trembled. "A video—trending. It's horrible."

Sam's phone buzzed against her ear. "OK," she said, "I'll watch it now."

"Also," Cynthia said. But then the phone went painfully silent. Sam guessed she was swallowing a sob. Tightly, Cynthia continued, "The police found his car. It was towed from Ozone Court at eleven forty-five last night. He's officially missing!"

"Give me that," Donald grabbed the phone. "Don't worry, Cindy!" he shouted. "We're close! We'll find him."

Sam heard a tinny "My name is Cynthia! Let the police do their job—"

She took back her phone. "Maybe you should postpone the bar mitzvah."

"There's no postponing!"

"OK, OK. We're in Venice, and we'll keep looking," Sam said, before realizing Cynthia had already hung up. "Rude," she said. Then she tapped on the link from Harper, and she and Donald huddled over her phone to watch the video.

12

"VENICE BUMBATTLE FAIL" opens with a few seconds of thrashcore and a surprisingly sophisticated animated title sequence. "Venice" and "bumbattle" slide in from opposite sides of the frame and swirl around each other before settling in the middle, where a red "FAIL" stamp smashes them to pieces to the sound of shattering glass. The pieces dissolve into a wide shot of a stubble-headed man in a Lone Ranger mask. Dressed in black, the man stands spotlighted in a dim space, dark figures moving behind him.

The man shouts from a smirking mouth, "For our next bout," he points, camera whip-pans, adjusts to low light to focus on a portly white man with thin, graying hair, "he's shoeless, he's clueless, but he obviously ain't been foodless. He's Fat Jack! From some shit-stained alley!"

The Lone Ranger holds for applause, receives none. The portly man grimaces, shielding his eyes with his hand. His dress shirt is dirty and torn at the shoulder.

"And his opponent," the masked man shouts, "from some piss-perfumed sidewalk, weighing, like, a buck-thirty if he kept down his last meal, with a known history of biting . . . Sticky!"

The camera swings wildly across more darkened space to a

classroom skeleton dressed in rags. There's a smattering of cheers and a whoop that may be sarcastic.

"*Why* is he called Sticky? Syrup addiction? Poor hygiene? Or does he have needles in his pocket? Let's find out! Betting closes in twenty seconds!"

The music gets louder.

Voices off-screen shout, "Nickel on the Fatty!" and "I'll take that!"

"Wait!" The camera pans back to "Fat Jack"—clearly Jack Waxman—looking frantically around the room. "Please! I don't want to fight! I'm a peaceful man!"

Crackling laughter and shouting as the camera zooms in on Jack's terrified, darting eyes.

"OK!" the MC cries. "All bets are in! Ding fuckin' ding!"

Dizzying swing back to Sticky, the classroom skeleton, who flashes crooked, corn-colored teeth. His face disappears, the lens widens and finds him again, coming at Jack, pulling his right fist way back.

Jack sees the punch coming, ducks.

Sticky whiffs, stumbles into the crowd. A man in a balaclava pulls him up, shoves him back toward the camera. Sticky can't find his feet, lands facedown right in front of Jack.

The crowd goes wild.

"Kill him!"

"Squash him, Fatty!"

"Eat the Biter!"

"Bite the Eater!"

"Kick him!" the Lone Ranger commands from off-screen. "He's down!"

"No!"

Jack looks right at the camera, then at the crowd around him, and shouts, in a breathless but loud voice, "I don't kick people when they're down." He gasps for air, adds, "As Jesse Jackson once said, 'Don't look down on someone, unless you're helping him up!'"

The boos are so loud they crackle. Jack leans over Sticky, holding out his hand. Sticky lunges, grabs Jack's legs just below the knees. Jack loses his footing on the shiny floor, falls over backwards. The camera dives in close beside Sticky. His face is near Jack's calf, his mouth open. His tongue is purple.

A high-pitched scream, and Jack's bare heel catches Sticky in the nose. Sticky falls out of frame. The camera finds him on his back, both hands to his face.

The crowd cheers, and the angle widens.

Back on his feet, Jack raises his hands in surrender. He shouts, "You can't treat people like this. We're human beings!"

More deafening boos. Something—empty beer can?—bounces off of Jack's stomach. He backs up, and balaclava-clad spectators step aside to avoid other projectiles thrown at him.

A full beer can explodes against a blank gray wall behind him. The crowd calls him "Pussy!" and "Faggot!" and exhorts Sticky to get up and kill the Fatty. The camera moves from Jack to Sticky. The MC helps Sticky to his feet, hands him a knife that flashes in the spotlight.

Jack on the move. Glimpse of motorcycles in the shadows behind him. Sticky tests the weight of the knife, bounces on his toes. Bouncing seems to make him dizzy. He charges crookedly toward Jack.

Jack turns away, grabs something—a stick?—from out of frame, turns back. Sticky runs into the end of it. Blood cascades. No—red fabric, a flag. A Confederate battle flag? Which hangs in the air over Sticky writhing on the floor with both hands pressed to his face again.

Jack drops the flag, rushes to Sticky's side. He says something inaudible. Noticing the spotlight on him, he turns wildly to the camera, "It was an accident! I didn't mean—self-defense!"

The Lone Ranger yells for Sticky to get up.

People yell at Jack, "Finish him! Finish him!"

Eyes wide in his red face, Jack rises from Sticky's side. He closes his eyes, mumbles, *"Shema Yisrael, Adonai—"*

Stepping into the spotlight, the Lone Ranger punches Jack in the face, sends him crumpling to the floor next to Sticky.

The crowd roars with laughter. The thrashcore starts playing softly, and the Lone Ranger shouts, "This fight is called a draw! Due to one guy being a diseased weakling and the other guy being a giant pussy! Stick around for the next bout and find us on the dark side for more live streaming and betting. We take bitcoin, we take Ethereum, we take fuckin' Magacoin. War!"

The pounding drums and bass and screaming get loud for a few seconds as the camera twirls downward toward an empty beer can, zooming in on the mountain stream logo before fading to black.

13

In Sam's shaking hand, the video ended, and the *Up Next* window appeared. The options were three other "bumbattles."

The world was past redemption. Sam's panic had nowhere to go, but she thought throwing up might help. When her dad had stood up to them and quoted Jesse Jackson, she'd felt a stab of love for him, for his stupid quoting tic, for his stubborn principles.

Donald had been confused by the elaborate title sequence and irritated by the self-conscious camerawork. Once he understood that his son was being forced to fight, he just felt rage. (Though he was overjoyed by the boy's successful dodge of that junkie's punch, just like Donald had taught him in the old days—or was that Ward and the Beave?) Then, when Jack refused to finish his opponent, Donald felt a familiar frustration. Did the boy think this was some kind of tea party? It almost served him right to get sucker-punched like that. (Though Donald vowed to put the hurt on the Masked Man for such wanton dehumanization of any person, and especially the flesh of Donald's flesh.) Donald tried to think. He had to stay rational and clear-headed, study this video as new evidence containing potential leads.

"All right, kid," he said, "what do you make of it?"

"What do I *make* of it?" Sam hadn't yet committed to not throwing up. "What do they do with them? Dad might be dead!"

"But he probably isn't. Remember, he called your mother earlier today. When was this posted?

Donald was right. It had been posted around three a.m. by someone calling himself "skllfkkkr420."

"Any idea who these people are?" Donald asked.

Sam shrugged. "Westside skinheads? Ancient Rome LARPers?"

"What?"

"I don't know."

"What was that guy talking about when he said to check them out on the dark side?"

"The dark web? It's like the black market of the internet, but I don't know anything about that." Sam felt like she couldn't get enough air into her lungs. "What are we going to do? What can we do?"

"Keep looking."

"The police are on the case now. They might be able to do something with the video." Out of curiosity, she looked at the URL, but bonkersvidz.omfg didn't tell her anything useful. She closed her eyes and imagined herself in bed, listening to Cat Power in the dark.

"You listening to me, kid? Could be a couple days before the cops even get around to assigning someone to the case. We gotta keep going, and we gotta go hard." He held her gaze until she looked away. "But first," he said, scanning the storefronts, finger to lips, "restroom and quick drink. For fortification."

Sam agreed. Maybe they could just get drunk and stay drunk until the police found her father, or his body. The closest bar was Kapua's, a paint-chipped, surfadelic relic of a more aloha age. An extra-large man with long, wiry hair blocked the door. His goatee looked like a black guinea pig had bitten his chin and hung on.

While he checked Sam's ID, she noticed hairy white skin showing through blunt-sized holes in his Malice t-shirt.

Other than two stoics sitting at the far end of the bar and a young Asian couple by the front window, the place was empty.

The bartender was a rail-thin rocker with wispy blond hair and a yellowed t-shirt that said *Certified Mammographer*. "Christ," he muttered, "we got grampas comin' in here now?"

Donald headed back to the bathroom while Sam scanned the paltry whisky selection and ordered two Johnnie Walkers on the rocks.

The bartender nodded and went to work. Sam looked outside, where the last bit of pink in the sky had faded to blue. Maybe if she concentrated hard enough, her dad would just walk through the door of the bar. She tried for a few seconds but forgot about it when she remembered there was something she wanted to do.

She hopped onto a stool and searched "853 Ocean Front" on her phone. Sure enough, Venice Renewal Venture, LLC, had recently bought it. Googling VRV revealed that it was a wholly owned subsidiary of SoCal Property Partners, itself held in partnership by Qualicore and Gredan, Roch and Missler, both—or was it all?—of which were owned by SBT. The information for 847 began with a different LLC but ended in the same place.

Soon, Donald was back, groaning onto the stool beside her.

"It's Vigor, all right," Sam said.

Donald took a sip of whisky, paused a moment before swallowing it. "What's Vigor?"

"Trying to redevelop the whole block. But I don't see what it has to do with my dad. Maybe it's just a coincidence." She noticed the bartender hovering nearby, listening, so she called him over. "Have you seen this man?"

He leaned over the bar to get a look at the photo on her phone. Sam noticed a constellation of broken blood vessels above his eye. The right half of his mouth curled up. "What's it worth to ya?"

"Dude," Sam said, "he's missing. He's in danger. Can't you just tell us if you've seen him?"

"It's worth ten bucks," Donald said.

The bartender scratched his head. "Not twenty?"

"Screw this guy," Sam took back one of the two dollars she'd left on the bar for the tip.

Donald said, "We can do twenty." He nudged Sam.

Sam nudged him back. "I'm out. You pay him if you want."

Donald sighed, nodded, pulled out a full money clip, peeled off the outer twenty. Sam made a mental note to demand some reimbursement later.

"Ah—thank you," the bartender said, cramming the bill into the pocket of his tight jeans.

Sam and Donald leaned forward, eager to hear what he knew, but the bartender just picked up his rag and went back to wiping the counter.

"Well?" Sam shouted.

"Hmm?" Now both sides of his mouth curled up. "Oh, right. Nope, haven't seen him." Smirking, he turned his full attention to his rag.

"You son of a bitch—" Donald lunged over the bar, but the bartender nimbly stepped back out of reach.

"Lawrence!" he shouted. "Lawrence!"

The enormous head of the man in the Malice shirt appeared in the doorway. "What?"

"Eighty-six these bitches!"

"They don't look like trouble."

"This asshole just conned us out of twenty bucks," Sam said.

Lawrence shrugged. "Give the money back, Spencer."

"Fuck no. They gave it to me to tell 'em what I knew. I told 'em what I knew. Also, we can't encourage geezers to hang out in here."

Sam said, "I'm sorry—are we driving the junkies away?"

Donald lunged over the bar again. This time the bartender wasn't quick enough, and Donald's fist caught him in the mouth.

"Hey!" the bartender cried.

Donald slid back to the other side of the bar, downed his drink.

The bartender touched his fingers to his mouth and looked at them. "You fucker! You cut my lip."

Donald smiled at him. "At least now I feel like I got something for my money. Come on, kid." He grabbed Sam's sleeve and turned to the door, which was blocked by the bouncer.

The bartender shouted at the bouncer, "Well, Lawrence? You gonna do your fucking job?"

The bouncer sighed deeply, hanging his head and sagging his shoulders. Then he straightened up and tapped Donald in the stomach. Donald fell to his knees.

"What the fuck—you . . . poor man's Hagrid!" Sam tried kicking the bouncer in the balls, but he moved and her foot just glanced off of a thigh that was like a concrete pylon. He wrapped a hand around her arm and squeezed so hard Sam felt like the bone was going to snap. She screamed. With his other hand the bouncer grabbed Donald by his coat and pulled him to his feet. "Come on," he said softly. He dragged them both out of the bar, his goatee swinging scrotally above Sam while she shouted, "Let go!" over and over again.

Outside he let go of Sam and gently released Donald to his hands and knees.

"Spencer's an asshole," the bouncer said, "but I can't let you do stuff like that. Don't come back." He resumed his position standing in front of the bar.

Sam rushed over to Donald, who coughed and spat, still on hands and knees. "Are you OK? Is anything broken? I'll call an ambulance!"

But Donald shook his head and swatted her away from him.

What was wrong with her? She was an idiot, that's what. Endangering an old, demented man just to cure her boredom. Unemployed, drinking during the day, *smoking. Again.* She had completely failed to become an adult, and this—grandfather injured, potentially fatally, father missing, potentially fatally—was the result.

"Stop blubbering," Donald commanded. He got to his feet and put a hand on her shoulder. "Come on, kid. Pull yourself together."

Sam needed a tissue but had to make do with the hanky Donald stuck in her hand. "I shouldn't have brought you here," she said. "This is exactly the kind of shit I shouldn't be doing."

"What are you talking about? We came here together. We're partners."

"No. You don't know what you're doing. And that makes me responsible, and I don't want you to get hurt."

"I know exactly what I'm doing, kid. That goon was big, but that was just a love tap."

"Can you not call me a goon, please?" the bouncer said from his post. "I'm standing right here. And I have feelings."

Sam tugged at Donald's sleeve. "Come on. We're done. We're not good at this. We have to let the cops find him."

This time Donald didn't argue. In the darkness, they walked north toward the car. The wind had picked up, thinning out the tourists, blowing sand across the boardwalk. Donald didn't say anything when Sam walked past a group of skaters without showing them the photo of Jack, but Sam had counterarguments ready anyway. She was tired, cold, hopeless. Her dad was not here.

PART II

14

HAPPY, relaxed Jack Waxman sailed into the SBT office right on time. He and his team had met the first benchmarks for the Venture Charter program, and Jack believed the thoroughness and intelligence of their work would blow Vigor away.

So what if his coat was unbuttonable to due to several months of stress eating? He'd start working out as soon as the program was off the ground.

Unfortunately, Jack's irresistible positivity met the immovable indifference of the beach volleyball player sitting behind the reception desk. She smiled with her teeth only and told him to have a seat.

Consciously maintaining optimism levels, Jack sat and counted to ten before pulling out his phone. He worked through the thirteen emails that had arrived during the drive, replying, forwarding, and archiving as needed. He glanced at the latest headline—"Senator Proposes Affirmative Action for 'Aryan-Americans'"—and felt his chest tighten. But Jack was an optimist. He just had to keep doing his job, teaching his fellow citizens the values they didn't get at home or from popular culture. He needed to get *Be GRREAT!* programs into as many schools as possible.

Jack noticed he'd been waiting for twenty minutes, and he felt a slight stirring of negativity. His time used to be worth eight hundred dollars an hour (in late '90s dollars), and he had other things to do. Giving Season was just around the corner, so he needed to craft a personalized letter to the few top-level donors he had left. Then he had to review resumes for Samantha's replacement and finish revising the daily writing exercises for Venture Charter, which Samantha had really messed up toward the end there. He recalled one writing prompt of hers for the Empathy Key: "Is the death penalty ethical? Explain." Directed at third graders!

He also had to update his sexual harassment training presentation, *Bad Romance: How to Stay Cool in a Hot Workplace*, which he hadn't touched since that winter when Sophia played that Lady Gaga song over and over again. What else? He checked the to-do list on his phone. Of course, in red urgent font: "BM Speech."

Oy. What to say about your only son becoming a man? Jack liked it better when Immanuel was little. He snuggled, kissed goodnight, happily came along on Saturday trips to the car wash and dry cleaner. Now Jack knew his son mostly as a surly, cracking voice behind a closed bedroom door.

At twenty-four minutes, Jack stood up. Just as he did (as if maybe that was her cue?), the long-limbed receptionist told him to follow her down the hallway.

In his huge corner office, Vigor boomed from his treadmill, "Jack! Sorry to make you wait!" He did his primal alpha-male thing, holding out his hand and waiting for Jack to walk all the way over to shake it. "How are you, my friend?"

Jack smiled, "I'm well, thanks. As Babe Ruth said, 'It's hard to beat a person who never gives up.'"

"Good one!"

Jack tried not to be distracted by the wall of windows and the long shadows the setting sun cast over Koreatown. On Vigor's disconcerting wall of weapons, the shiny blades of the crossed swords reflected the orange sky.

"I've got lots of great material to show you," Jack said. "Sample writing exercises, class activities, field trips. Also, we were thinking, in light of recent events, of this bleeding into the mainstream of so much hate and disrespect, that we might begin the year with a Respect and Empathy boot camp."

"Respect and empathy?" Vigor mused while he strolled. "Yes, those do seem to be in short supply these days."

Jack set his satchel on Vigor's conference table and opened it. "Should I set up over here?"

"Actually, no, let's hold off on the charter school project right now. There's something else I want to discuss. Have a seat." Vigor gestured to one of the jagged pop art chairs.

Jack had hated these chairs for two years, since the first time he tempted fate and sat in one. That meeting had led to his teaching an ethics class for SBT managers with multiple OSHA violations.

Now, lowering himself slowly, he asked, "What is it, Nick? Not another SBT scandal, I hope."

"No, nothing like that. I wanted to talk with you about your work on the Historic Preservation Commission."

"Oh?" Jack grinned. He was proud of his seat on the Commission, loved talking about it.

"Yes, it's come to my attention that one of our subsidiary's recent acquisitions has been nominated. Are you familiar with 847 Ocean Front, in Venice?"

"Sure, the old Caffe Carnevale building. We're voting on it next week."

"That's the one," Vigor said. "Did you read the 'Friend of the Commission Brief' our lawyer submitted?"

"*Your* lawyer? You're SoCal Property Partners?"

"More or less."

Jack didn't like the general direction of this conversation. "I think I skimmed it," he said.

"And?"

"It's a complicated case."

Vigor's voice went up an octave, "Is it though? There's nothing architecturally or historically significant about that building. It's home to roaches and rats, an overpriced wine bar, a bong shop."

"They said it was a 'gift' shop!" Jack joked. "Anyway, it's a historical site. That wine bar was once a cafe that hosted readings and jazz. Allen Ginsberg and Jack Kerouac performed there. If I remember correctly, the previous owner pulled up some old wallpaper and found a poem written by Stuart Perkoff himself, the greatest of the Venice Beats."

"Purported." Vigor pressed a button that slightly accelerated his stroll. "I don't think we've seen credible evidence confirming the handwriting. Nor is it much of a poem. 'Crunch the bones'? 'Suck the marrow'? I'd call that graffiti. Also, is there anything other than rumor suggesting that Ginsberg ever spent time there? And even if he did, wasn't he into young boys?"

"Let me stop you right there," Jack leaned back a little in the lightning bolt chair, felt the muscles in his neck beginning to knot. "I don't think it's appropriate to debate the merits of the building with you."

"You're right. I know you can make an independent, impartial decision. I didn't mean to pressure you."

"Good! Thank you."

"You're welcome. But, just quickly," Vigor pressed the stop button and stepped off the treadmill, "I need you to tell me you understand that, in the case of 847, a vote for preservation is a vote *against* progress, *against* the very process of civilization."

"Nick, the whole reason I'm on the commission is to serve as its 'ethical conscience.' Those were the mayor's exact words when he appointed me, and I take that charge seriously."

"Exactly!" Vigor walked around the desk and hovered over Jack. "So just think about it: wouldn't preservation serve to glorify a bunch of law-breaking, drug-addled deviants who happened to do heroin in the bathroom fifty years ago? What this community needs is development, capital infusion, job creation. An influx of a more, let's say, economically *significant* population. That's the ethical choice." He took a deep breath, drank from a plastic water bottle.

Jack said nothing, refused to meet his eye.

"OK, Jack," Vigor said, brow furrowing, "I'll be honest with you. If you're the kind of person who would vote to preserve that building, well, I'm just not sure you're the kind of person I want to work with."

"What?" Adrenaline suddenly burned through Jack's arteries. Through the windows, the sky had turned an apocalyptic shade of deep red. He saw the Venture windfall slipping away, saw himself letting more employees go, moving ever closer to total institutional dissolution. "Was that a threat?"

Vigor said, "Yes," without hesitation.

Jack was stunned. What seemed to be happening couldn't really be happening. "Can't we keep our focus on the students? All those kids who are going to lead good, successful lives, who are going to solve the complex problems of our world?"

"Exactly, Jack. You focus on that. Let me worry about the real estate."

"This is beginning to feel like a conflict of interest," Jack heard panic in his own voice. "I'll just recuse myself."

"No," Vigor ran a hand over his shiny head, looked Jack in the eye. "I didn't want to do it this way, but the fact is, I need you to vote against landmark status. If you vote yes or abstain, we can't do business together."

Jack knew his laugh sounded forced. "You're kidding, right? It's hard to tell when you're kidding."

"I'm not kidding."

"We have a contract!"

"With plenty of escape clauses."

"But—the kids!"

"I'm sure they'll get by with one of your competitor's programs."

Something in the back of Jack's mind pushed its way to the front: the Venice Beat Community group nominated 847 Ocean Front for preservation in early September. Then, not even a week later, Jack got the first phone call from Vigor.

"Nick, did you . . . is the only reason you brought me in—"

Vigor smiled. "We have a motto here, Jack. 'YCBTC.' *You Can't Be Too Careful.* We do our research. We triangulate."

Jack stood up so they were face to face. He felt his heart thumping. "Nick, this is unacceptable. It's just—it's unacceptable. I don't even know—you should take some time, reconsider the moral ramifications—but I'm going to leave."

He made a tight quarter-turn to push the chair back so he could walk out, but Vigor clamped a hand on his shoulder. No one had touched Jack this aggressively since he was robbed at gunpoint in a parking garage twenty years ago. He froze, feeling another adrenaline surge.

"Oh, Jack," Vigor said again, "I *really* didn't want to do it this way." He stepped back, but only so he could slide around Jack and close the door. Then he plucked a tablet computer off of the conference table. "See, I know a few things about you—personal and private things—that could easily become public."

"Blackmail?" Jack laughed in disbelief. This was beginning to feel so much like a bad dream that it couldn't possibly have real-world consequences.

"I'm not joking."

"But I don't have anything to hide." Jack believed this to be true. Obeyed all laws, paid his taxes, paid the housekeeper (who had a green card) over the table, used no substances stronger than aspirin, remained faithful to his wife, even avoided viewing pornography—on principle, sure, but also because he simply didn't need it. He took care of his needs in the absolute privacy of his shower, occasionally thinking of Bo Derek in *10*, or Katharine Ross in *The Graduate*, or, come to think of it, Ann Bancroft in *The Graduate*. But most often it was Cynthia he imagined, her body and their encounters usually fresh in his mind. Though, when was the last time? Six months ago? Close to a year? He'd been working so hard he couldn't remember—and this was all beside the point. The point was that Jack had nothing to be ashamed of, except maybe the occasional pint of ice cream he polished off alone in the car while listening to Paul Simon's *Graceland*.

Vigor tapped a couple of times on the tablet and turned it toward Jack. It was a video: convenience store parking lot at night. A Tesla the same dark color as Jack's fills the screen. Camera zoom on the front window, partially open, behind which a heavyset man eats ice cream out of a pint container. He bobs his head joyfully. Very faintly, "Diamonds on the Soles of Her Shoes" plays.

"Oh, my God!" When had his face gotten so fat? But he had to focus. "How petty do you think I am?" he said. "Go ahead, put that on the internet. Who cares?"

"Oh, that one's just for fun." Vigor tapped on the tablet a few times and turned it back toward Jack. "How about this?"

Large, warmly lit hall—a hotel lobby. The camera work is a little shaky, but a woman, Cynthia, walks right through the frame alongside a handsome young man. The camera follows them to the elevator, zooms. She stands close to him but doesn't touch him. The elevator arrives, they get in, and just as the doors close, they come together for what has to end in a passionate kiss. Unless it's a slo-mo chest bump. Yes, maybe a chest bump is what it is: a meeting has gone well, and, unbeknownst to Jack, Cynthia has adopted the customs of bro culture at work!

"How . . ." Jack started, but that wasn't right. "When . . ." wasn't right either.

"Know him? Young lawyer, reports directly to your wife, which I'm pretty sure is a no-no, from an HR perspective."

Jack did know him. Jim or Tim or something. Boyle or Dolan? Met at the studio holiday party. Charming, handsome kid. A little arrogant, maybe, but Jack had attributed that to his millennial sense of entitlement. Cynthia couldn't possibly be sleeping with him. He was a kid!

Vigor tapped on the tablet. "I've got some decent audio from another rendezvous, if you'd like to hear it. Cost me a pretty penny to get it—"

"No!" Jack pushed the tablet away.

"OK, take my word for it," Vigor said. "So we're good then? I don't need to show you the videos of your children?"

"You videotaped my children?"

"Let's just say they've got problems. Do *my* kids have their own problems? You bet. But not like yours. When was the last time you checked your son's browser history? The bar mitzvah boy is really into hentai porn. And that stuff is . . . raw."

Jack didn't know what that was. He barely heard Vigor over the sound of blood rushing in his ears. Tiny circles floated on the wall across the weapons.

"And your daughters," Vigor said, looking down at his tablet. "Harper: tenth-grade pothead; Sophia: the school slut; and your eldest, Samantha—well, as sex tapes go, it's not—"

Jack snatched the tablet from Vigor's hands, threw it onto the floor, stomped it with the heel of his shoe until it cracked and crunched and came apart.

Vigor smiled. "You're not really a 'tech' guy, are you? Because, obviously, that's all in the cloud. You should calm down. A guy your size . . ."

Seeing not red so much as purple and yellow spots, Jack

looked at Vigor's smug face, desperately wanted to pummel it. He'd never hit anyone in his adult life. He was a peacemaker, a mediator, a man who had thanked God more than once that he was allowed to go to college instead of Vietnam. But now he saw himself pulling one of those ridiculous antique swords off of the wall and splitting this man's head open. And then splitting the pieces into smaller and smaller pieces.

Meanwhile, Vigor talked in soothing tones, and his words started to sink in. He was telling Jack to think rationally about what he wanted to happen. Jack could easily vote against landmark status, allow the redevelopment plan to go through—which really would help clean up the neighborhood—and Jack could quietly handle his wife's infidelity and his kids' issues. Or, he could let Vigor ruin his business and his family and find another way of getting what he wanted.

"Really," Vigor assured Jack, "I hate to involve them, but you're such a boy scout, you left me no choice in how to leave you no choice."

He looked Jack over, probably noted his clenched teeth and clenched fists. "Let's talk at the end of the day tomorrow. I know you'll come around, and then we're going to be *grrrreat* together!"

"Never," Jack said.

Vigor pretended he hadn't heard him. He just mounted his treadmill again and tapped out something on his keyboard. Jack stood there, body frozen while mind raced, thinking punch face, strangle veiny neck, thrust bullet head through window, shove body out, watch fall down.

Before he could act on any of these ideas, Misty or Christi or whatever her name was took him by the arm and led him down the hallway.

Jack found the restroom. He splashed water on his face, looked into his own wild eyes. Should kick open the door of the nearest stall, dump all of the toilet paper rolls into the toilet, kick open the door to the next stall, do the same thing.

But who would that hurt? Not Vigor; just the poor soul who cleaned the toilets every night.

Instead Jack wiped his face with paper towels, looked again into his own eyes, now less wild, though certainly old and tired. He dabbed at his forehead, picked off pieces of paper towel that had stuck. He took some deep breaths, evened out his collar, and left the bathroom.

The elevator came almost instantly. Jack tried to see it as a sign that things were looking up. No stops on the way down to the garage—he was on a roll now!—and he found his car and wound his way to the exit.

In a little box by the gate, a round-faced, pencil-mustached cashier checked the back of Jack's ticket, noted the lack of validation, and announced, "Seventeen dollars."

Jack Waxman never swore, even in his head, but right now he barely restrained himself from screaming, "FRACK!" He considered going back up, but no way. He couldn't trust himself not to get violent. He handed the man a twenty, was ready to shout, "Keep the change!" as his engine roared and he zoomed out of there. But the gate didn't go up. The man picked at a folded corner of the bill, placed it into the tray, counted out three dollars—"Eighteen, nineteen, aaaaaaaaand twenty!"—and handed over the money and receipt. Then he stepped out of his little box and manually lifted the gate. And then, finally, Jack's Tesla did not roar. It glided forward silently, and only for two seconds, before Jack had to brake and wait, and wait, *and wait*, for an opening in traffic.

15

JACK DROVE west in a rush-hour stutter of red lights, surrounded by dangerous idiots. People failed to signal, ignored the signals of others, denied merges, seethed alternately at people they tailgated and people who tailgated them.

At least Jack had a good excuse for driving like a jerk: he was being blackmailed. He could go to the police, except he had no proof. And then there was Cynthia: how long had she been cheating? Was that Tim or Jim as young as he looked? Was he the first, or just the latest? Would Cynthia lose her job, which she loved, and which was currently their primary source of income? Would she leave him? Or he her?

His divorce from Samantha's mother had been the worst experience of his life, and he didn't want to go through another one now, with three kids involved. But he'd spent decades building his reputation as "a man of character." Does such a man tolerate unfaithfulness? If no, what does he do about it? If yes—well, is he even a man?

He'd always taken for granted that she'd tell him if she were unhappy. They'd get counseling, work it out like adults. As her former professor and unofficial mentor, he was pretty disappointed by her decision-making here. He thought he'd done a better job. Then again, look what his kids were up to. Maybe there was something about him that encouraged bad decision-making and skillful deception.

He'd been mindlessly crawling down Olympic. Half the store signs were in Spanish and the other half Korean. La Olita, a little stand that had the best ceviche in the city, came up on the right. Jack signaled, paused at the next corner to make sure no one was crossing the street—got honked at for pausing—turned, and found a spot halfway down the block. Ceviche, and a couple or three tacos, was just what he needed.

He found five people waiting in line ahead of him. Over the general engine din on Olympic, the grinding gears of a dump truck did a call-and-response thing with the squealing brakes of a crosstown bus. Headlights of passing cars lit up a few street characters huddled along the block. One once-handsome lunatic said to everyone, "Buy me a Pepsi? Buy me a Pepsi?"

The wind smelled of grilling meat and frying tortillas. Jack's stomach growled, but the line didn't move. *Why* wasn't the line moving? The menu was right there. Surely people could have the details of their order ready when they got to the window. And why those terrible cars, one after another, gigantic trucks and SUVs with deafening engines? Why the super-loud motorcycles? Those guys didn't have a leg to stand on, ethically. Or maybe they were all just hearing impaired, had no idea they were the aural equivalent of a swarm of locusts, just laying waste to the soundscape, killing all joy and peace for a half-mile radius.

"Buy me a Pepsi?" the guy said to the man in front of Jack. "Buy me a Pepsi?" Like the others before him, the man ignored the Pepsi guy. Jack thought the Pepsi guy looked familiar, wondered if his headshot might still be stuck in some casting agent's notebook. He, Jack Waxman, would buy the man a Pepsi. And he would not obey his urge to jam the whole can down his throat.

When he finally made it to the window, Jack had to wait for the old cashier to finish retrieving extra salsa for another customer. Then, two punks just showed up out of nowhere and cut right in front of him.

Jack was stunned. These kids were Latino or Filipino or . . . something. Their race didn't matter—why even remark upon it? One was short. He had a smooth, babyish face that didn't fit with his bulging muscles and weird lobe-stretching earrings. The other was tall and thin, with darker skin and a dusting of a mustache. They seemed to vibrate with menace as they blocked the window.

Suddenly the Pepsi requester was deeply interested in lining up the labels of the hot sauce bottles on the counter.

But Jack was annoyed. "Hey, guys, there's a line."

They both looked at him, and the short one with stretched earlobes said, "Chill, man. We'll be fast."

"No. I was here first," Jack insisted, more loudly. "You should go to the back of the line?" The question mark was unintentional.

The tall one looked him up and down before looking away.

That was all Jack needed to launch excitedly into a righteous speech. "Just think about it," he said, raising his voice so every person in the line could hear him. "If everyone went out of turn like you two, no one would be able to order. No one would even get to the window because everyone would rush it, and there'd be wrestling matches in front of the cash register. There wouldn't even be any food here because the delivery trucks wouldn't be able to drive the streets because every intersection would be clogged with car accidents. We'd be completely lost. We wouldn't be able to grow or transport food, get clean water, guarantee our own safety or that of our loved ones. Only the strongest and cruelest would survive for long. Is that the world you guys want to live in? Is that the team you want to be on?"

Jack turned to the people in line behind them. "Am I right? We've all got to play by the rules!"

Some avoided Jack's eyes. Others stared right back at him. Nobody pumped his fist. Nobody said, "Right on!"

"Maybe we can't really blame them," Jack said, still hoping to win over the crowd. "Because we've failed to educate them *for character*." He looked at the short one with the stretched lobes. "They're living by the laws of the street instead of . . ." Jack lost track of his sentence as Earlobes leaned into the window and said to the old cashier, "*Gracias, Yayo. Hasta mañana*." The kid handed over a set of keys, and the two punks walked away, shaking their heads and laughing.

Shame washed over him, rinsing the invincible rage right out. The cashier looked at him. Jack couldn't remember his order. The cashier waited, wearily. Finally, Jack remembered: ceviche, three shredded beef tacos (because forget Cynthia and her "No Red Meat Mid-Week" rule), Diet Coke.

"Buy me a Pepsi?" The homeless guy was back, close enough for Jack to smell his sourness.

"Sure, pal." Jack nodded to the cashier, who set one on the counter.

"That's a Coke. I want a Pepsi."

"He wants a Pepsi," Jack said.

"We have only Coke," the cashier said.

"Coke or nothing," Jack relayed unnecessarily. The guy took the Coke and walked away without saying thank you. Jack felt another flare of rage, but he shook it off and paid. He sat on a bench and took out his phone. He knew he should tell Cynthia where he was. But he couldn't bear texting her, let alone talking to her on the phone.

"Yack!" the cashier shouted, and Jack heaved himself up and retrieved his food. Three fragrant flowers bloomed on the white paper plate, tortilla petals enveloping barbacoa pistils, bedewed with sour cream, salsa, lime juice. In his mouth the mixture blended alchemically into Baja sunshine. He chewed, and his brain did what it always did when he ate, which was go on vacation. All the street noise fell into the background, and Jack's spirit lazed in a hammock swinging in a warm breeze. He chewed slowly and thoroughly, swallowed, took another bite. He could stay here forever, or at least until they closed. Just place order after order, eat and eat and eat. Happy.

He was midway through taco number two when the clouds rolled in over his hammock. The traffic noise reasserted itself, the intense pleasure faded, and he bit, chewed, and swallowed automatically while his mind wandered.

Forgetting about Cynthia and the children for a minute, what was he going to do about having partnered in business with a sociopath?

Back in Vigor's office, he'd taken a principled stand in the heat of the moment, and that had absolutely been the right position, *then*. But now, with his heart rate out of the red and glucose jazzing up his bloodstream, he found a little more clarity. This principled stance could ruin him. If Vigor canceled the contract, the Institute probably wouldn't survive another year. If Vigor posted the videos, or paid someone to write a damning story contrasting Jack's parental and marital failures with his advice on parenting and marriage, Jack's reputation would suffer considerable, potentially fatal damage. He'd just become a punchline.

And the internet would make it permanent. Jack had written a Waxim once about how omnipresent camera phones and surveillance cameras meant that one's worst moments could easily become part of the public record. His primary example was Michael Malone, the actor (and Jack's freshman-year roommate, buddy, and fraternity brother) who'd been caught driving drunk with a prostitute and a couple grams of cocaine in his car. It was late 2003 or maybe 2004, when everyone was trying to escape from the Iraq disaster by watching cute cat videos and a reality show in which a fake CEO fired his fake employees. Michael Malone was sort of a poor man's Richard Gere—or maybe just a more self-destructive man's Richard Gere. In the famous mugshot, his normally combed salt-and-pepper hair jutted several directions, with one strand nearly covering his right eye but really just drawing attention to the fact that the eyelid sat at half-mast. A lipstick smear blurred the corner of his mouth, making him look like he had some kind of rash. His expression was one of sullen acceptance, as if even then he knew that website slideshows of "classic" celebrity mugshots would never fail to include his. Poor guy. Since then he'd recovered, been forgiven, and even got himself attached to a hit sitcom for a few years. But no matter what Michael Malone did with the rest of his life, when you searched his name, you'd find that mugshot.

Jack was out of food. The Pepsi guy was back, hovering near the counter, reciting his mantra to each customer. Maybe he was on the payroll: demand Pepsi, get a Coke, go around back, return it, demand Pepsi, get Coke, go around back.

Jack looked over his plate's sad remnants, picked at a few lettuce shreds. Then he collected his trash—and other trash some inconsiderate person had just left—and chucked it all into the nearby can.

Those darn punks. If one of them had just turned to him and said, "Excuse me, I need to return my grandfather's keys," he would've said, "Of course!" and stepped aside. Would that have been so hard? It wasn't his fault they just rudely stepped in front of him.

He walked back to his car, glancing over his shoulder just in case they were hiding somewhere, waiting to jump him. He acknowledged that he was being paranoid and racist, that not every poor kid with bad manners was a violent criminal. Probably not even five percent of them. Enough soft bigotry of low expectations. Until we expect more of our youth, they'll fail to give us more!

Jack opened the car door and climbed inside. He needed to solve this sudden personal crisis before solving the societal crisis.

Wasn't admitting defeat and going along with Vigor, on the whole, the more attractive solution? Sure, it would cost him a little in the integrity department, and maybe a piece of Los Angeles history would be destroyed, but wasn't that always happening? Wasn't it the nature of a living city to constantly rebuild itself? Especially this city, where people came to change their names and fake their way to fame and fortune? Where so many of the buildings looked like set decoration, flimsy facades a strong wind could topple?

And Vigor, despite being an obvious narcissist, had a point: who *were* these Beat poets who gathered there? Jack had never read any of them. In college he'd heard Michael Malone reading Ginsberg and Kerouac to girls he was trying to lay. To Jack, those writers seemed self-obsessed, drug-addled, and totally lacking in practicality or discipline. So what did he care if the place was torn down?

Of course, Jack told himself, it wasn't ethical to designate landmark status only to places that mattered specifically to oneself. If others valued the work of these poets and wanted to remember them, who was he to say they were wrong?

But, himself replied, would those people be severely injured or made severely unhappy by the redevelopment of this building?

Not likely. In fact, the unhappiness would be minor and diffused among many. Whereas Jack's unhappiness, were he to vote for preservation, would be acute, localized, and potentially permanent.

Maybe he just needed to talk to someone, get another perspective. That someone was Cynthia, his counselor, his comforter, his best friend—but going home would lead to high emotion and a sad rearrangement of the sleeping situation. He wasn't ready for that. Who else did he have?

Danny Schacht, his oldest buddy, was dead. And anyway, Danny had moved to Arizona twelve years ago, and they'd drifted apart. Jack had known he was sick, had emailed and called, had directed Bonnie to send lemon cakes, had sworn he would visit. But then, just as the Institute entered its darkest hour, and Jack scrambled to keep it afloat, he got the news of Danny's death. Danny's son called to invite him to the funeral, just as Jack was beginning to facilitate a four-day police ethics conference. He couldn't risk sending a subordinate and losing the business, and he'd already cashed the check, so he just sent his condolences and more lemon cake.

It served him right that he now found himself so alone.

Jack considered the other four historic preservation commissioners. Two of them had to be in Vigor's pocket, but which two? None of them had been interested in getting to know him. They didn't like that he wasn't an architect or urban planner, and they saw his appointment as a political move by the mayor to demonstrate his administration's anti-corruption focus. Whenever Jack talked at the meetings, discoursing on the ethical implications of their actions or comparing deontological and utilitarian perspectives, the other commissioners visibly slouched in their chairs and played with their mechanical pencils.

Jack did his best to ignore their slights. He took the job seriously, felt it was a natural outgrowth of his mid-career switch to ethics. By now, several years into that switch, he was used to being dismissed as a bore or a scold.

He tried hard not to be boring, and if he did scold, it was in service of the greater good. Which, how could he abandon that service now?

An idea formed, or a question containing an idea: *Could* he just *try* to forget Vigor's demand, or at least send it to the back of his mind and judge the building on its own merits? He'd been so busy that he hadn't given any thought to it yet. Hadn't even gone on the building tour the Venice Preservation Committee organized—he'd had a scheduling conflict: a meeting with Vigor to review the contract. (Now even the timing of that meeting seemed awfully suspicious.) So maybe Jack just needed more data. Needed to go to the beach, look at the building, see it in all of its mediocrity and insignificance. Then he could vote against landmark status with a clear conscience, and just sort of by-the-way avoid public embarrassment.

With renewed purpose and a delicately compartmentalized mind, he started the car and plotted his route to the beach.

16

A FREE PARKING spot at the beach was as rare as a clear conscience, but Jack found one on Ozone between the retirement home and the Jewish Family Service Center. The Center's wall was covered in a Chagall-inspired mural of flying fish, winged people blowing trumpets, a fiddler on a roof. Jack smiled. When in doubt, find the Jews!

The sign said no parking after ten. His phone said it was 8:09, and Cynthia had texted: *Where are u?* Feeling ventricular pain, Jack slipped the phone back into his pocket. Let her worry a little. He had to stay aware of his surroundings anyway, as the night seemed to swallow the lamplight whole.

Hands in pockets, holding phone and keys in left, wallet in right, he made a wide arc around a man muttering to himself and rummaging through a shopping cart. On the boardwalk, the salty wind carried the white noise of the surf. Tents and tarps and lean-tos lined the grass strip along with bags, suitcases, backpacks, upended bicycle frames with no wheels, stacked wheels with no frames. A shirtless, tattooed, tightly muscled young man puffed angrily on a cigarette between pools of streetlight.

When he was very young, before his parents' divorce, Jack's

mother took him to the beach all the time. She and Aunt Lillian would sit on a blanket, smoke cigarettes, and play cards while Jack built sand castles on his own. His older cousins wouldn't let him help build their castle, just because he had once tripped and flattened it. It was true that, as soon as he saw how tall it was, he felt an urge—almost a need—to wreck it, but he hadn't wrecked it, then. And when later he did wreck it, it was an accident. After that, the most he was offered was moat-digging duty, and only if he stayed outside the moat.

They always went to Santa Monica—never Venice, which his mother said was for "hippies, Mexicans, and blacks." He was in high school before he learned that the city had bulldozed Latino neighborhoods for the 405 freeway when he was a toddler in the late 1950s. Most of the displaced people moved west into Venice, which had once been the only place on the Westside where African Americans were allowed to live. The African American gangs didn't exactly welcome the Mexican American gangs.

Now it seemed every burnout and mental case in the country had washed up on the Venice shore, but Jack told himself he wasn't afraid. Being afraid only encouraged predation. One had to walk confidently through the night. Also, he couldn't remember the last time he'd read about a violent crime down here. So, even though the streets looked bad, they were safer than they used to be. We're not perfect, he thought, and we have our little hiccups— like the new wave of hate crimes spreading across the nation—but we get better. The arc of the moral universe is long but just!

He walked past a bar with cafe tables out front and an old guy playing John Lennon's "Imagine" on a chipped Telecaster. How many times had he sat with Cynthia at similar cafe tables, listening to live music? Appreciating, if not the music itself, her insistence that live music was of critical importance? Appreciating that she gave the music to him like a gift?

And now she was giving her gifts to someone else.

Just past the bar, at the base of a nearby palm tree, a girl with blue, silver-streaked hair knelt on a skateboard before a shrine. Flickering prayer candles and dead wildflowers framed a sun-faded photo of a smiling, brown-skinned young man in a dark knit hat.

The girl stood up, still staring at the flames. For a moment, Jack thought she had a bead of mucus gathering under her nose, about to drip, but it was just one of those silver septum rings glinting in the candlelight. Jack asked her if she knew what happened.

"Yeah." She turned her red eyes toward him, and Jack saw that one half of her head was shaved. "The pigs shot him. He was a sweetheart. Give you his last dollar if you asked for it."

"Why'd they shoot him?"

She shrugged. "They were looking for a black guy who'd stolen a bike from someone's yard. Darryl just happened to be the first one they saw. He was at the bar, but he was too wasted, so they made him leave. But he forgot his purple hat—he always wore that gross thing—and he tried to go back and get it. The bouncer wouldn't let him. There was, like, one second of struggle, and that's when the cops showed up. They yelled something at him and he was like, 'OK, don't need my hat that bad,' and he was leaving, and that's when the cop shot him. Just like that. Not threatening them or anything. Walking away. Right here."

"I'm so sorry. Why haven't I heard about this?"

"No video," she sniffed. "Happened so quick, no one had their phones out."

Like a lot of older, well-off white guys, Jack had only gotten "woke" to the extent of police violence against black men in the last couple of years, as killing after killing made national news. How many more never made the news because no one was around to film them? For how many people was the so-called "Land of the Free" as unjust and capricious as a third-world dictatorship? And why had he not written a Waxim about that?

Because he didn't want to alienate the police departments who paid him to do workshops on police ethics, of course. It would be a tightrope walk, but if he acknowledged first the fact that he believed most cops to be good and decent people who obeyed the law and treated everyone equally, then he might discuss the psychology of implicit bias, and strategies for recognizing and countering one's own internalized stereotypes.

The girl still stood next to him. "Man," she rubbed her flat stomach, "I'm really hungry. Can you spare a buck or two so I can get a bite?"

"Of course." Jack usually didn't give to panhandlers. He and Cynthia gave to organizations, and he'd spent the last eleven years devoting all his energy to his nonprofit, so he didn't feel too guilty. But this girl couldn't be more than a year or two older than Sophia. Living on the streets. Friends with people who were killed by the police? Even if she'd just use the money to buy drugs, he felt he had to give her a couple of bucks.

The girl took the bills with a flash of eye contact and mumbled thanks. She dropped her skateboard onto its wheels and hopped onto it. Jack watched her go, thinking again of his daughter.

For the most part, he'd handled Sophia's pregnancy scare like a pro. That night, a little over a week ago, when he came home from work and she tearfully told him she was late (he said, "For what?" and she said, "My period!"), he didn't indulge his anger or distress. He told himself the numbness in his left arm was psychosomatic, drove straight to the pharmacy, searched up and down the awkward aisle—noticing, even in his distress, that he lived in a golden age of lubrication—collected one of each brand of pregnancy test, and presented them to the elderly woman behind the register. She looked down at them and breathed hard through her nose.

"Please, withhold your judgment," he told her. "You don't know the story."

She rolled her eyes. "No story could make it OK for a man your age to buy these."

"They're for my daughter," Jack said, and realized she was right.

On the way home from the store, he contemplated the ethics of abortion. He came of age in the '70s, considered himself a feminist, but he'd joyfully brought four people into the world. He believed those lives, and all life, to be a sacred gift. Thus, the termination of any life was morally wrong. (Any *human* life, that is. Cows, chickens, fish, and other delicious creatures were obviously here to be humanely butchered and eaten.)

Once home with the pregnancy tests, Jack sent Sophia straight to the bathroom with the whole bag. Harper and Immanuel were in their separate rooms with their doors closed—she apparently smoking pot and he looking at porn. While he waited for Sophia to take the tests, Jack sat at his desk and took out his legal pad.

Following his own advice to his listeners, he drew a T. Above it he wrote, *Abortion?* On the pro-abortion side, there was Sophia's future; the future of Zach, the sudden boyfriend and potential father; the difficulties of growing up as the child of a teenage mother; Jack and Cynthia's having to support and care for Sophia and the child; the bad optics for him and the institute when the news got out. (People would love to read about the teenage pregnancy of the daughter of a highly respected ethicist.) On the con-abortion side, all Jack could think to write was, *Sanctity of life?* A few seconds of thought later, he drew a caret between *of* and *life* and added *potential.* A few more seconds later, below *Sanctity,* he added *Grandfatherhood,* but this was immediately canceled out on the pro side by *Too young for grandfatherhood?* Which, he quickly recognized, was false.

But none of it mattered. While he justified to himself the reasonableness of his position, his daughter burst through the door and cried, in equal parts sob and song, "Negative!"

He hugged her, but then he held her at arm's length so he could deliver an extemporaneous lecture on the importance of self-respect, responsibility, and long-term goal orientation, concluding with the decree: "Grounded until graduation!"

Solid parenting. And his muse rewarded him with an idea for exactly the kind of bold, controversial Waxim Samantha had been begging him to write before she completely betrayed him.

Closing the door to his home office, Jack sat at his cluttered desk and spun the straw of Sophia's story into Waxim gold. For the Sophia of Greatest Potential had died and been reborn, and she brought back with her an affirmation of his belief that abortion must be kept legal and accessible. His daughter's life was more important than any potential life inside her. He loved her, and he couldn't stand to see her future compromised by a broken condom. For both of their sakes, he made sure to change her name and disguise their relationship, describing her as "Sarah, the daughter of a friend." He read it through twice, found nothing he wanted to change, and then he hung the soundproof foam sheet over the door and recorded himself reading it.

Late that same night, after he uploaded the audio file to the radio station's FTP server, he found Cynthia in the bathroom brushing her teeth—likely washing out the taste of her boy toy. But then, in his innocence, Jack just leaned against the wall, told her about Sophia.

Cynthia was oddly furious. "What's wrong with her? You'd think she'd at least take a pregnancy test *before* telling you."

That wasn't the first thing Jack had thought of, but she had a point. Cynthia considered the situation for thirty more seconds and declared that the non-existent period was due to Sophia's intense training for cross-country. The morning sickness was not morning sickness, but simply the result of her recent decision to become a coffee drinker and/or her obsession with a French-Indian fusion food truck, and/or the fact that white men were constantly attacking the bodies and rights of women, so every feminist in America was having trouble keeping down her breakfast.

"But I didn't even know Sophia was having sex!" Jack practically shouted.

"At least someone in this house is," Cynthia muttered.

Jack felt like he'd been slapped. "I'm sorry," he said. He reached out, brushed a strand of hair away from her eyes. "Do you want to . . . ?"

She smiled coldly. "Not in the mood, thanks."

"Work's just been crazy, but I think we've weathered the storm. Let's plan a date night. Or a weekend away." Recovering his focus, "Did you know she was sexually active? *And* she drinks coffee?"

"Oh," Cynthia rubbed cream into her cheeks and forehead, "don't be so old."

She knew just where to strike. He'd never been completely comfortable with their age difference, and he'd only grown more insecure as his body sagged and spread its way toward senior citizenship, while hers seemed ageless, barely altered by three pregnancies. Maybe that contributed to his reluctance to get in bed when she did, to initiate intimacy. He was grotesque to himself.

The conversation, like so many they had in recent months, ended abruptly with her pecking him near the lips and leaving the room. He went back to his office to send one last email. She was asleep by the time he got into bed.

One day later, when children and wife ganged up on him for accidentally saying "Sophia" instead of "Sarah" one time on the radio, which "basically ruined her life," as Harper put it, Jack got defensive. He felt terrible, of course, but it was an innocent mistake, an error of excitement, of his single-minded devotion to writing the best Waxim he could write.

And Cynthia could take some blame, couldn't she? After all, why hadn't Sophia gone to her, the mother, the natural choice for such a delicate issue? Was it because Cynthia hadn't been available, emotionally or physically? Too busy at work, or doing yoga or Pilates, or something called HotCycle? All of which, Jack now suspected, were alibis for sexual rendezvous?

Snapping back into his body, which walked along Ocean Front beneath streetlights that illuminated waves of rolling fog, Jack realized he'd found his destination. He'd have walked right past the building if a candlelight vigil weren't happening right in front of it.

17

A VISUALLY UNREMARKABLE building in the "commercial vernacu-
lar" style, 847 Ocean Front was a two-story, brick-sheathed box
with rounded corners and two dozen people gathered in front of it.
Most of them held their phone screens up to show GIFs of flickering candles. A few tried to keep actual candles lit in the wind,
which carried bits of a man's voice to Jack. The man, silver-haired
and slender, stood in the middle of the crowd, his back to the wine
bar's windows, reading aloud from a small book.

Jack couldn't make out the words, but the man had a familiar-
sounding baritone. He wore jeans and a gray sweater, and a lock of
silver hair fell over his forehead. With a gasp, Jack recognized it as
the lock of Michael Malone, the very same freshman-year roommate, talented actor, and coked-up mugshot celebrity Jack had just
been thinking about. Kismet!

Michael finished reading and bowed his head while people
tried to clap with phones and candles in their hands. Michael
looked as handsome as ever, had become more of a rugged
Harrison Ford type than a Richard Gere. When the scattered
applause faded, he said, "That concludes part one of Allen Gins-

berg's 'Howl.' See you tomorrow night for part two. First we save this building, and then we save the rest of this desperate country!"

Slightly more enthusiastic applause, and then the candles blinked out or were blown out, and the crowd—mostly old hippies—began to disperse.

This wasn't going to be the piece of cake for which Jack had hoped. Why did actors always have to be so dramatic? Though he had to admit, Michael still had charisma. Jack could feel the magnetic power of celebrity drawing him in, causing him to want to get close, to have people see him standing next to someone so significant, because then Jack, too, would be significant. People would see how he drew the celebrity's attention, would think, "*We're* all looking at the celebrity, but *he's* looking at *that* strong-looking man there!"

Jack approached behind a few selfie seekers, said hello.

"Jack Waxman!" Michael grinned and pumped Jack's hand. "On the boardwalk! I had no idea this kind of thing was on your radar. Let me introduce you to the people in charge."

"No, no. I don't want to meet anyone. I just came to check out the building. I'm on the preservation commission."

"No shit? You've really branched out."

Humble shrug, "It was a favor for the mayor."

"Big shot!" said the man who was way more famous than the mayor. "You know which way you're going to vote, right? I mean, it's pretty obvious the place needs to be saved."

"Well . . ."

Michael grabbed him by both shoulders, looked him intensely in the face. "Jack. Jackie Wax! Brother Mother!"

Jack laughed at his old nickname. He'd been dubbed "Brother Mother" when everyone realized he was the go-to guy for soberly maintaining order at parties. He drove the too-drunk home, offered bandages for cuts and ice packs for bruises. He negotiated with irate neighbors, police officers, and, once, the owner of a dog that had been painted Bruin blue and gold.

"I'm not sure how I'll vote," Jack said. "That's actually why I'm here."

"Jack, this is an easy decision. You know what happened inside that building?"

"Sure."

Michael looked into Jack's eyes, "And? You get how badly we need to celebrate a place like this, right? Especially now?"

"Well . . ." Jack broke eye contact, "maybe I don't know enough about what happened here."

Michael nodded, "Then read up. Do your homework and you'll see that this is a piece of history we should be celebrating. I'm gonna head on home."

"Wait." Jack really didn't want to go home yet. And, from an ethical standpoint, the vigil had only complicated his utilitarian calculation. "I don't have a lot of time. Can you help me understand this better? Give me the short version, the elevator pitch, for why this place is still relevant?"

Michael thought about that for a minute. "Have you read any Venice West poets? Seen any of the art?"

"No."

"Then come on over to my place. I've been collecting their work for years. You can see for yourself how important it is to revive their spirit."

"I'd love that," Jack said.

First, Michael had to shake a few more hands and pose for photos, but then he patted Jack's shoulder and led the way southward. "I'm just a few blocks that way."

They walked past one of those marijuana dispensaries that had popped up all over the city, neon green cross glowing in the window. Jack knew his was an unpopular opinion, but he thought it idiotic to allow the legal sale of drugs, from storefronts, with prominent signage, sending impressionable children and teens the exact wrong message.

"I know 847's style is nothing special," Michael was saying, "but that cafe helped give this neighborhood an ethos. The Caffe group proved that community can transcend those old boundaries of race, class, and religion. Over fifty years ago, they knew these basic things that forty percent of this country still hasn't figured out. And they weren't materialists or consumerists. They weren't TV watchers. They were doers and makers."

"But didn't they spend their not-watching-TV time strung out on drugs? *Consuming*, if you will, those drugs?"

"They were trying to get out of their heads, undo the conditioning of our culture."

"Or they just wanted to get stoned."

"Can you blame them? I can't."

Jack chuckled. "*Obvs*, as my daughters say."

"Fine," Michael said, "but there's another reason to preserve that building: we need to keep the land from being developed into super-luxe housing for tech executives with, like, an Odysse watch store in it. You know how much those things go for? Their entry-level piece is like ten grand."

Jack did know that. He'd briefly researched the watches after admiring one on the wrist of the private equity guy who sat in front of him at Lakers games.

"Just walk around," Michael went on, as he steered Jack left up a dark, narrow walk street, "and you'll see how they're trying to scrub the history of this place, clean it up so the money feels comfortable. Which is a real fuck-you to the people who made Venice a community that celebrated creativity and welcomed everyone with love."

They passed a white-clapboard Cape Cod, and Jack glanced behind them to make sure no one followed. "Considering all those tents on the sidewalk back there, it seems to have remained pretty welcoming."

Michael nodded. "Yeah, the homeless issue is tough. I can't blame people for wanting to live here, but I don't love having to wash human shit off the sidewalk in front of my house."

They passed two softly lit Spanish stuccos, and a huge glass-and-concrete modern. Trees in the yards made a dark bower over the walk.

"Is it dangerous around here?" Jack asked.

"Nah. Lots of stolen bikes and surfboards . . . stuff junkies can sell quickly. Every now and then someone gets mugged late at night." Michael unlocked an iron gate, led Jack down a gravel walk between two Japanese pines. Under one tree a low stone bench faced a stand of waving bamboo and a life-size smiling stone Buddha, lit gently from below. A narrow, white-painted, two-story house with a flat roof was nearly hidden by another wall of live bamboo.

It occurred to Jack that he'd never been to this house. "How long have you lived here?"

"Just a few years. I'm as much to blame for the skyrocketing prices as anyone. Bought just after the fourth season of *Special Ops Pop*."

Michael unlocked the weathered front door, "It's so good to be home. I got back from a silent retreat yesterday."

The thought of a silent retreat gave Jack a sick feeling inside, so he said nothing in reply. Michael led the way to the living room, where a beige couch and chair bordered a Turkish rug of swirling blue and green. He offered Jack the couch. Behind it, a huge painting of primary-colored blobs and black lines covered the whole wall.

"That's a Venice West painting right there," Michael said. He left the room, and Jack forgot to count to ten before pulling out his phone. Another text from Cynthia: *Everything OK??*

He felt guilty, so he replied, *Fine, home soon.*

Then Michael was back, setting down a milk crate filled with books, dog-eared literary journals, and loose photographs.

"Take a look at these. You can take home whatever you want if you promise to bring it back. All this stuff is out of print." He turned toward the kitchen, "I'm going to have some dessert. Are you hungry?"

"I could eat," Jack said automatically.

"Great. I've been thinking all night about this killer açaí."

Jack didn't know what açaí was, so he just nodded. He was flattered by Michael's attention, amused by his clichéd embrace of Eastern spirituality. And it was sort of pleasant, forty years on, to reassume the role of student of Michael Malone, "Curator of Cool."

While Michael was in the kitchen preparing the food, Jack dug into the crate. He pulled out the Bible-sized *The Holy Barbarians* by Lawrence Lipton, with its black-and-white cover photo of two young men and a beautiful young woman on a bed. The woman smiles, holding a cigarette, and one man sits cross-legged next to her, smiling at her, while the other man reclines between them, legs jutting into the foreground. Both men are shirtless. Copy in the bottom corner gushes, *At last the complete story of the 'Beats'— that hip, cool, frantic generation of new Bohemians who are turning the American scale of values inside out.*

Jack put it back without opening it. He pulled out a much thinner book, Stuart Perkoff's *Love is the Silence*, flipped to a middle page:

> if this is the wrong road
> (surely this is the wrong road!)
> which is the right one?
> if this is not me
> who am i?

am i you?

Oy. Jack agreed that sometimes, like now, it was hard to know which was the right road, but how could *i* be *you*? And why did poets have to be so dismissive of standard capitalization? It was so childish. Jack just didn't understand poetry, and he didn't like the feeling of not understanding.

It was the same out-of-the-loop feeling he had freshman year, 1971, when Michael showed him the Mayday Tribe's manual, with cartoon people raising their fists on the cover and the slogan, *If the government doesn't stop the war, we'll stop the government.* Inside were intricate plans describing which government buildings in Washington the Tribe would shut down through nonviolent protest.

Michael had thrown socks and underwear into a gym bag and said he'd be back in a week if he didn't get arrested and his car didn't break down.

"It's going to change everything," he promised. "We'll be out of Vietnam in a month!"

Jack didn't think so. Change, as far as he could tell, came from working within existing structures, through discussion and compromise. Later that week, he wasn't surprised when Cronkite gave the Mayday protest barely a minute of attention. The police had gotten hold of one of the manuals, so they knew exactly where and when everything was going to happen. Nixon called in the National Guard, and they tear-gassed the longhairs on sight and herded them into giant holding pens. About 13,000 people were arrested, and all the mainstream journalists declared it the biggest failure in the history of protests.

But when Michael and his older yippie friends finally got back to campus, after missing a week of classes, they weren't treated like failures. They were war heroes, and their tales of suffering ("Tear gas is a drag, man!") and loss ("Had to barter my belt buckle for a couple sandwiches!") made them campus celebrities.

Jack was jealous, but he thought they were all style and no substance. Just like his father and his "radical" writer friends, they'd never accomplish anything. Jack had read biographies of the great leaders of American history, and he knew you had to trace a middle path, bring out the moderates on both sides, build consensus.

"Sorry—had to toast the coconut flakes," Michael was back in the room, handing Jack a bowl and a saffron-colored cloth napkin.

"'Venice!'" Michael pronounced. "'Holy ground, stained with the blood of poets. City which lies beneath the breasts of birds, guarded by cats. Behind every corner, the Muse, Angel of Surprise. Poems, out of pavement cracks.'"

Jack didn't know what to say, so he said, "Nice."

"That's by Philomene Long. 'The Queen of Bohemia,' they called her. Her words are carved into the Poet's Monument near Windward."

"There's a Poet's Monument?"

Michael sat down next to Jack. "Even if not many people read them anymore, these poets are a crucial link in the chain. They got these ideas out there. Anyway, please enjoy."

Jack spooned up some golden curls of coconut, a banana slice, and some deep purple slush. Tart, sweet, and icy. There was neither cream nor chocolate in it, so calling it "dessert" was a stretch. "Mm," he said, to be polite. Then, "When you say, 'They got these ideas out there,' what ideas do you mean?"

Michael swallowed. "Jack, these people lived through the ramping up of the military-industrial complex, the poisoning of America's soul with consumerism and its body with . . . poison. They saw that the only response to a world fucked up on an industrial scale was total rejection of it." He dipped his spoon into his bowl but didn't bring it to his mouth. "Violent revolution was no good, and political revolution just wasn't happening, thanks to TV and advertising—so they just *lived* it. They said no to violence, racism, sexism, and unrestrained capitalism." At Jack's skeptically raised eyebrow, Michael conceded, "OK, some of them said yes to sexism."

Jack found himself laughing.

"What?"

"Nothing," Jack said. Then, "I'm just tickled to hear all of this from the man who played a soldier on a network sitcom that sold, what? Pick-up trucks? Soft drinks? Potato chips!"

"Also the short-lived Cronurrito—may it, and the people it sent to early graves, rest in peace."

"Those were good," Jack recalled.

"Look, I fully admit that show was evil and spiritually damaging to anyone who watched it. But without it, I wouldn't have had my own spiritual awakening."

Jack swallowed his "Ha!" They finished the so-called dessert in silence. Then Jack set the bowl down and turned to study the blobby painting behind him. It was a mess of shapes and colors. If Jack squinted, it looked kind of like a smudgy angel in profile, straddling a giant purple wine bottle.

"The brilliant John Altoon," Michael said. "Tragically short life."

"Drugs?"

"No! Enough with the drugs, Jack. Drugs aren't the problem."

"And what, in your learned opinion, is the problem?"

"That's easy: we think we don't matter. Even though we *feel* like we're the center of the universe, we really think we aren't worth squat. Just a watery sack animated by electrical impulses that give us the illusion of self. Which, if you think that, then when you're dead, you're just dead."

"I don't think—"

"Sure, you go to temple, tell yourself you believe in some sort of New Agey non-personified God-as-energy or whatever, but you don't believe in a life after this life. Not if you've been educated in the Western scientific tradition. Not if you consider yourself a rational person. Your brain thinks heaven, or reincarnation, is a fairy tale, so why *not* be an asshole in this life? Why *not* grab all you can for as long as you can? What do the kids say nowadays? 'YOLO'? That's the screwed-up thinking underlying our whole society."

"Not everyone—"

"Right, maybe you like to think of yourself as a good person, so you don't do greedy or violent things, but you decide you have to be *the most* good. You'll gain immortality by winning everybody's love, making sure everybody remembers you when you're gone."

"I don't think that."

"You sure?" Michael's smug smile made Jack fantasize about violence for the second—or was it third?—time that night. Nothing major: he just wanted to fling his empty bowl at Michael's face.

"Jack, I think this is exactly the thing that's screwing up your decision-making."

"*Me*? What did I do?"

"I read that essay your daughter wrote."

"You still read my blog?" Jack couldn't help but smile at the implicit compliment.

"No. Someone emailed it to me."

Jack thought about it for a moment. "To laugh at me? The guy who can't even control his daughter?"

"No, because she was right! You should have listened to her. You're running out of time to take a stand. But I don't blame you. You're afraid of dying and becoming nothing, except, you hope, this precious legacy you always talk about. You can't do anything to jeopardize that. You're so stressed out, of course you're acting like a dick!"

Jack stood up. "I just remembered that I don't have to listen to this. Thanks for the whatserjee."

"Ah-sigh-*ee!*" Michael said, also standing up. "Maybe that didn't come out right. Come back. I haven't gotten to the good part."

But Jack was on his way down the hall, wondering why he always forgot that Michael was a jerk. He paused at the front door, shouted, "Good night!"

Michael shouted back, "Aw, come on, Jack. I didn't mean to hurt your feelings. This isn't going to affect your vote, is it? We need to save that building!"

In the yard, Jack blew a raspberry at the Buddha and flung open the front gate. The street was all shadows, but the lights of Ocean Front weren't far away.

18

WHILE HE RETRACED his steps down the walk street, Jack defended himself against Michael's attacks. He wasn't wrong to stay out of politics; he was trying to save his company from ruin, and one surefire way it could be ruined was through the loss of its nonprofit status. And he *did* believe, truly, that there was more to life than just this mortal coil. He'd felt, when he first fell in love—with both of his wives, with each of his four children—the feeling of his soul joining that of his beloved. Total immersion of self in other. Didn't last, but even now, for brief flashes, he felt so connected to the kids that their joy and pain was his. That love was God.

Sure, "God" could just be a serotonin surge or dopamine release in his brain, natural selection motivating him to produce and protect offspring to further his genes. And maybe he did have serious doubts about his consciousness taking up permanent residence in some heaven or hell. But there were reasons to behave well toward others apart from protecting one's eternal soul. Jack wanted to be a good person because, as Abraham Lincoln so perfectly put it, "When I do good, I feel good."

At the end of the block, a pile of discarded clothing suddenly stood up and lurched across the sidewalk into Jack's path.

The guy croaked from beneath his rags, "Can ya spare a dollar? Help me get my boat outta dry dock?"

"Sure I can," Jack enjoyed the thought of this little man with a yacht just a dollar short of setting sail. He pulled out his wallet, spotted three singles remaining among the twenties. "Here, take two!"

"God bless you," the man said to Jack's back.

Jack waited for a white BMW to pass on Speedway, the alley that ran along the backs of the Ocean Front buildings. The car's headlights plastered every surface in cold light as it stopped briefly near the green-lit back door of the marijuana dispensary before continuing past the recycling and trash bins of the neighboring building.

Feeling uneasy, Jack hurried across Speedway, thinking Ocean Front would be more populated. But before he even turned the corner, he heard people shouting.

Angry bass: "I told you!"

Tenor: "No, you didn't!"

Bass: "Trust me. I fucking told you!"

Tenor: "No, you fucking didn't!"

Bass: "Yeah, motherfucker, I fucking did."

Tenor: "You just call me a motherfucker, motherfucker?"

Bass: "Yeah, motherfucker!"

Tenor: "Fuck you!"

Bass: "No, fuck you!"

Jack turned around. He could walk down Speedway just as easily. A bit darker than Ocean Front, but it was free of angry people with awful argumentation skills.

He hurried past the dispensary, thoughts turning toward home, toward facing his dear, faithless wife. He walked past the back of the apartment building and the huge bins.

Something rustled behind him—something hard slammed into the back of his head.

Jack saw red and yellow sunbursts and fell into a deep, dark pool where the street was supposed to be.

JACK WAS AN INFANT AGAIN, tugged roughly from his crib, slipping out of his mother's arms, falling hard. The pain in his head aged him sixty-two years.

"Fucker's heavy. Get on his other side."

Now two sets of hands gripped him by his upper arms, jerked him upright. Jack groaned.

"He drunk?"

"He's fuckin' barefoot."

That explained the airy feeling in his toes. Lifting his head a little to see where he was being dragged and who was doing the dragging, Jack made out the silhouettes of men: one big, one small.

"Not drunk," he managed to say. "Mugged."

"Well, we got you now," the big one said. He had blond hair, and his name was Bam-Bam, Jack decided. Bam-Bam took one hand off of Jack's arm, slid open the side door of a minivan. Both men pushed Jack onto a seat covered in dusty blankets. Jack smelled the funk of unwashed bodies. Felt for wallet, phone, and keys, but of course they were gone. Tried to sit up, too dizzy. Bam-Bam slammed the door behind him and got into the front passenger seat. The small man got in on the driver's side, and Jack got a brief look at him: red buzzcut hair, freckles across his nose.

"Please, take me home," Jack tried. "I can pay you."

"With what? Empties?" Freckles snickered. "What's your name?"

"Jack. What are your names?"

Freckles didn't answer. They crossed Lincoln into the eastern, slightly less gentrified part of Venice.

"Where are we going?"

Freckles suddenly swung the car to the left. Jack, unbelted, slammed shoulder and head against the door—another explosion. He lay dazed, stuck between the seat and the door.

"Stay down and keep your mouth shut."

Jack reached up and tried the door handle. He'd rather jump out than go wherever these guys wanted to take him. But the child lock was engaged, and Bam-Bam caught him in the act and smacked him in the mouth.

Lip stinging, ears ringing, face pressed against a rough blanket that smelled like ancient farts, Jack felt the van decelerate. He listened and labeled the sounds: window rolling down, electronic beeps, grinding of a gate opening. The van moved forward, and then they stopped for a moment, and continued through a garage door that began to close behind them.

Jack raised his head, risked a glance out the back window before the door went all the way down. Parking lot. Chain-link fence behind it. Through the side windows, he saw a cavernous room, some kind of warehouse? Music was playing, but it sounded less like music and more like an old smoker clearing his throat into a microphone while someone threw drums, guitars, and amplifiers down a flight of stairs. Then Bam-Bam flung open the door and dragged him out.

It was a dimly lit airplane hangar, with a small office area on the right wall, and a green-lit emergency exit door on the left wall, near several parked motorcycles. Bam-Bam dragged Jack past a bunch of leather-and-denim-clad men standing around some kind of ring, cheering, laughing, "head-banging," perhaps even "moshing." They were Caucasian, to a troubling degree, and the words EARTH SHAKERS or POSEIDON'S PROGENY were stitched across the backs of some of their jackets.

Before Jack saw anything else, Bam-Bam dragged him toward the office. He flung wide the door and threw Jack down on the industrial carpet.

"Sit until you're picked. Make any noise, touch anything . . . you're fuckin' dead." He slammed the door behind him.

Next to Jack, a man straight out of concentration-camp-liberation films sat with his back against a filing cabinet. With his skeletal arms wrapped around knees, he rocked back and forth, muttering, "He's gonna die and she's gonna die and I'm gonna die and you're gonna die—"

A slap across his face stopped him short. The slapper, an older black man with dreadlocks and a curly white beard, said with Caribbean rhythm: "Sorry—but I'm sure I'm not the first to slap that face."

"Nope he slaps me and she slaps me and you slap me—"

Another slap. "You done?" the Jamaican asked.

The slappee nodded.

Gingerly probing the throbbing spot at the back of his head, and then his swelling lip, Jack looked at his fellow hostages. Aside from the Jamaican, the slappee, and himself, there were three others. Two seemed to be grungy teenagers, their beards short, clothes not yet faded to that uniform gray-brown. The last was a man Jack originally mistook for an off-kilter coat rack behind the desk. Only when the rack moved—fingers coming out of a sleeve to scratch under the low brim of the old straw sun hat—did Jack notice the frizzy gray hair, the scabbed nose, and patchy beard. Thin, blueish legs showed through the holes in baggy pants shredded at the cuffs.

"Does anyone know what's happening?" Jack said.

"Human sacrifice!" Slappee shouted. "They pull you off the street, take you somewhere and make you disappear, forever!"

"Don't be so dramatic," the Jamaican theatrically enunciated the final syllable. "Man said we fight, whosoever wins gets twenty

dollars. Man said win or lose, we go to Skid Row. And no goin'
back to the beach. We go back to the beach, they kill we."

Outside the office, the boos and laughter grew louder. Jack
looked around the room. There was a desk, a few chairs, the filing
cabinet, but nothing else. Not even a window.

"OK, we don't have a lot of time. Let's turn over the desk. See if
the legs unscrew or if we can break them off. Is that cabinet
empty? We can use it as a battering ram."

No one moved.

"They've got guns," one of the teens said.

"And, like, a willingness to torture," said the other.

"Maybe some of us would get away," Jack tried.

"I may be fucked up," the second teen said, "but I bet I can run
faster than you."

"I'm surprisingly quick for a big man." Jack had been making
this claim for forty-five years. Only now did he consider that it
might no longer be true.

"Bumbaclot idea," the Jamaican said. "Fight pretend, get hurt
pretend. Live to see the sunrise."

"Sure," the coat rack finally spoke up in a high, rasping voice.
"Long as I win. That twenty bucks is mine, even if I have to kill one
of you for it."

"Sticky," the Jamaican said, disappointed, "that's the junk
talkin'. Babylon uses it to control your mind. I-and-I got to resist."

"You-and-you can go blow each other," Sticky muttered.

Outside the door, the cheering and booing rose to a crescendo
and then faded. A loud voice shouted something Jack couldn't
decipher. Then a general murmur.

"Shit-shit-shit, here they come!" Slappee said.

"Everyone attack as soon as they enter, OK?" Jack crouched
and said, "Let's roll!"

But he was the only one who popped up and rushed the door
as it opened. A mountain of brown hair and black leather walked

in, said, "Ooh!" and swatted Jack in the stomach with a giant paw. "You're an eager beaver, aren't you? I like that!"

Jack fell, breathless and wheezing, while a second mountain of hair and leather stepped inside and looked around the room. His eyes stopped on Sticky. "You! You're a cranky sonofabitch! Lean and mean versus fat and soft? How 'bout it, Clem?"

"Hell yeah, Clyde." He grabbed Jack's arm and hauled him to his feet. "Fifty on Fats here."

"You're a fat chauvinist, you know that?"

They dragged Jack and Sticky into the main hangar. Only a few ceiling lights were on, but they bounced off the shiny chrome of the motorcycles parked between the closed garage door and the emergency exit. From the back of one bike, a limp red flag dangled from a pole.

A bass-and-drums approximation of machine-gun fire blared from speakers somewhere. Several men stood around shouting and laughing, drinking and smoking.

Jack wasn't sure how hard he'd hit his head, but he wasn't convinced any of this was real. It was all too stupid. Homeless gladiator matches? And they thought *he* was homeless because they found him without shoes and a little beat up? These slacks were Hugo Boss. He was eighteen years into a mortgage, in Brentwood!

The bikers were mostly tattooed men in leather and denim, but there were a couple of clean-cut, military-looking guys like Freckles. One broad-shouldered, business-casual man sat on a folding chair far back in the shadows, youngish face glowing in the blue light of his laptop.

Freckles dragged Jack to one corner. Bam-Bam basically carried Sticky to the other corner, shouting, "Whatcha gonna do? Whatcha gonna do?"

Jack didn't catch the answer because Freckles demanded attention. He twisted Jack's shirt tightly, pulling out a few chest hairs in the process. The liquor on his breath made Jack's eyes water.

"How you feeling?"

"Afraid—confused," Jack said. "Is this the Santa Monica Airport?"

Now Freckles was confused. "The fuck you know about the Santa Monica Airport?"

"N-nothing!"

Freckles pulled a flask from his pocket and held it up to Jack's mouth. "Drink, shitbag!"

Jack turned his face away.

"I—I don't drink."

"I will drown you in a fucking bucket of grain alcohol if you don't drink this."

Jack drank, and it burned all the way down. He coughed. Freckles wiped the flask and tipped it into his own mouth. Then he shouted in Jack's ear, "You're angry, not afraid! You hear me? Angry!" He paused to let it sink in. "Now, *what* are you?"

Jack wiped the tears from his eyes and the spit from his ear and tried to control his voice, "Still pretty afraid!"

Freckles raised his fist. Jack flinched. Freckles waited for Jack's eyes to reopen, flicked the tip of Jack's nose. Jack cried out, and again Freckles flicked.

"Please," Jack begged. "Please!" He tried to pull away, but Freckles held on, made him take another swig.

Freckles asked Jack if he was angry now. Jack, always a good student, said yes. Did Jack want to hit something? Jack said yes. Did he want to fuck someone up? Get some payback for all the people in his life who fucked him up?

"No!" Jack couldn't help himself. "I don't want to eff anyone up. And I don't like that language."

Freckles said, "Then prepare to get yourself fucked up!"

"I don't believe in violence," Jack said quickly. "I've never even been in a fight!"

"Well, Sticky is gonna fight *you*. And he looks like he needs a fix, so you better protect yourself."

Somebody shut off the music and the bikers gathered together and covered their faces with ski masks or bandanas. Business-casual guy pulled a baseball cap low over his eyes. Someone else held up video camera with an attached spotlight. Freckles, now wearing a black Lone Ranger mask, shouted something at it. Then the camera turned, and the light blinded Jack.

He realized he might really be about to die. He saw the illuminated *EXIT* over the door, and several bloodthirsty men between him and it. He whispered to God, begged Him for deliverance. Revised that to mercy. (This was already too close to *Deliverance*.) Jack tried bargaining, swore constant and eternal repentance for his sins, offered the whole of his remaining days to God if He'd just get him out of this mess. He even found himself mumbling The Four Questions from Passover, the only Hebrew he could remember under the stress.

Still, Sticky came at him, sneering horribly, winding up a punch. Jack closed his eyes and ducked—and possibly screamed. Opening his eyes again and turning, he saw two bikers shoving Sticky back into the center of the circle. Sticky flew forward and landed face down right in front of him.

A primitive voice from deep in Jack's amygdala told him to stomp the head. Kick the face, jump on the back, twist the neck until it snaps. But Sticky in the spotlight was too pitiful a sight, from the scabby skull under the thin, matted hair down to the chalky heels. Jack took a deep breath and squared his shoulders, the better to bear the crowd's anger and impatience.

But then Sticky grabbed his legs, intending, it seemed, to bite, and whatever was civilized in Jack vanished.

19

CHEEK PRESSED AGAINST COLD FLOOR, Jack listened to stomping motorcycle boots and raised voices as people argued about who owed whom money. He was not dead—at least not yet. He'd hit the floor only about fifteen feet from the door under the *EXIT* sign. No one stood between him and it. He could run for it, but there was Sticky, lying on his side, moaning, hands pressed to his eye. Blood seeped through his fingers.

Jack didn't really do blood. When he was a kid, his mother used to call him her little doctor. She told everyone what a great doctor he was going to be. But then Duke, the dog, got injured in a fight with a stray. Jack took one look at the bloody gash on Duke's foreleg and fainted dead away. And had nightmares about it. From then on, his mother told everyone, "Jackie's going to be a lawyer— he can't stand the sight of blood."

Jack crawled over to Sticky, spat out a little of his own blood so he could speak. "Are you OK? Can you see anything?"

Sticky didn't answer. Jack crept closer, gently pulled at his hands. Blood trickled out of a gash above Sticky's eyebrow, but it didn't look like the flag pole had actually gone through the socket.

PHLERRRGHHH! Jack vomited next to Sticky, who jerked his head away from the spray.

"I'm so sorry." It was purple—internal bleeding! No, ah-sigh-ee. He wiped his mouth with the Confederate flag, offered a cleaner patch for Sticky to use to staunch the bleeding. "Use this," Jack pressed it into his hand. "I don't think the eye itself is damaged."

"Fuck off," Sticky said, but he took it.

Jack effed off. He took another look around, noticed everyone busy arguing. Two of the bikers had even begun trading blows, and now other bikers were making bets on the outcome of that fight.

"Let's go already!" Freckles shouted. "Who's next?"

"Let's roll," Jack whispered to himself. He scrambled for the door. Some guy, no taller and certainly much thinner than him, shouted, "Hey!" but Jack just lowered his shoulder like Larry Csonka and knocked him out of the way.

"Oi!" someone else yelled, as Jack reached the fire extinguisher hanging by the door. Jack yanked it off the wall, turned it toward whoever came at him. Before he could think about how to work it, *bap!* a hole sprang from the side of the cannister. A white cloud filled the air, and fluid spewed onto the floor. Second and third shots sparked off of the wall behind Jack's head. He dropped the canister, hurled himself out the door.

Jack ran left for no reason past parked cars. He darted around the corner of the building into an alley between hangars. He heard the door fly open again, but he kept running the length of the building. Deeper into the airport. Stupid! Or brilliant? They wouldn't expect deeper.

By the next corner, his heart felt like it might explode. He found cover between a huge SUV and a gleaming black boat of a luxury sedan. Over his own stifled gasps, he heard shouts and the starting of horribly loud engines. From the other direction, foot-steps and a man talking on his cell phone, maybe twenty yards from the car.

". . . no, man. No, I'm not putting pressure on you. I just figured, I'm back in town, I'm in your hood, maybe you can show me what you been doin' . . ."

The sedan's lights flashed, the door lock clicked just above Jack's head, and the trunk whooshed open. Down the block, un-muffled motorcycle engines rumbled to life.

The man's voice got louder as he neared the back of the car, "Whatever issues you're having, I can give you some advice, or just talk it out with you."

The open trunk blocked the rear window's view into the back-seat. When the man started talking again, saying, "I know, I know, but this isn't pressure—" Jack reached up, eased open the rear passenger door and scrambled in, "—it's an offer to help you, man, to support you." At the exact moment the trunk slammed shut, Jack closed the door behind him.

The motorcycle engines grew louder. Jack's whole body shook with fear.

"The fuck's going on here?" the man said, coming around the car, phone blocking his face. "Listen, man, I don't care what you're in the mood for. I'm getting in the car now. See you in ten."

The man opened his door, got into the driver's seat. Sniffed, then glanced behind him, saw Jack, jumped out of the car. "What? The fuck!"

He was middle-aged and he wore wire-rimmed glasses and a sports coat, but he was black, and Jack instinctively covered his head with his hands. "Don't hurt me—I've been abducted!"

"Hurt *you*? Get the fuck out of my car!"

"No—please!" Jack whispered. "You have to get me out of here! They shot at me!"

"I'll call the cops, man!"

"Yes! I *need* the cops!"

Jack heard one of the motorcycles approaching, flattened himself as much as possible. Over the din, a man shouted, "Hey, brother! You seen a big white guy around here?"

"No, *brother*, I haven't seen anyone."

"Don't use that tone with me, *boy*. We're takin' our country back!" With an ear-splitting, bowel-loosening roar, the motorcycle took off.

The man got into his car, shut the door, and said to Jack, without looking at him. "You come up front in a minute. I'm not your damn chauffeur."

"Thank you! And please, I'm not like them. They kidnapped me. I'm Jewish! I have black—I have a black friend."

The car came to life, but the engine was so quiet the only sound was the perfectly equalized funk assault on Jack's ears. The man backed out of the space and drove through the parking lot, glancing often in his rearview mirror. Jack kept his head down, a good thing, since they passed two more motorcycles on their way to the gate. He scarcely breathed until after the gate opened and they were out on the streets.

"Anyone following?"

The man checked his mirrors. "No."

"Want to call the police?"

"No, I don't want to call the police." He drove another few blocks down Pico and pulled over. "Now get up here."

Jack reached for the door handle, thought better of it. He wasn't going to give this guy a chance to drive off and leave him a sitting duck. He crawled forward over the center console.

"What the fuck!" the man complained, but he didn't want to touch Jack, so he gave him room. "Damn, man! Is that blood or vomit? Did you piss yourself?"

"All three, I'm afraid," Jack admitted. "I'll reimburse you for any cleaning costs."

The man rolled down all of the windows, brought wind swirling into the car. He looked more closely at Jack's rapidly swelling face. "I know you?"

"Jack Waxman, founder and CEO of the Waxman Ethics Institute. I do radio pieces on KORK?" He held out a shaking, bloodied hand, but the man only glanced at it.

"Did you used to work in music?"

"Sports law, and I taught Contracts and Ethics."

The man shook his head. "Your kids at Hancock?"

"Yes!" Jack said. "Daughters in ninth and twelfth, son in seventh!"

"I have twin daughters in eighth."

Then Jack recognized him. "Yes! 'Killer V.' Williams!"

"Nobody calls me that anymore," Williams said coolly. "Where you live?"

"Brentwood."

"All right. I'm in Beverly Hills—north of Sunset—so you're on my way. I just gotta make a quick stop first."

"You're a saint! Thank you," though Jack noted they were heading west, in the opposite direction of home. "Where are we going?"

"The beach."

Williams said nothing more, but Jack couldn't handle the silence. It allowed him to think about violence and blood and pain. He tried to make conversation, talking loudly over the wind and the music: "What is this beautiful car?"

"It's a Kingpin. They only made fifty of them. See the little logo here?" Williams pointed to the glowing golden-crowned bowling pin in the center of the steering wheel. "It was a gift from my wife. As you might imagine, I'm getting pretty hard to shop for."

"Yes! I think I recently heard one of your songs, 'Jelly' by Princess Playa? Featuring . . ."

"Big Chichi? Yeah, I produced that."

"Yes!" Jack said. "I was reviewing the playlist for my son's bar mitzvah. That one has some nice hooks!" He didn't really know what a hook was, but he hoped it applied.

"Thanks," Williams had turned left on Lincoln and now they were heading south.

"Just one question," Jack said. He just couldn't help himself. "What was that line, 'No jelly 'til you fill my belly, no . . . ?'"

"'*No booty grindin' 'til I get my diamond.*'"

"Yeah, that. What do you think young girls and boys are taking away from that?"

Williams exhaled loudly through his nose. "First, I didn't make it for kids. Second, you're missing the point. It's about female empowerment."

"Really?" Jack stroked his chin, winced at the pain in his bruised jaw. "Because when I heard it, I thought, 'Wow, this could really contribute to the objectification of women.' You're basically saying that women can be bought."

"Everyone can be bought. Let's drop it, all right? My fourteen-year-olds have already told me I'm a misogynist. They think I'm greedy enough to vote Republican just for the tax break. I don't need any shit from an old white dude whose ass I just saved."

"I'm sorry," Jack said. "All three of my daughters are angry with me too. Maybe all of us men need to listen more to the women in our lives."

A Waxim Alert went off in Jack's concussed brain. He could write a public apology to Sophia, could remind Cynthia why she loved him, or had loved him. Yes! Acknowledge the different—in some ways superior—intelligence of the women in his life, underscore the importance of noticing and working through one's ingrained sense of male privilege. In a way, the events of this terrible night—the events of the last terrible century—could be blamed on male privilege.

"Man, you don't know anything about the women in my life," Williams turned right on Rose, past the huge Whole Foods and the mandatory Dollar Store, putting them squarely back in Venice.

"By any chance do you have a pen and paper?" Jack asked, looking around his seat, seeing only leather and burled wood. He had to get this idea down before he forgot it.

But Williams was still thinking about his song. "And who are you to judge what's good pop music, what's good poetry?"

"Well, I don't think it's talking about trading sex for food and jewelry."

"Maybe it's a protest song. Maybe it reflects the sad reality for poor and uneducated women in this country."

"OK," Jack said. "I didn't get that, but I guess you're right. Think there might be a notepad and pen in the glove compartment? How's it open?" He couldn't find a latch, but there was a touch screen between them, not totally unlike the Tesla's. Jack pressed it, looking for the menu.

Slowing to turn left off of Rose, Williams glanced over. "Hey, don't touch that. I haven't figured everything out yet."

But Jack thought he saw what he was a looking for, a little passenger seat icon and an arrow up icon in front of it, where the glove compartment would be.

"No, don't do—" Williams swatted at Jack's hand as he made the turn.

But Jack had already pressed it.

"—that."

All at once: seatbelt unbuckled, door flew open, seat just kind of sprang up on the left side, launching Jack out of the car. Briefest moment of flight. Then, rolling on rocky macadam, whirling streetlights, trees, buildings, and banging knees, elbows, shoulders.

Jack came to rest inches from the crooked bumper of a parked car. *BERNIE 2016*, a faded blue sticker read. The Kingpin screeched to a halt about fifty feet down the road, idled for a few seconds, and accelerated down the street.

20

"HOLY SHIT!"

"Is this a TV show? Which one?"

"Where's the craft services at?"

Jack could only groan.

"Don't badger him! And for the last time, they aren't shooting a damn TV show."

A dark-eyed woman leaned over him, her silver hair hanging in shiny curtains from her heavily lined face. "You hit the ground like a bag of dead cats. Anything broken? C'mon, Bo. Help me get him out of the road before the coyote starts pickin' at him."

"Who is he? Why'd he just get tossed from the Batmobile?"

"Eh," the woman shrugged. "Prolly just more of the new brutality."

Together the woman and an elderly man hauled Jack to his feet. They managed to support him as far as a little sidewalk campsite, where they let him down on a pile of flattened cardboard.

"Medic," Jack managed to croak.

"Sorry, brother. Ambulances don't come to this address."

Jack raised his head, saw in the streetlight tents pitched on the sidewalk, trees, chain-link fence, and behind that some kind of windowless two-story building. It was a mini-Skid Row. "Where am I?"

"Third and Sunset," the woman said.

"A.k.a., Dingleberry Lane," the man said. "This is the ass crack of Venice, and tomorrow they turn the hoses on to get rid of us."

"Shush, Bo! I'll fix you up," the old woman said to Jack. "I'm Cassandra. You just lie down on this nice, soft cardboard . . ."

Jack did as he was told. He accepted the blanket that fell over his legs, and he maintained consciousness long enough to raise his head for the bundled sweatshirt that was offered as a mildewed pillow.

HE WOKE to the smell of alcohol and then the sting of it on his brow. He was under a blanket. A cool hand pressed his forehead, distracted him from the throbbing pains in right knee and shoulder, swollen left cheek and bottom lip.

"Listen," the old woman leaned over him, "I cut off those ruined clothes, but I got this big bathrobe might fit you. Can you sit up?"

Jack knew he should feel alarmed at finding himself naked, but he had no strength for it. After several attempts, he managed to get the robe around himself. Also mildew-scented, it was a little tight in the belly, but it would do.

"Thanks," he whispered.

"Now go on back to sleep. It's all gonna be OK."

Jack closed his eyes again, heard whispering, "Such a fine, handsome man . . ."

Didn't like the sound of that. He began to sit up, but she pressed his forehead back down and made little cooing noises. He dozed. Dreamed of discovering snakes slithering under the couch in his living room, wrapping around the legs of the coffee table, even sleeping coiled beneath pried-up floorboards.

He woke to the pleasant warmth of a hand rubbing his chest and then, in a slow arc, curving up over the crest of his belly and down the other side. The hand kept going.

"Shush," she whispered, though Jack had said nothing. "I know what I'm doing."

Dreaming again? It seemed unfair that his dreaming mind would stick him with a possibly schizophrenic crone instead of a sexy-but-age-appropriate yoga instructor.

"Don't worry," she whispered. "He's an idiot and so's his dog. I just want a touch. It's been so long . . ."

"I'm married," Jack said.

Her breath hot in his ear, "Your wife knows what you need, but I know what you want."

Jack wasn't sure either statement was true, but she pressed hard against him, and he found himself responsive.

It had been so many months. He just never found himself in the mood. Too busy working, desperately trying to build something that would last. *He* certainly wasn't going to last. Just like good old Danny Schacht, who ate right and exercised (neither of which Jack did), and who now was just gone. Alive in the memories of a handful of people, but they'd all be gone soon enough too.

And what would Jack leave behind? Despite his best efforts, he was no world changer, nobody to be particularly remembered. Even his wife and children didn't seem to appreciate him, would probably not talk much about him after he was gone. The Institute would go under in a month, maybe two. Eventually they'd take down his little Wikipedia entry, and it would be as if he'd never existed.

Poor Cynthia. Probably thought he couldn't get it up anymore. Probably thought he'd aged out of their marriage. Though, if she thought that, why hadn't she suggested an erectile dysfunction medication? Maybe she was afraid of hurting his feelings. Maybe she no longer found him attractive. He certainly couldn't blame her for that.

But here, in the calloused hand of Cassandra, Jack Jr. was alert and curious. Encouraged, she stroked more rapidly. Her breath rushed hot and sickly-sweet over his cheek.

Jack raised his head, saw her other hand down her pants. She was going and going, brow furrowed, mouth open. She was missing a lower incisor. Still, sexy, in a kind of naturalistic way. Good cheekbones, passionately knitted brows. Probably around Jack's age.

That said, she was starting to chafe him. He gently pulled at her hand, and she released her boa-constrictor grip. "Can I help?" he asked.

She guided his hand into her pants, and Jack, always a sensitive lover, negotiated the wiry bush and slippery, soft folds until he found the spot. He began slow, and gentle, allowed her to lead. She urged him to keep going. She seemed close. He thought, "Now it's time," was wrong. Thought, "*Now* it's time," was wrong again. Finally, with a soft groan and a great shudder, and totally erotic contractions around his fingers, she came.

She collapsed next to him, heaving, forehead sweaty and smelling like mushrooms against his neck. She stuck her hand inside Jack's robe, rested it on his penis. She shyly looked her question at him.

"Oh, don't worry about me!" he assured her. "I'm fine."

"You sure?"

"Yes!" He took her hand in his. Then, so as not to hurt her feelings, "Long day."

She pressed herself against him, slurred, "Mind if I lie here a while?"

"No, I like it." Her body was warm, and her hair smelled like a campfire. He closed his eyes again and immediately fell back asleep.

. . .

JACK DREAMED he was a thin lad in dark sack coat, Bowlered head swimming with lust and terror. Gaze shifting all over the square, failing as before to find the object of his lust, the subject of his terror. But in his coat, a promising, perfumed letter pressed against his heart. Last time he'd waited for twenty minutes, pulse quickening idiotically at every approaching girl, thinking each one might be she. He recreated her in his mind: bold, amused eyes, tresses more red than brown, the magical way she looked up from her work at the exact moment he passed Finn's. She'd turned her face to him like a buttercup to the sun, and he rose right out of his body, eyed them both from up high and slightly to the side, heard his own tumbling nonsense about she being a blooming flower and her neat retort, "Aye, one that won't be plucked by the likes of you."

How not love her instantly and forever?

There—hurrying down Merrion Street, face flushed, *embonpoint* heaving, eyes and mouth smiling her yes to his will she come. Yes, her eyes said, yes, her crooked smile.

Skip several pages—her mouth on his yes her tongue yes over his yes—but what's this—finger? In his—no!

Actually, yes.

Jack attained complete waking awareness roughly one second before Cassandra's mouth and finger brought him to an orgasm in which every muscle in his body contracted just shy of snapping.

Again, darkness exploded into color, orange bursts turning purple at the edges. Snowed by bliss, entire limbic system on the fritz, Jack made vague plans: collect wits, find feet, run away. But sleep crushed him like a rogue wave and carried him swiftly out to sea.

21

Оннн. Oh, ohhhh.

Pigeons moaned in the palm trees. Jack blinked at the cinderblock wall inches from his face, thinking James Joyce, Leopold Bloom, Max Bialystock, Zero Mostel. He'd fallen asleep next to Cynthia while she finished that Joyce documentary—last week or ten years ago. Then he remembered the other dream, for surely it *had* been a dream, and he had not actually received oral pleasure from a homeless woman in the middle of the night. He felt himself under the—oy, *something* had gone on down there. He realized that he wore a robe, and his robe was open, and this greasy blanket was touching his—

"Cooties!" He struggled upright, tried to forget about his forever-tainted penis. Blood throbbed intensely in his head, faintly in his anus. The woman, Cassandra, was gone, thankfully.

Never speak of her, of this. Never think of it.

Of what? himself said.

Exactly!

What time was it? The sky was an indistinct gray. Flaps were closed on nearby tents. Across the street, vaguely human-shaped bundles. A man wrapped in a blanket sat on the curb and dumped the remains of a potato chip bag into his mouth and beard.

Jack struggled to his feet, discovering new injuries with every movement. He had another small freak-out when he realized all he had to wear was this filthy robe, which, he now noticed, was pink, with two cigar-shaped burn holes around the left nipple. He shivered, tried to think positively: after all, he wasn't naked.

Flashing blue and red lights suddenly bounced off the windows of the apartment building at the corner. Thank God.

Re-knotting his belt, Jack limped to the end of the block, found the patrol car parked in front of a boxing gym. Next to it, two uniformed officers patted down a filthy, yellow-haired man with some kind of rash on his face. One officer was a post-millennial reincarnation of Poncherello from *CHiPs*, with thick black hair and a compact Latin swagger. The other was more like a late-career T. J. Hooker on steroids. Body armor bulged beneath their blue-black uniform shirts.

Ponch had the yellow-haired man leaning against the trunk of the patrol car with his hands and legs spread.

"Hello," Jack called to T. J. Hooker from fifteen feet away. "Can you help me?"

Hooker briefly assessed Jack's threat level, found it beneath his attention. "We're busy. Move along."

"I can wait!" Jack tried to convey cheerfulness and respect. He stepped back a few feet, watched the policemen shove the yellow-haired man down hard on the curb. T. J. Hooker stood over the man while Officer Poncherello took his ID card to the squad car.

Hooker suddenly looked at Jack. "What? You want me to write you up for loitering?" Bulging his eyes, "And indecent exposure?"

"No, sir," Jack futzed with his terrycloth knot. "I'd like to make a report. Last night I was mugged, kidnapped, brutally beaten, and forced to participate in some kind of underground gladiator match. There is a violent gang of criminals at large, and you need to do something about it."

T. J. Hooker took a closer look at Jack, who became self-conscious about his wild hair, bruised and unshaven face, filthy Pepto-colored robe, and bare feet. "Listen, pal, we're busy right now, so why don't you go down to the station and file your report?"

Jack took a deep breath. "I can wait until you're done here."

The cop said, "Better yet, go back to the mental ward and tell your doctor."

"Get out of here," the yellow-haired man whispered to Jack. "These guys are dicks."

"What's that?" Hooker snarled. "Where did you say you were born?"

"Right fuckin' here, man."

Jack backed away, more shocked than angry. He knew there were a few bad apples who brutalized and killed unarmed black men and boys, but for him, police had always been a welcome sight. Now they seemed like just another species of predator.

Jack limped down the street a couple of blocks, turned right toward Main Street, thinking pay phone. He reached the sidewalk, looked right, saw only the severe concrete-and-steel lines of new live-work lofts. He looked left, saw, jogging toward him only a few yards away, a young woman in running clothes. Maybe she knew where he could find a phone. He hobbled toward her, "Good mor—"

SPRRSHHHHHHHHHHHHHHH!

Mist exploded in Jack's face, and he found himself engulfed in flames.

22

ON HIS KNEES on the sidewalk, Jack realized that he'd been pepper sprayed. It felt like drowning in Tabasco sauce, like having hot pokers shoved into eyes, nostrils, and mouth all at once. In one night, he'd become so grotesque that people treated him like a rabid dog or Occupy protester.

"You OK, big man?" Gentle male voice, nearby.

"Water!" Jack croaked, blindly clutching at the hood of a car.

"Follow me."

Jack extended a hand in the direction of the voice. The man sighed, and then fingers gripped Jack's arm and pulled him across the street.

The light dimmed. Was he being led into another alley to be further abused? Jack stopped short, tried opening his eyes again. The tears were helping, but he only saw a beige blur over a gray blur.

"It's OK, man," said the voice. "I got you. We're just on a walk street."

A seagull screamed from not far away, and the strong hand on his arm pulled Jack straight into the bright light. The Pacific wind hit him with the smell of brine and bacon, and the sidewalk became sandy under his bare feet. Again, with the beach?

The man stopped Jack short as something fast and whining—motorized skateboard?—flashed past them. Then they moved forward again, but Jack tripped. He stumbled and landed palms first on a patch of grass that seemed to appear from nowhere.

"Whoa—Harold Ramis? Back from the dead?" This was from a deep, African American-sounding voice. Was that thought racist? No, but the flash of fear Jack felt definitely was.

Jack's rescuer said, "Guy got pepper sprayed. Got some water?"

A plastic bottle bounced off of Jack's side. He groped for it, got it open, poured it over his burning face, let it run into his eyes and nose. He coughed, poured more water on and into himself, and coughed some more.

When the world came back into focus, Jack found, to his dismay, that he was back on Ocean Front, maybe a few blocks south of 847. On the horizon, the Pacific Ocean was a thin navy strip sandwiched between gray haze and khaki sand. The board-walk buzzed with runners, stroller pushers, dog walkers, and people on bikes, skateboards, and even a single diehard roller skater. The darker shape that had provided the water turned out to be an African American guy sitting on a blanket. He had an Afro on its way to becoming dreadlocks, scraggly beard, and he was carving something with a small chisel. He looked like a soldier on the losing side, too thin for his frame, veins branching down in his neck and arms. Before him on another blanket lay small, carved figures of lizards, snakes, birds, mice.

Next to the man with the Afro, the lighter shape that had been Jack's guide turned out to be a stocky, youngish, bushy-bearded white guy. He wore a black hoodie and loose, paint-spattered jeans. Paintings on canvases, paper, and pieces of wood were spread out on the sidewalk and stacked one in front of another against a dolly. The painting closest to Jack was at least five feet tall, technically masterful, conceptually deranged. In the fore-ground, a vampire-clown dentist jackhammered the roots of a giant oak tree, while three naked hermaphroditic fairy-hygienists floated around him.

Jack rubbed his eyes again, wondering if they were working correctly. They seemed to be. In the background of the painting, silhouetted hunchbacked figures bent over glowing devices.

The bearded guy followed Jack's gaze. "That one's called *Root Banal*. On sale today for five hundred. Oh, Fuller," Beard held a paper soup container out to the man with the Afro, "almost forgot your breakfast. Thanks for watching my stuff."

Fuller took it and pulled off the lid. "Oatmeal? I look like a fuckin' horse?"

Beard said, "You can't eat stale pastries every morning and expect to live a long time."

"Who's trying to live a long time? Shit." Fuller replaced the lid and set the container down next to him. He picked up a small chisel.

"If by 'shit' you mean thanks, then you're welcome, or, in your parlance, 'Go fuck yourself.'" Beard turned his attention back to Jack, "You look like you've had a rough night. I'll give you that painting for four-fifty."

Jack spat out some more peppery phlegm. "I'm sorry I—I can't—"

"Negotiate?" Beard said. "No problem, man, I'll do it for you. Four hundred?"

"I don't have any money." Jack was still stuck on the jogger, on the pointless violence she'd done to him. "I can't believe . . . that woman."

Beard squinted at him, his eyes creasing at their corners. "Yeah, you aren't the first. You get a look at her?"

Jack shook his head. Pain shot down the side of his neck. "Young? Athletic? Blonde?"

"Narrows it down to about a third of the women in L.A."

"I hope it was that same one," Fuller said. "Otherwise we got an epidemic, a plague of pepper sprayin' Caucasian ladies." He gestured toward Jack with his chisel, "Including you, that's four people we know of in the last week been pepper sprayed."

"But, *why*?"

Beard guffawed. "You're obviously new here."

"Shit," Fuller cleared his throat. "We already got coyotes roaming the streets, people setting fire to buildings . . . gettin' apocalyptic out here."

"Speaking of," Beard said, "any more word on the fire?"

Fuller shook his head. The baby dreads shivered. "Rumors. Phil thinks it's Big Pharma."

"That dude is a broken record."

"Rocky thinks it's another pot doc, trying to muscle in on Dr. Hoff. Or an insurance thing. Maybe Dr. Hoff saw the writing on the wall—end of prohibition as the end of his business model."

"Too bad," Beard said. "Dr. Hoff had the best jingle."

Together both men sang, to what might have been the tune of the old *Spider-Man* cartoon theme:

> *Dr. Hoff—feels your pain*
> *Dr. Hoff—know all the strains*
> *Dr. Hoff, he's the man to see*
> *Dr. Hoff, he's hassle-free*
> *Come ON!*
> *Into Dr. Hoff's!*

Beard giggled, and Fuller allowed himself a smile.

"Why haven't the police arrested this pepper-spray woman?" Jack asked.

That made both of them laugh. Beard said, "She's probably

paying five grand a month to live by the beach. We're just the local color."

Fuller said, "Jesse, how long you think this guy's been out on his ass? I'm guessing three-day bender."

Beard—Jesse—stroked his beard. "I don't know. Looks like he shaved more recently than that. Two-day blackout?"

"Who, me?" Jack was indignant. "I've never been on a 'bender' in my life! Last night I was mugged, and kidnapped, *and* forced to fight. For sport! They filmed the whole thing."

Saying the words, Jack understood their significance. "Oh my God! It's probably on the internet already!"

"Wow. I was way off."

"Do you have a car? Could you drive me home?"

Jesse said, "Sorry. My van got booted last week. I sorta forgot to make the money to pay some parking tickets. Just a couple sales short of a return to mobility. Hey," he cocked an eyebrow, "Fuller, man, you hear Smithy the other day? Talkin' about how he ran into Old Pete at the bus station?"

Fuller shook his head. "B. Smith? Or Kyle the Smithy?"

"B., I think. Said Pete's face was all fucked up and he was totally freaked out. Sleeping at the bus station, spare-changin' sixteen hours a day trying to get fare back to Detroit. Detroit! Said some guys told him they'd kill him unless he fought this bridge troll in some crazy death match. Old Pete actually won. Worried he may have killed the guy, or at least put him in a coma, not to mention exposed himself to MRSA."

Fuller shrugged. He appeared to be a difficult person to impress.

Jack said, "Sounds like the same guys. This Jamaican fellow said they'd kill us if they saw us back at the beach."

Fuller said, "No offense, but maybe you oughta sit a little farther away from me."

Jack nodded. "None taken. I'm getting up anyway. Unless one of you has a phone?"

"Out of minutes," Jesse said.

Fuller just shook his head.

"Do you know where there's a pay phone? Are there still *any* pay phones?"

Jesse dug paint-stained fingers into his pocket and pulled out two quarters. He handed them to Jack. "Two blocks down and to the left. You'll wanna give that receiver a little wipe first."

"Thank you for your help. At least there are a few decent people left in the world."

"He just call us *decent*?"

"I think he meant it as a compliment."

Jack groaned to his feet just as an unmuffled motorcycle started up somewhere and set off a car alarm. The world spun, and he sat shakily down. His heart raced. "You don't think those guys would come after me in broad daylight, do you?"

Jesse shook his head. "Probably too many witnesses."

"But we thought the coyote only struck at night," Fuller said, "'til the day he snatched a parrot right off its perch. It was just chillin' on the front porch, and . . . *squawk*-snap!"

Jack's blood sugar was dangerously low. He looked at the little container of oatmeal that still sat uneaten in front of Fuller. "Excuse me, Mr. Fuller, but are you going to eat that?"

"I look like I own a fucking brush company? It's just Fuller. Go ahead, man, it's all yours."

"Ingrate," Jesse said.

"Thank you!" Jack snatched the container and greedily spooned lukewarm oats, liquefied brown sugar, and raisins into his mouth. Breathing while chewing was difficult, since his right nostril was clogged with bloody snot, but Jack got the first bite down and felt better. He spooned in another mouthful, chewed and swallowed, repeated until it was gone.

As soon as he swallowed his last oat, his problems surged forward, clamoring for attention: cheating Cynthia, blackmailing Vigor, wayward children, business failure, possible concussion, potential internal bleeding, penile cooties—

"Where you guys from?" Jack asked, just to stop spiraling.

Fuller ignored him.

Jesse said, "St. Louis, originally. But I've been here over a year now. Fuller, you've been here for, what, four years? When did you come back from Iraq?"

"That's none of his business."

"Thank you for your service," Jack said. "I've always been a strong supporter of our troops. Where were you stationed?"

Fuller just slit his eyes at Jack.

Jesse said, "Baquba, dude. Like, Al Qaeda headquarters."

"I don't wanna talk about it."

"He doesn't like to talk about it. I've tried to tell him he's got benefits coming to him, but he won't listen."

"You don't want your benefits?"

Fuller looked right into Jack's eyes. "When I came back after my third tour, Chaplain says to the whole unit, 'Anyone havin' any issues?' CO answers, real quick, real loud, 'Nope!' Two weeks later I'm choking my girl half to death in my sleep. Feeling like the roof's about to cave. Driving to the store thinking a Muj is tailgating me, but it's just one of the big-bearded hipster motherfuckers that took over my neighborhood while I was gone. No offense," he said to Jesse.

"*Some* taken."

"I finally went to the VA. Spent half a day in a waiting room with a buncha other fucked-up vets—each one looking like he's ready to throw himself off the roof. They give me Paxil, which don't do shit for the nightmares and paranoia, but do turn my dick into a piece of rope. So then my girl leaves, because it's one thing to wake up getting choked but another thing to get no dick."

He took a very long, very deep breath, let it out slowly. "Weed worked pretty good. But when you're caught smoking weed, you get a less-than-honorable discharge."

"Sounds like it stings," Jesse said with a straight face.

"No benefits. Cheap motherfuckers looking for any way they can to throw everybody out on their ass." Fuller picked up a tiny wooden turtle and said brightly, "But it's all good. I'm just chillin' here, making almost enough from my art therapy to survive. My grampa taught me how to do this. He was a master woodworker."

"Hey-O!" Jesse said. Jack wondered if he had some mild form of Tourette's.

"Grampa claimed to have Tlingit totem carver blood in him, but he was a drunk and a liar." Fuller smiled, revealing a missing canine surrounded by straight white teeth. "He made all kinds of animals, and he gave me these tools and taught me how to do it."

Fuller set the turtle down and picked up a fist-sized armadillo. "So this is what I do."

"Just that?"

"Yeah. I'm retired from everything else. Army, VA, job, car, bills, taxes, fuckin' 'smart' phones—all that shit. Women, too, but that's just an unfortunate side effect."

"No," Jack found himself near tears. The last twelve hours had wreaked havoc on his emotional suspension, and he was bouncing all over the place. "You're too young to write off the whole world. I'm sure we can get you benefits, therapy, a place to live. I'm a lawyer, I can help you."

"Nope! All this," Fuller waved a hand over the whole of civilization, "is fucked. Killed my friends, ruined their relationships, repo'd their cars, even repo'd their fuckin' *homes* while they were out defending the home*land*. Killed half a million Iraqis, not that anyone kept track. And I'm sure we'll start another bullshit war just as soon as we can."

He let out a bitter, one-note laugh. "Fuck this rigged, racist, world-destroying country, man. I may need to live here, but I'm doin' it off the grid. At least until they shoot me for no reason."

"Right on, Full," Jesse said. "Art is our country, the great muse our president. And I'll happily act as your honky human shield. I'll wrap myself around you like a . . . like a fuckin' cracker barrel."

"You guys can't just give up!" Jack said. He had nothing against artists. In fact, he was a huge supporter of the arts—he'd paid for Samantha's useless master's degree in fiction writing, hadn't he?—but society couldn't afford to lose any kind people, and these two were clearly kind. A quote popped into his head, and he shared it: "As Harriet Beecher Stowe once put it, 'Never give up, for that is just the place and time that the tide will turn.'"

"Yeah, well," Jesse said, "I believe it was Jeffrey 'The Dude' Lebowski who said, 'Fuck it, man.'"

Fuller nodded. "We're good here. We're not hurting anybody. What's wrong with that?"

"Nothing. But life is so much richer, so much more rewarding, when you help others. William Penn said it best: 'I expect to pass through life once, so if there's any kindness I can show, or any good thing I can do for someone, let me do it now, because I won't pass this way again.'"

Neither replied to that. Jack knew his quoting was a bad habit, resulting as often as not in this awkward silence. He just couldn't help himself.

"OK." Jack rose, managed to stay on his feet this time. "I'd better walk. Thank you for the oatmeal and conversation."

"Peace."

"Happy trails!"

Jack ensured the tightness of the robe's belt, tried to walk without limping. He ignored the stares of the joggers, fought the urge to invade their personal space, to beg, "Help me, please! I'm one of you! Just hear me out!"

In fact, he'd often been on the receiving end of the "Let me tell you my story!" characters. He usually looked them in the eye to show that he saw them and empathized with their plight, said, "I'm sorry!" and kept walking, fleeing with as much dignity as one could flee. The few times he didn't flee, then he was really sorry. To have to stand there and listen to the elaborate stories: *My wife and baby are in the car around the corner, and we're out of diapers. Can you just give me, like, five bucks, to buy some diapers?* Or, *I was on a date with this guy, and he tried to get fresh with me. I stopped him—I'm not like that—but he grabbed my purse and just ran off. Can you give me ten bucks to catch the bus home to Palmdale?*

And now he was one of those desperate people, just another vendor at the hardship bazaar, except more so, because his horrible story was true, and he was wearing nothing but a pink bathrobe. A less stable man might snap under such an experience, might begin to wonder if he was still himself anymore. Certainly nothing in Jack's sixty-two years of life had prepared him to be in this situation. Even his face felt to his fingers like someone else's face, with a strange new topography of cuts and bruises, dried blood and stubble.

He told himself it was going to be OK, made it a mantra. Somehow he would find value in this experience, would learn something that he could impart to others. Yes! Now that he thought about it, this could be good for a whole raft of new Waxims. Jesse and Fuller were good for at least one, about how it's just not OK in this era to disengage from public life. Mental note!

For now, though, he just had to call Cynthia, beg her to come get him. Then he could take a scalding hot shower, call the police, head to the office. Then, call Vigor, tell him he'd vote against landmark status as long as the checks kept coming. Then, begin plotting his revenge.

He found the phone outside of a convenience store, used the sleeve of his robe to wipe something gelatinous from the receiver.

He was ready to call Cynthia, even if it meant facing the fact of her infidelity.

Jack dropped in the coins and dialed his home number. It just rang. It must have been later than he thought, and everyone was at work or school. The housekeeper—Maria? Thelma?—was instructed to let the machine get it.

The machine! Jack hung up before it picked up and took his money. He waited for the quarters to fall out, lifted the receiver again, reinserted them. Dial tone, but he just stared blankly at the keypad. For the life of him, he couldn't remember Cynthia's cell or work numbers. Had the repeated blows to his head damaged his brain? Maybe, but he'd never been good with numbers, and he'd never had to learn any phone numbers because Bonnie had programmed them into all of his phones for the last fifteen years.

He tried the Waxman Ethics Institute's main number. Rescuing him and driving him home wasn't exactly in Bonnie's job description, but neither was planning the family vacations, and she did that.

Bonnie didn't answer, even after four rings. Again, he feared losing his money, so he hung up before voicemail took the call. Bonnie hadn't been sick in probably a decade, so where the heck was she?

Quarters back in hand, Jack realized he didn't know a single other number, except the one belonging to Susan, his ex-wife. Her home phone was the same one they'd shared when they were married, in the olden days when one had to know phone numbers. He dialed, and glanced up as the phone began to ring. A young woman pedaled past on a beach bike, holding the strings to six shiny Mylar balloons that trailed above and behind her head, each emblazoned with the face of a different Disney princess. She wore a blouse and skirt, heels, and the defeated expression of the personal assistant ruing her life choices.

Distracted by the cyclist and the bobbing, big-eyed, big-haired faces on the balloons, Jack had forgotten to hang up in time to save his money. His ex-wife was telling him to leave a message.

After the tone he said, "Susan, it's Jack. Sorry to bother you, but yours is the only number I can remember. I'm in Venice—Beach—and I need help. I was kidnapped and robbed—and beaten . . . I imagine you don't mind any of that too much—ha-ha—but can you . . ." What was there to ask her machine to do? He didn't know. "Sorry. I'll just call you later."

He hung up and the box swallowed the coins for good. What now? He could try to find Michael Malone's house, but he couldn't remember which street was his, and all the walk streets kind of looked alike. Also, he was angry with Michael. Justifiably or not, he blamed him a little for this whole nightmare.

Jack picked up the receiver again, dialed 9-1-1. It rang twice, paused for a few seconds, then rang several more times until a woman finally said, "9-1-1, what is your emergency?"

"Yes, hello! I've been robbed, kidnapped, and assaulted, and I'd like some assistance."

"OK, just hold on a second, sir. Where are the kidnappers now?"

Jack hadn't expected that. "I don't know."

"You're calling from 989 Ocean Front?"

Jack looked around but couldn't see any address. "Sure."

"So you're not currently being held against your will?"

"No, I . . . got away."

"Do you require immediate medical attention?"

"Uh—"

"Are you currently having a heart attack or stroke? Choking? Bleeding excessively from the head or a major artery?"

"No. I'm pretty badly bruised though."

"Sir, this line is reserved for emergencies. What you're experiencing is a non-emergency. To report an assault and a robbery that occurred yesterday, please hang up and call the non-emergency number."

"Are you serious?"

"Yes, sir. Please free up this line for another call. Have a good day."

"No—wait!"

But the line was dead, and there was nothing for Jack to do but hang up.

23

JACK HEADED NORTH on aching knee and blistered feet. He ignored the stares from people who held their to-go coffees in front of them like handles of invisible shields, First milestone would be the Santa Monica Pier. He could see the Ferris wheel at the end of it, a little hazy circle a couple of miles away. Then he'd turn east to climb the bluff, continue north along Ocean Avenue all the way to San Vicente, another mile. Then, three meandering, tree-lined miles east to Brentwood.

San Vicente was a thoroughfare, and someone in the parade of Rovers and Porsches and Benzes might recognize him. They were his cohort. Or worse, they *wouldn't* recognize him, and they'd call the cops on the crazy man in the pink robe, so high he staggered into the wrong zip code.

He stopped to pull a sticky ice-cream novelty wrapper from the bottom of his foot. Nearby, a group of bedraggled young people sprawled on and around a bench. One dreadlocked blond kid dangled a long fly rod in front of every person who walked past him. A small blown-glass bottle hung from the line, and a torn piece of cardboard propped against the boy's knees read *FISHIN' FOR NUGS.*

"What are nugs?" Jack asked him.

"Grass, I think is what your generation calls it. Got any?"

"Doesn't fishing require bait?"

"Ha. Guess that depends on the brains of the fish and the skill of the fisherman."

"What about a dollar?" asked a fleshy, sunburned girl who sat next to the boy. "You got a dollar?"

Jack shook his head. "I could give you a hundred dollars, upon arrival, if you had a car and could drive me to Brentwood."

"And I could give *you* a hundred dollars if you gave me two hundred dollars first."

Jack forced a laugh. "Seriously though, do any of you have a car?"

"Sorry," said the girl. She scratched under the strap of her tank top, which she seemed to have made with a stapler and motel curtain. "We're broke as fuck."

"Know anyone around here who *does* have a car?"

Another boy, the most heavily pimpled person Jack had ever seen, said, shakily, "What about that pissed-off old guy? Doesn't he have a truck?"

"Oh yeah," the blond kid said. "Phil. You see him last night? Yelling about how people need to rise up? Didn't stop until he saw the police lights."

"He's right, though. The pigs ran over some dude sleeping in the sand," said a very thin, very pale girl in a fisherman's sweater.

"Well, now," Jack began, "'pigs' is not—"

"And they shot and killed this lady's dog—and fucking wounded the lady," another kid said. Jack couldn't tell if they were a boy or a girl, but the side of their head was shaved and tattooed with a stenciled *PRIVATE PROPERTY / KEEP OUT!* "They're just trying to get us to leave, like they did in La Jolla and Del Mar and Newport, but, like, where are we supposed to go?"

Again, Jack felt his emotions getting the better of him. Because his knee-jerk answer was, "Inland?" but he didn't say it. Because why should you have to be a millionaire to see the ocean every day? His pity for these kids transcended the cold stares, body odor, bad skin, potentially lice-infested hair, travesties of tattoos and piercings, complete lack of Ambition, the crucial Fifth Key to GRREATness. He saw little hope for them, and he had no idea how he might help.

"What do you guys do?" he asked. "When you're not fishing for drugs?"

"*Nugs*," the girl in the motel curtain corrected.

"We live," the blond kid said. "Skate, surf, find food. Repeat."

"By 'find food,' you mean, you panhandle until you have enough to buy food?"

"Pretty much. Or people give us stuff they're throwing away. Dumpster-dive if we have to. Americans waste, like, forty percent of our food."

"You don't want to do something meaningful? Contribute to society in some way?"

The kids groaned in unison. Private Property said, "Wasn't that, like, Hitler's pitch?"

"I don't think so."

"It's kinda true," said an elfin girl in a threadbare sweater. "Like, the Inquisition? Slave trade? The Holocaust? Hiroshima? Vietnam? Iraq? All those guys—and they were all guys—thought they were fixing everything!"

Jack felt out of his depth. His previous research into homelessness hadn't extended much beyond the ethical response to panhandling. He told his listeners to give if they felt like it, but absolutely to help through community service and charitable contributions to organizations that serve the homeless. That way they'd be sure their money didn't go to drugs or alcohol. But he'd never studied the issue or thought deeply about actually solving it. His audience were the middle- and upper-middle-class people who'd bought into the system, who'd succeeded in it, or at least survived in it. Their improvement of their position—or at least maintenance of it—was practically a given. They sent their children to schools that could afford character-education programs. And the hope was that those kids would shape a better society. But in the meantime, what do you do with the kids who didn't have a chance to succeed? Who were abused, or rejected for being gay or trans or non-binary, or just given no reason to trust in civilization or in any kind of happiness beyond a donated "nug"? At least artists like Jesse and Fuller were doing some kind of work.

"Can someone explain to me, please," Jack said, "what's so bad about working, saving, maybe starting a family? Owning property?" It occurred to him that he'd said almost the same thing, verbatim, to Michael Malone, forty years ago.

The punks all talked over one another, but everyone stopped to listen to the waif in the sweater, who addressed her speech mostly to the woven bracelet on her thin wrist: "We won't just go along with a system that ruthlessly exploits entire, like, peoples, and destroys resources. Just so, like, a handful of super-rich white guys can hold onto their global hegemony or whatever. We're on strike, and we'll stay on strike until the rich white guys stop ruining the planet and fucking over everyone else. And every *thing* else."

"OK, well—"

"And if they don't stop, we're just gonna chill out and watch the motherfucker burn," Private Property said.

"And feel pretty fuckin' smart for not busting our asses at some shit job that barely covers rent," Dreadlocks said.

"Amen!" Private Property and Dreadlocks shared a complicated handshake that ended with Private Property's finger gun mowing down—with sound effects—all the fingers of Dreadlocks's hand.

"I should go," Jack said. "Do you have any idea where I might find this Phil guy?"

The girl in the curtain looked south, the direction opposite Jack's home. "I think he's at the skate park, like five blocks that way. Just look for a crazy bald guy shouting compliments at people."

Jack looked north. The pier was so tiny in the distance, and when he reached that, he'd only be a third of the way there. He looked the other way. "Skate park? Five blocks? You really think he'd help me?"

"Totes. He's, like, an angry, hairless Jesus," the waif said.

The kids turned their attention deficit disorders to likelier game, a middle-aged European couple in pastel-colored shirts and loafers.

"Hey," the blond kid shouted at them, "*Sprechen sie Deutsch? Tun sie kiffen?*"

As he retraced his steps, Jack kept thinking about those kids, in particular the waif. Likely a neglected boarding-school girl, too smart and strange for her set, or too spoiled to follow the rules. He wanted to go back, ask her about her parents—ask all of them about their parents. Of course, he knew people, good people, whose kids became addicts, dealers, thieves. A whole group of kids a year ahead of Samantha had dropped out of college to follow a "jam band" around the country. The scandal had greatly disturbed the whole Hancock community. Most of those kids had straightened out eventually, but they had resources, stable homes, parents that would always take them back.

These kids, by contrast, seemed abused and neglected, failed by family and the state. What would it take to make up for that? Short of a complete transformation of society? He had no idea, but maybe this topic was something the Institute ought to investigate. No money in it, but it could do immeasurable good and be totally worth whatever compromise of his integrity Vigor required.

OK, God, he thought, addendum to previous deal: get me home, and I'll try to help as many of these kids as I can.

An engine revved nearby. Jack tensed, but it was only a motor scooter. He re-tightened his belt and hurried southward in search of the skate park.

24

THE SUN BURNED off the haze, and the street came to life. Jack walked past dancers, musicians, tumbling brothers, a man preparing to juggle axes. He walked past Jesse and Fuller, but he didn't want to disturb them. Both were deeply engrossed in their work. Jesse sat nearly motionless, staring at his canvas for a long time before dipping his brush and adding a single daub. Fuller was a flurry of movement, chipping and digging and scraping the palm husk in front of him.

On the next block, a man in a tattered plaid shirt had put a red G-string bikini and sunglasses on his dog, an old pit with big nipples and lolling tongue. Crumpled bills were stuffed into the thong that stretched across her mottled pink belly, which rose and fell steadily. Next to her, a cardboard sign suggested a dollar donation per photo. Jack felt a fleeting kinship with that poor dog. He knew what it was like to feel betrayed and humiliated, toyed with by powerful forces for unfathomable reasons.

He finally saw the huge metal beams soaring into the sky. He'd forgotten about that sculpture. Not quite a V, and not quite a K, it was just another example of the unknowable. Nearby, the concrete skate park was crowded with spectators and the occasional rising

and falling skateboarder. On the grassy rise near that, there were
scattered tents and tarps. Jack headed that way, past an upright
piano that listed in the wet grass like a wrecked chariot. Going up
a small slope crowned with a single palm tree, he entered an
encampment of tightly clustered blankets and a couple of tents.
Through one tent's open zipper, Jack saw the knotty spine and
deeply bruised back of a curled-up shirtless man.

Some people sat at the base of the palm tree talking and laughing. Jack counted two graybeards, one bald man, and three
younger men with beards of varying bushiness. Behind them the
grass dropped off a couple of feet to the bike path, and beyond
that, the sand stretched for a hundred yards to the water.

Everyone looked up and stared at Jack, either because he was a
new face or because that face was bruised and swollen and resting
atop a dirty pink bathrobe. At the center of the group, the bald
man crouched on a molded-plastic classroom chair. He had a
beaklike nose and small ice-blue eyes. He held a three-foot length
of white plastic pipe at his side like some kind of holy staff. Neck
twisting as his eyes tracked a woman running on the bike path, he
stood on the chair and cried down to her, "THANK YOU FOR
GRACING THIS BEACH WITH YOUR BEAUTY TODAY!"

The woman kept running without even a glance in his
direction.

Jack approached warily. "Are you Phil?"

The man jumped out of his chair, grinning. "Nice robe, man! I
recently lost one just like it!"

"Oh," Jack instinctively took a step back.

"Just kidding!" the man said. "Phil Anderson. What the hell
happened to you?"

"I'm Jack. It's a long story. I was just talking to those kids down
there, the, uh, nug fishers?"

"Those useless dirt punks? Who wouldn't lift a finger to help
themselves or anyone else?"

"They told me you had a car and you might give me a ride home? It's just fifteen minutes—twenty at the most. I have no cash on me—I was mugged—but I can pay you once we get to my house."

"Sure, sure. Sounds great." Phil sat back in his chair, "But first, I'm curious to know your story, Jack. Who are you? How'd you end up down here, in such a . . . vulval shade of pink?"

"It really is a long story," Jack felt tears rising, and he didn't want to weep in front of these strangers. He sat down on the grass, mainly out of exhaustion. He tried to cross his legs without exposing himself, didn't totally succeed. "I haven't even processed it all yet. You promise you'll take me home?"

"You got it."

"All right," Jack took a deep breath and tried to begin. "I was kidnapped. No. First I got mugged—no, *first,* a client threatened to blackmail me." Jack scanned the men's rough faces, "You're probably wondering why I'd do business with a man like that."

They shook their heads.

"I didn't know he was totally unprincipled. I mean, in retrospect, there were signs, but I guess I willed myself not to see them."

"Skip to the mugging," one of the younger men said. His eyes glittered in the small strip between his fishing hat and his huge, dark beard.

"Sorry. Let's see . . . I was at my friend Michael's house—you guys know Michael Malone? The actor?" Some heads nodded, others shook. "Not important. Anyway, I left his house last night, was just walking down the street when I got hit from behind. I never even saw the guy."

The men traded glances with each other, seeming to ask, *Was that you? No, you?*

"Next thing I knew, two guys were picking me up and throwing me in the back of a van, like this is Mexico or Brazil or something. Except, it wasn't for ransom, like normal, twentieth-century kidnapping. It was to be impressed into a gladiator corps, as punishment, I guess, for being unconscious on the street. I'm a pacifist! But I was forced to fight a sad, broken-down junkie in the last stages of addiction—" Jack broke off, overwhelmed by the injustice of it all, the casual cruelty, the fact that a really great man, the man he'd always wanted to be, wouldn't have hurt Sticky. He'd have found some other way out, or just taken the beating, turned the other cheek. "I hurt him!" Jack cried. "Self-defense, but still, it was savage—"

"It was those Sons of Poseidon fuckers, wasn't it?" Phil said. "The Earth Shakers?"

"Yes! How—"

"So what happened? How are you *not* in Skid Row?"

"You know about that?"

Phil nodded. "Poor Bob over there," he used his length of plastic pipe to point to the green tent, "took him two days, but he walked all the way back here, to warn us." Phil paused, pounded his staff into the grass a few times. "Must be a lot of money in staging fights on the internet, but there's something I can't figure out. The whole enterprise seems like a lot of work for a buncha closet cases who mostly just do drugs and tattoo each other. And I can't figure out why they're forcing people out of the neighborhood. Especially if these people are their quote-unquote *talent*?" Phil spat furiously into the grass. "But I digress—how'd you get away?"

"*Did* he get away?" the youngest man asked, stroking the wispy hairs of his struggling goatee. "Or is he a fuckin' spy?"

"Spy? For whom?" Jack said.

"Not the bikers, with that syntax," Phil said.

"I just got lucky," Jack explained. "The fight was in a hangar near the Santa Monica Airport, and I got away, and hitched a ride with a guy getting into his car. He happened to be Vince Williams—"

"Killer V. Williams? Saved you?"

Jack nodded.

"You're kind of a name dropper, aren't you?"

"He really did, sort of. I accidentally ejected myself from his car on Third and Sunset. I don't know why he didn't come back and check on me. I guess he was afraid he'd killed me. Or maybe he was annoyed that I got blood on his upholstery. And criticized his music. Anyway, a . . . a Good Samaritan helped me, let me sleep on her cardboard, gave me this robe."

"More than some people got," said one of the graybeards. Jack noticed for the first time that, under his jacket, the man wore an Iron Man bedsheet as a toga.

"Granted," Jack said. "But when I woke up, the nightmare continued. The police refused to help me, and a jogging woman pepper sprayed me in the face!"

Phil gritted his teeth, "We're aware of the pepper-spray jogger and are planning an ambush. She doesn't follow a predictable route, so until we have more data, until we can establish a pattern, it's pretty much a needle-in-a-haystack situation."

"What'll you do if you catch her?"

"Gut her!" Phil said, eyes glittering. And then he laughed, "No, I'm kidding, of course. Ha-ha!"

"Heh-heh," Jack forced a couple uncomfortable notes.

"Seriously though, we'll interrogate her, figure out why she's doing what she's doing, and then consider the proper punishment. And execute it."

Jack opened his mouth but no words came out.

"Look. We're under siege, Jack, and we don't even have a wall to hide behind. It's circle the wagons and watch out, because if they aren't criminalizing our existence, they're preying on us!"

"Listen, Phil, I really need to get home now." Jack wondered how much cash was in his closet safe, "I think I can give you two hundred dollars as soon as we get there."

Phil laughed, tapped the keys that hung from a hemp cord around his neck. "I will absolutely take you home, as promised, but I don't know exactly where my truck is right now. Our young friend Nate borrowed it, but between parking it and returning the key, he forgot *where* he parked it. He's out looking for it, because he knows if he doesn't find it before it gets ticketed, I just might bash his skull in with this rebar I've ingeniously concealed here." He rattled his plastic pipe. "So, I guess the gods aren't ready to let you leave the beach."

"The who?" Jack wanted to close his eyes. The hope and positive energy that he'd mustered, thinking himself finally on the verge of deliverance, disappeared.

"You obviously have work left to do here. Tell me, what line of work are you in?"

"I run a nonprofit ethics institute—"

"No way!" Phil leapt out of the chair again, held his hand out over Jack's head, waiting for the high five it took Jack way too long to give him. His pupils were black pinpoints in ice fields, and he said the scariest thing yet: "Jack, you're my new bestie!"

"Oh?"

"Ethics is exactly what I've been talking about! We have so much work to do together. Greed has totally corrupted us. We gotta rise up and fight this bullshit, or stick a fork in the human race! Wait a second, are you on any meds?"

"Just baby aspirin for blood pressure, and a statin for cholesterol."

Phil laughed. "OK, stop that shit. Big Pharma's trying to turn us all into slaves. Just smoke a little ganja, and eat health-promoting fruits and vegetables, and you'll be in great shape and ready to stand up in violent revolution against these corporate cunts!"

Jack couldn't help but flinch at the C-word. "But you know, I really do need to get home."

"Just be patient, man. I'll get you there. And you can help us fight back—what are you worth?"

Jack considered trying to run away.

"Savings? Stocks? Bonds?" Phil leaned in an inch for every inch Jack leaned away. "I gave away all I had, sixty thousand bucks! At least that's what my bitch wife—excuse me, bitch *ex*-wife—claimed in the filing. I didn't keep track myself. I just couldn't take it, driving past the same people every day, begging at the off-ramps, begging in front of Starbucks, getting nothing from people driving luxury cars and buying five-dollar coffees. Not even getting an acknowledgment of their existence? A 'Sorry' or 'Wish I could help' or even a 'Get a job!'"

Phil spat on the grass. "You pass them every day, and you start to ask yourself, 'What are we doing about it? What's anyone doing about it?' Well, I did something. I brought a few home. Fed 'em, let 'em use the shower, call relatives. I paid for clothes, groceries, glasses, doctors, bus tickets ..."

"That's really noble," Jack said.

"No!" Phil shouted. "It's humane! That's what I realized, once I stopped taking that poison they told me would 'help' me. As if I was the one who needed help! You know what they mean when they say you're bipolar, right? They mean you're threatening *their* bullshit system. You're spreading the Good News, the Goddamned Gospel of Jesus Fucking Christ, and they can't have that! After all, they killed Christ, didn't they?"

"Um, *who,* exactly, do you mean by 'they'?" Jack braced himself for an anti-Semitic rant.

"You know, the people who have money and power! Same ones who killed Martin Luther King, Jr., Bob Marley, John Lennon ... Jimi Hendrix ... Bill Hicks."

"Bill who?"

"But with Citizens United, with fucking Facebook, they've

managed to get total control of government. They're going to start a few more wars, wring the last of the fossil fuels from the earth, take even more from the poor to make themselves richer. Man, I didn't realize until my money was all gone that I should've spent some of it on weaponry. Because, make no mistake, a war is coming. And it ain't the War on Christmas!"

Phil turned suddenly to the tourists flowing down the boardwalk in the distance. "WAKE UP!" he screamed. "TIME TO RISE AND SHINE, PEOPLE! STAND UP TO YOUR CORPORATE OVERLORDS!"

"So . . ." Jack said, once he was sure Phil was done shouting, "do you have any idea when your friend might be back?"

"Nate?" Phil raised his eyebrows, perfectly calm again. "Unfortunately, the Purple Amnesia we're using to treat his anxiety lengthens the time it takes him to perform the simplest of tasks."

Jack looked on the bright side: it was probably for the best that Phil not know where he lived. He struggled to his feet, felt wind on his crotch and realized his robe was askew. "Excuse me." He straightened it. "Before I go, does anyone have a phone I might borrow?"

"For a hundred dollars? Next time you see me?" Phil laughed. "Just kidding! Here," he pulled an old flip phone out of his pocket, held it toward Jack, pulled it back.

"Keep it brief, though. I don't have a lot of juice."

"Thanks, you're a real mensch." Jack began dialing his office.

"YOU ARE DIVINE!" Phil shouted over his shoulder.

Jack looked up, saw, behind the jogging woman at whom Phil had just yelled, a fit man in a clingy synthetic shirt and running shorts, his silver hair peeking out from under a baseball hat.

"Michael!" he called, half-suspecting him to be a mirage. "Michael—it's Jack!"

Michael recognized Jack and stopped short, causing a three-skater pile-up behind him.

25

JACK GAVE the phone back to Phil. "Thank you, but it looks like I'm saved."

"Oh, no!" All the lines in Phil's face tilted downward. "Jack, you need to stay. We need to rap about ethics. In particular, the ethics of righteous violence."

"I'm sorry, I really have to go."

"Was I wrong about you? Are you one of *them*?"

"No, no, of course not," Jack said quickly. "You're an inspiration! I just—I need to get home as soon as possible."

"Well then hit the road, Jack!" Phil held up his staff, rattled it at him.

Jack bowed his farewell to the rest of Phil's court and limped toward Michael, who'd just finished apologizing to the skaters. They met at the edge of the grass.

"What the hell happened to you?" Michael looked into Jack's eyes, held onto his shoulders in case Jack fainted. "Are you OK?"

Jack just nodded, struck dumb with relief.

"Can you walk?"

Jack nodded again, and Michael guided him homeward.

Behind them, Phil shouted to someone, "THANK YOU FOR YOUR LOVELINESS!"

They walked past the shops and street performers and wandering tourists. Once Jack regained control of his emotions, he told Michael how he'd been mugged, abducted, forced to fight. He told him about his daring escape, his sudden launch from Vince Williams's car, his pepper-spray assault. This telling, he thought, improved on his first, tentative attempt with Phil and his friends. He was more confident in his material, and he slowed down a little, added color and sound, used his hands in his description of the fight with Sticky. Also, he found himself telling Michael about his strange sexual encounter with Cassandra. He thought he'd struck it from the record, but Michael had always enjoyed a lurid tale. His reaction here didn't disappoint.

"You got a Pompeii Wake-up Call?" he cried. "I've dreamed of that my whole life. Once I tried to pay for it, but I was so excited it took me forever to fall asleep. I woke up alone, with no wallet, and she'd raided the minibar on her way out." He shook his head, "*And* she played with your ass? Very hot! What'd you say she looked like?"

"Can you lower your voice please? And keep walking?"

"Yeah, sorry. But don't worry, Jack, everything's cool now. I'll get you home."

"No, nothing is cool."

Jack told Michael about Vigor's blackmail threat and Cynthia's cheating. He figured, once you've described sidewalk anal play, what's off limits?

Michael took it all in without saying anything. They passed a shop with a female mannequin out front wearing tiny shorts that read, on the rear: *Dave's Booty*. Below that, a handwritten sign: *Personalize it! Let everyone know who owns that booty!* Jack felt offended on behalf of all women.

Michael said, "But you're still going to vote for preservation of 847, right?"

"What? *That's* your response to all this? 'How does it affect my pet project?' Selfish, Michael."

"Oh, no. You're going to vote against it, aren't you?"

Jack sighed. "I'm sorry, but it's got to go. I made a deal with God." He felt Michael's eyes boring holes into him, but he refused to meet them. "Sometimes you have to lose a battle to win the war."

"What the fuck does that mean? You let this Vigor guy win, and you'll never be able to look yourself in the eye again."

"You know something? After what I've been through, maybe redevelopment is exactly what this place needs. It's too dangerous!"

"No, Jack. What happened to you isn't typical. There are some crazy people around, but this is still a community. Don't you see it?" Michael grabbed Jack and turned him so Jack had no choice but to look at his stupid handsome face. "Come on, Brother Mother. I've never been mugged or kidnapped here, and I'm on these streets all the time. Maybe there's something else going on here."

"What do you mean? You think I've been targeted? You think I've done something to deserve being beaten and robbed?"

"No! As my former friend Clint Eastwood once said, 'Deserve's got nothin' to do with it.'" Michael took a deep breath and said, with great solemnity, "But karma, Jack. Maybe you—the deepest you there is—*needed* all of these new experiences to open your eyes a little wider."

"You're seriously talking to me about karma right now?"

They passed the marijuana dispensary, where a curvaceous young woman with an eyebrow ring checked IDs and medical cards. She looked up and her red eyes met Jack's for a second. She looked exactly like Harper looked a few weeks ago when she claimed she was having an allergy attack. Jack filed that away for later. He followed Michael up his street.

"Right there," Jack said, as they crossed Speedway. "That's where I got mugged."

"I'm sorry," Michael scanned the street. "Maybe this place really is going to shit—but that's all the more reason to fight for it."

"Can you just call me a car, please?"

Michael unlocked his gate, waited for Jack to enter the garden first. Jack wondered if he'd been too blunt. But then Michael said, "Do you remember the Waxim you wrote about me, about my . . . thing?"

"Your arrest? That thing?"

"Yeah. You got on your high horse and offered me forgiveness if I could just turn my life around? You said you chose to care about me rather than judge me?"

Jack didn't like where this was going. "Of course I remember. It was true, I did care about you."

"But you never thought about how hurtful it was to turn me into one of your little homilies? Using my name, and my personal problems, to publicly congratulate yourself? Assuming your forgiveness was something I wanted or needed?"

"It was all a matter of public record. And I thought you'd see the logic of my argument. Do we need to talk about this now?"

Leading Jack down the path, past the offended Buddha, Michael said, "Yeah. You see that it's a form of using, don't you? Turning the personal lives of friends and family members into self-aggrandizement?"

"That wasn't my intent at all. Your addiction was killing your best self, and I loved that best self, so I was angry. Truly, I'm sorry I wrote that Waxim."

"Thanks. I forgive you." Michael unlocked the front door and led the way inside. He removed his shoes before stepping onto the deep-blue-green Turkish rug, looked down at Jack's dirty bare feet. "It's OK, you can come in. But you're not getting in my car until you're showered and wearing something that doesn't smell like garbage."

"Great," Jack realized he was weak with hunger. "Do you have anything to eat? All I've had today is oatmeal."

Michael paused, then said, "Actually, I have a special smoothie concoction in the fridge. I'll split it with you. Here," he handed Jack a cordless phone, "Call your wife, tell her you're safe, you're with me, and I'll make sure you get home."

Michael went into the kitchen, and Jack stood there staring at the phone in his hand. He began to dial the office line. Bonnie could give him Cynthia's number. But he didn't have the strength right now to talk to Bonnie, to listen to her shrieks and rapid-fire questions and fussy Monday-morning quarterbacking about what he should have done. He put down the phone.

"Drink up," Michael came back with two glasses brimming with a dark purple-green liquid.

Jack drank from the glass, and it was cold, sweet, and tart. "This more of your ahasi?"

"Nah. Blueberries, blackberries, kale, orange juice, and special probiotics."

Jack felt something fibrous between his teeth and pulled it out. "What's this?"

"Eat it, it's good for you. And hit the showers."

HALF AN HOUR LATER, showered and wrapped up in a white, quilted robe (the only thing of Michael's that fit him), Jack found Michael standing in his kitchen, now wearing loose-fitting cotton pants and a fleece sweater. He studied Jack's bruised, sunburned face. "You look like hell, but that's a comfy robe, right? From now on you are Jack, The White!"

Jack felt strangely shaky, wondered if it was a PTSD symptom. "Ready to go?"

"Actually, I'll call you a car. They're always close by." Michael started to say something else, stopped, started again, "I know you don't want to deal with criticism right now, Jack, but I feel like this is a crucial moment, a moment of real spiritual potential."

"Not now, OK?" Jack created a little more space between them.

"Just listen to what I have to say. Yesterday, I didn't make the right case. The question is what's the point of life?"

"Please no."

"It's to evolve. To open up, to be as compassionate to other beings as you can, to give as much love as you can and relieve as much suffering as you can."

"Enough with the mumbo-jumbo, all right?" To avoid Michael's eyes, Jack picked up a clementine from the fruit bowl, feeling its pebbled surface against his fingertips. He thought about eating it, but the smoothie had given him a slight stomachache. "I'm not interested."

"I know! And the reason you're not interested is that you think everything outside your body is The Other, The Big Bad World, which sucks, because then it's always you versus the whole world. You lose every time!"

Jack smiled, which made his lip sting. "Michael, I've been through a lot in the last day, but I think hearing what you just said was the worst part." He pretended to look to the corners of the room for hidden cameras. "Am I being pranked?"

"I'm totally serious. Your Waxims should be about how we're all connected. Each one of us depends on the whole world and the whole world depends on each one of us. If we understood that, we'd all be better to each other. You should be teaching mindfulness, meditation, and service. Leading people to the realization that we're all one. What's so funny?"

"This," Jack said, suddenly aware of his own laughter. "Being told how to run my ethics institute by an abuser of drugs and prostitutes."

"Hey, I always treated my prostitutes with love and respect. But speaking of drugs, since you seem to be obsessed with them, taking the right ones at the right time, in the right place, can lead to real awakening."

"Nope. No way. At best, they're a distraction. At worst, suicide." Jack felt a twitch in his eye and a painful rumbling in his stomach. Movement in his peripheral vision: Incredible Hulk at the window? He looked, half-expecting shattering glass, but it was just the bamboo leaves rustling outside. "So," he heard himself say, "can you call me that car?"

Michael sighed. "Listen, Jack, I know you've got to go home, and I'll make sure you get there, but I couldn't let you leave my presence without jarring you out of this rutted road you've been on for way too long."

"I'm not on a—*you're* the one on a rutted road!" Jack's tongue felt too big, or his mouth was shrinking.

Michael became Dr. Goldberg, offering his concerned, hospital-bedside face. "You look pale, boychick. Maybe you should go have a lie-down?"

That sounded like a good idea. Jack, suddenly feeling very cold and shaky, staggered into the living room, made it to Michael's swirling blue and green carpet, where he collapsed. "What'd you—"

"Shush," Michael was a chanteuse, climbing onto the couch as if it were the top of a grand piano, demurely tucking his legs under him. "Just relax. Lie back and close your eyes. You're safe here, just let yourself go."

Jack did lie back and close his eyes, but he felt very unsafe. "What's ... happening?"

"Ve fing is," now Michael was some kind of chimney sweep? "Medi'ation and good acks ain't ve only fings you need. In some cases, when a man's 'abitual fought pa'erns is so rigid, 'is mental ruts so deep and narrow-like, it 'akes years of solitude and silent medi'ation to pull 'im out."

Michael exorcised the unconvincing Cockney. "But fuck that, right? Because a sudden application of force can work too. All we have to do is manufacture a peak experience, easily done if you happen to have a few grams of magic mushrooms in the house, which I did, and which we just drank in our smoothies."

"Oh, no." Jack's voice sounded to him like it came from far, far away. The very air thrummed. "No no no!"

"Zat's your problem right zer! Try saying *oui! Oui oui oui!*"

On the other side of the humming glass windows, bamboo leaves smiled at Jack. But these weren't friendly smiles; these were leers.

26

CEILING PLASTER NIPPLING. That was the first thing Jack noticed when he stopped thrashing on Michael's rug and just accepted the demon eating its way through his stomach. *Rippling, not nippling.* Jack chuckled wryly at that, and the wry chuckle became a bark, and the bark became a giggling, a tee-hee'ing, a hooting and guffawing, which didn't stop until Michael suggested they go outside.

No, that wasn't what happened. Michael felt left out by Jack's inexplicable laughter. He turned up the music, two old-timey acoustic guitars, one riffing on the melody played by the other. A sad, dreamy-voiced woman sang about building a boat and going in search of her dear someone. The ceiling breathed with the music. Waves of red and yellow and blue built, crashed, receded.

The ache in Jack's stomach ebbed. All pain ebbed. He lost all sense of being embodied. The ceiling became an empty street blanketed in new snow, and he was not Jack but a shivering, rag-covered boy in a frozen ghetto, out of his mind with hunger. Reds, yellows, and blues undulated across the snow while he listened by the broken window, waiting for the old lady's wheezing to even out in sleep. He crept to the front, up the steps, pushed open the broken door. He strained to hear beyond his chattering teeth. The old lady snored. He crept through the kitchen, past the larder, empty in moonlight. Inched his head around the door jamb. It was darker, but there she was, so thin she hardly rumpled the bedclothes, curled up on her side facing him. She clutched something to her chest. He crept forward, crouching low. Close enough to smell her sickly exhalations. Breathing out of his mouth, he inched close enough to reach out, hook a thumb and forefinger around the reticule. Gently, he pulled. The crone's fingers did not give. Gently, he increased the force of his pull. He looked at the craggy face, met open, angry eyes. He screamed, tore the bag from her grip. She wailed like a siren, "*Ganef! Ganef!*" He ran back through the kitchen, out the back door, just as a light flickered across the street. Into the first alley, flying over snow, numbly wet inside flapping soles.

He collapsed behind a roofless, disused chicken coop, gasping for breath, heart hammering. Bag awfully light. He pulled the string, dumped the contents into his lap. Two shrunken potatoes, withered as the old woman's face. A meal for a mouse. Holding one in each fist, he hugged his knees to his chest and wept. Didn't hear the rats who'd followed his footprints in the fresh snow.

They jerked him up by his shirt. The potatoes made two small holes in the snow. He cried out, got the back of a hand, made a larger hole in the snow. The man who cuffed him jerked him upright. He had Michael Malone's eyes. But the eyes went dead, and he shoved not-Jack toward the South Gate, where the soldiers were. Without ceremony, without question, without even pause, one soldier pointed his rifle at his chest.

Blinding muzzle flash faded to slate sky. With shot still echoing, not-Jack's consciousness shed the costume of his body, instantly grew nine times more intelligent, traversed green worlds of divine giants radiating love and compassion, fire worlds of wrathful, thousand-armed deities with sharp teeth and tongues dripping with blood. He moved fluidly across space and time until he found the ruby-colored point of light that was his recently deceased—though also not-yet-born—friend Daniel Schacht, who told him without speaking (as neither of them had mouths, vocal chords, ears) that he'd been in Amitabha's Pure Land, where Schopenhauer and Shantideva were team-teaching a course on compassion, with guest lectures by Spinoza. A cosmic bellhop had alerted him of Jack's presence, and he had come "running." His message:

1. Jack need not fear death as he'd experienced it countless times on his crooked path from ignorance toward enlightenment.
2. He knew that Jack had failed to attend him in his final hours and missed his funeral, but he forgave him, hoped only for Jack to cease being afraid.
3. He knew Jack loved him, and he loved Jack in return and would see him in another life.

As the warm ruby light began to fade, disembodied Daniel added, *And should, in one of those lives, you find me to be your mother, go easy on the nipples! OK, Jack?*

"Jack! You OK?"

Snapped back into his body, Jack opened his eyes.

Michael Malone's concerned face hovered above him. "What was that about nipples?" Mandalas spun on the ceiling behind his head, a man with a voice of honeyed bourbon sang about careless love.

"Did you . . . is a car . . . coming?" Jack managed to get out.

THEN JACK and Michael were outside, in the loud and bright

world, waiting for a car. A truck roared down Pacific Avenue. A squirrel chattered on a power line.

Michael squinted at the luminous blue-pink sky through the trees, said in a bad Castilian accent, "The sun—she is setting. ¡Vamanos!"

"I think the sun's a 'he.'" Jack's toes bulged like risen madeleines around the thongs of the too-small flip-flops Michael had given him, but he hurried to keep up. Something bounced in his pocket: clementine from Michael's kitchen, though he had no memory of actually putting it in his pocket. He held it to his nose, sniffed. Citrus. Comforting. Returned it to the pocket.

So many palm trees along the boardwalk, so many thin, curvy-twisty trunks bursting on top. The closest one had a beard of dead fronds hanging beneath live spikes, spitting image of Barry Gibb circa 1972.

"Bee Gee in that tree," Jack observed. Then, awed by the next tree, and the one after that, "Bee Gees in *all* these trees."

"Thees way!" Michael shouted at Jack from twenty feet down the street.

Jack hurried to catch up in his tiny flip-flops. Two enormous bodybuilders approached from the opposite direction, muscles bulging obscenely. "Nice geisha!" one said to Michael.

"What?" Michael looked behind him. "*¡Dios mío*, Yack! Leave your mincing!"

"It's these sandals," Jack tried to kick them off but they were embedded in his flesh. He balanced on his right foot while he pulled the flop off of the left. Shifting weight to his bare left foot, he bent to remove the right, but realized that he hadn't pulled off such deft maneuvers in decades. He promptly fell over.

AND THEN JACK and Michael were sitting on the sand, halfway through the Sinai that was Venice Beach. Among other scattered sunset-watching humans and a whole flock of sunset-watching seagulls, they caught the sun floating on top of the ocean, watched it deflate and sink. It seemed to pause midway, glittering below the horizon, bursting yellow above it, pupil in the eye of God. Then it was a scythe of light. Then, a point. Then, gone.

Jack looked to either side of him, met Michael's eyes, and the eyes of other people, smiling and self-conscious for having briefly lost themselves. There was something heartbreaking about it. Was there a Waxim there? Maybe the subject was more suitable for a poem.

An old man trudged past in shiny tracksuit, bright white running shoes. Maybe Jack had given his own old man the silent treatment for too long. It was never about the DUI. It was her death. As if cancer were caused by decades-old absence, infidelity, divorce, failure to love. Also, Jack was afraid to lose his father too. He'd just made a preemptive strike.

He dug his feet into the sand, found the sun's heat buried beneath the cool top layer. He considered other preemptive strikes: denied his children a dog because he still mourned Duke, best pal from ages seven through eighteen; ignored Samantha's natural urge for independence by keeping her financially dependent on him; abandoned friendships, avoided making new friends because he didn't want to lose any more people; denied himself even the joy of making love to his wife because somehow that made him less afraid of losing her.

So many bad decisions! He laughed. Turned to Michael to see if he got the joke too, but there was no Michael.

Not anywhere. It didn't seem possible in the vast landscape, but Michael had disappeared. He was Jack's ride home!

And it was dark!

It was night!

Because the sun went down, who knew how long ago!

Which meant he was missing the Shabbat evening service!

He stood up, as if that might inspire the next step in a plan. Near the waterline, a clump of seaweed looked like a body. Was it a body? He approached; seaweed. The frigid, churning Pacific washed his sore feet. A wave shimmered darkly. He'd stood in water like this, cotton clinging to brown legs, beating a shirt against rocks. Next to him, brown-skinned girls singing in a strange language.

The memory faded as soon as he noticed himself noticing it, replaced by the distant sound of a trumpet or a car horn—*Tada! Tada!*—and the memory of holding one of his tiny daughters so they wouldn't get knocked down by a wave.

AND THEN HE HIMSELF, Current Jack, was in the waves, naked. Sixty-degree water clawed up legs, punched him in the nuts. Next wave broke, smothering him, jerking at his limbs. Seaweed, he hoped, touched his foot. He breached, gasped, tasted the salt. Found footing, dove under in time for the next wave, felt the thunderous rush over his back. Surfaced, grabbed another deep breath, dove under the next one. He did this for a long time, matching his rhythm to the waves, which was the rhythm of the moon, the sun, the mysterious center of the Milky Way.

He even bodysurfed some of the way back to the shore. Spent a few surprised, glorious seconds at one with the wave's immense energy, and then they were two again, and the wave spat him forward in a tumbling pile. He staggered to his feet, happily coughing salt water.

A blast of wind slapped him on the ass in farewell, and with it, he knew exactly what he was going to tell Vigor, and damn the consequences. Let the contract go, let Vigor smear him and his family all over the internet. They'd survive, just like the Racist Cops, Pottymouthed Sorority Girls, Donut-Licking Pop Stars, Refugee Kickers, Cat Torturers, Sexual Harassers, and all the other

victims of public shaming. The Waxmans would suffer the spotlight until the internet fixed its flighty gaze elsewhere, and maybe
they'd all learn a valuable lesson about cause and effect, action
and consequence.

But where *was* his robe? He looked to the distant buildings,
saw that he'd drifted quite a way down the beach. His entire body
shivered. His genitals had become mere suggestions. Walking
north, he sang through chattering teeth, for no reason he could
fathom, The Byrds' "Turn! Turn! Turn!"

He ignored the whirling, pulsating, multicolored lights of the
Ferris wheel on the Santa Monica Pier and focused on the ground,
hallucinating a white pile here and a white pile there. The fifth or
sixth was the robe. He snatched it up, snapped the sand from it. It
took him a few tries, but he finally got his arms into the sleeves,
pulled it over himself, and tied it tightly. He stuck his hand in the
pocket, was surprised to find the clementine snug inside, warm
with life between his frozen fingers.

Let Cynthia do what she wanted. Of course, she already did,
but he wouldn't make any demands. After all, he bore some
responsibility. Pushed her away, closed himself off from their life
in the vain hope of posthumous renown.

Walking, he told himself the story of their first date, which
wasn't really a date, a week after her graduation. She'd asked him
if she could buy him lunch to thank him for his guidance on her
law review article. She'd ignored nearly all of his comments, but
she said he'd forced her to clarify her arguments. At the time, he
was sad, rumpled, chalk-sleeved. Two years divorced, he saw
eleven-year-old Samantha on weekends only. As Cynthia's professor, he found her beautiful and charming, but he didn't even allow
himself to fantasize about romance. After all, by then he was
teaching Ethics.

But, as they ate their salads, and she met his eyes and held
them, he realized she wasn't his student anymore. She was a hot

doctor of jurisprudence, passionate about ending hostile work environments while maintaining a firm pro-business stance.

The Supreme Court had just decided *Harris v. Forklift*, and Cynthia got an angry kick out of every icky detail that made its way into the case law. She couldn't believe that, as recently as 1987, a man thought he could call a coworker a "dumb-ass woman" or drop stuff around the office and demand she pick it up. "That's a twelve-year-old boy's way of telling a girl he likes her. A real man knows to wait for a woman to give him signals."

"Like what kind of signals?" Jack asked.

"Like touching his arm." Cynthia leaned over and gently squeezed his forearm. "Or holding his gaze for just a second too long." She locked eyes on his.

Dizzy from the flirtation, Jack fantasized about kissing her, touching her, being further touched by her. To cover his befuddlement and distract himself, he asked her if she'd had similar experiences of sexual harassment.

She laughed. "Nothing I couldn't handle. Law school was just like that movie *Groundhog Day*, you know? Same old lines from the same old guys, day after day after day!"

"I love that movie," Jack said. He'd seen it by himself, on one of his first nights as a divorced man, and it led to some deep reflection. Forced to relive the same day infinitely, Phil Connors figures out what he really wants, once he's exhausted his carnal desires. What he wants, it turns out, is meaning, a sense of purpose, love. Jack excitedly told Cynthia about his favorite moment in the film: when Phil casually saves a boy from falling out of a tree, just part of his daily "errands." Jack told Cynthia that *Groundhog Day* might even have contributed to his decision to teach more, to pull away from the contract law racket.

By the time they finished that first lunch, Jack was infatuated. And then, while they waited for the valet to bring their cars around, she kissed him. She, this lovely woman in full bloom who could kiss whomever she wanted, stood there, in public, in broad daylight, and kissed *him*.

He belonged to her from then on. Never really won an argument, and didn't mind, because she was so beautiful, and her mind so marvelous and infuriating to watch in action. Later, to see her mothering their children with such fierce-tender love, he never doubted his own feelings.

What changed?

In his heart, nothing.

In hers, he didn't know.

AND THEN JACK was back on the boardwalk, watching two scruffy country-music-legend lookalikes square off on the sidewalk in front of a bar called Kapua's. Their only audience was a large man sitting on a stool by the door. He had what appeared to be a beaver's tail glued to his chin.

"I'm tellin' *you*," the musician who looked like Merle Haggard said, "there wudn't nuthin' here."

"Ah-ha!" the one who looked like Willie Nelson pointed with a crooked finger, "Changin' your story! A second ago you said there was nothin' there but a plastic bag filled with sand."

"So?"

"So I *filled* that bag with sand and put it there to hold my place."

"A bag of sand is garbage."

"What—you expect me to just leave my amp sittin' here while I go take a piss?"

"Both of you guys fuck off!" said a very thin man with a fat lip from the doorway. "Nobody wants to listen to your hillbilly shit!"

"My brothers," Jack found himself standing between these men, holding up his hands, enjoying the expansive drape of the robe's sleeve, "be good to one another!"

"Who's this nut?" Merle asked Willie.

"Dunno. But you gotta admire his commitment to casual dress."

"Hey!" the thin, fat-lipped man said. "You're that guy!"

Jack smiled. Had he finally been recognized as the semi-celebrity he was? "Jack Waxman, nice to meet you," he said.

"Whatever. Your dad's a fucking maniac. And your daughter's a bitch."

"Excuse me? You must have me confused with someone else."

"Lawrence! Eight-six this fatso!"

It didn't seem to matter that they had the wrong guy or that Jack wasn't even inside the bar. The large man with a huge goatee began to rise from his stool.

Jack backed away, "I don't know what you're talking about. All I'm talking about is being the person who starts the giving. Putting aside selfish desires for the brotherhood of man! 'We may have come on different ships, but we're all in the same boat now,' as the Reverend Dr. King once said."

The bouncer took a step toward him, and Jack hurried away, protectively clutching the clementine inside his pocket.

A few blocks down, a young woman sang beautifully about these being the days of miracle and wonder. Paul Simon! Jack couldn't believe it. He walked right up in front and swayed softly to the music. She was a young African American woman dressed in a patchwork hippie dress, with dreadlocks tied up in a pile on her head. She smiled at him and sang right to him, and he saw these bright rays of light coming from her—a halo, almost, around her head—and twinkling lights on her guitar. When she sang those last words, "*Don't cry, baby, don't cry,*" Jack cried. He cried, clapped, and exhorted the jaded bar patrons to clap too.

The girl looked at Jack, and said, "Thank you!" Then, to everyone else. "Does this man belong to someone? Sir? Where is your massage therapist?"

People laughed, and Jack ran away.

Surely Michael would have made it home by now. Just had to find his house. Fortunately, he'd remembered to pay attention to Michael's address the last time he was there, and he managed to make it to his gate without being attacked again.

But still, five minutes or an hour after he'd begun ringing the bell, there was no Michael at Michael's address. Jack had no idea what time it was. It seemed to have been dark for a long time. He gave up on the bell, tried shouting Michael's name a few times.

"Shut up and die!" someone suggested from a window.

Maybe he'd find him on the boardwalk. Jack stepped cautiously onto Speedway, on the lookout for attackers. The street was still and silent but for the revving of a car engine in the distance. Jack smelled marijuana, but it was mingled with the rubbery, vinegary, choking scent of things burning that weren't supposed to burn. He looked to his right, saw down at the end of the alley a taxi just beginning to turn onto it, FOR HIRE light illuminated. A good old-fashioned taxi! He could hop in, refuse to get out until he was driven home. But he heard a baby crying, and something crackling.

He turned toward the sound, saw an orange flash in the back window of the brick building that faced Ocean Front. It was the building with the green light, the dispensary. There was the flash again, a flickering. A flame. The baby wailed. He looked back down Speedway, saw the taxi idling. He wanted to go to it, wanted nothing more than to go to it. But there was that baby's cry again, and no denying its location.

Jack yanked open the broken back door, turning away from the rush of heat and smoke. He took a deep breath, ran inside.

PART III

27

TRUDGING up Rose a block away from the car, Sam and Donald approached a parked, booted van with its doors flung open. A cloud of smoke billowed out and rose into the lamplight. Inside, a weird samba played softly.

"Nah, man," someone said, "I don't think I'm ever gonna get it."

"C'mon, give it a chance!"

The song was Phish's "Fee," and it reached into the back of Sam's brain and yanked out a memory: she was stoned for the very first time in Lisa Kline's bedroom, thinking she could totally, like, *see* Paige's piano solo, while Lisa stared at herself in her closet mirror and said, "Am I talking right now? Seriously, am I talking? I *see* my mouth moving and I *think* I hear sounds but am I really making sounds?"

Sam slowed and glanced inside the van as she passed. One guy was black, with young dreads sprouting like question marks from his head. The other was white, with brown hair and a big red beard. They crouched on two stools, surrounded by canvases and boxes of paint tubes, and the white guy was passing the black guy a joint. They both looked up at her.

"Go Phish!" Sam said, and immediately regretted it. That just wasn't a thing people said.

The white guy grinned at her and held out the joint.

"Oh, no thanks."

"Now, now," Donald stopped her. "That might be just the ticket."

"Oh, come on, Pop."

"I'm serious. My tooth is killing me. Is that strain analgesic?"

"Lamb's Bread, man. It was good enough for Bob Marley." The white guy held it out.

Donald took it, puffed elaborately before taking a deep drag. He blew out the smoke, croaked, "That'll do."

Sam was horrified by his casual willingness to swap spit with random guys in a van. But she was no square either. She discreetly checked their lips for mouth sores before taking a polite puff. The next song from the album began. It was a wandering instrumental, and it made Sam think of a summer road trip up the coast with Stephanie, to meet Lisa in Santa Cruz for some music festival in the redwoods.

"This is the music of my youth," Sam said.

"Mine too," the white guy said. He was a little rumpled, but he had kind, laughing eyes above the big beard. "I'm trying to turn him on, but—"

"It ain't gonna happen," his friend said. He met Sam's eyes for a second. His were brooding, soul-tired. "I need lyrics that make just a *little* sense."

"I'm with you," Donald said.

"Well," Sam pulled Donald's arm, "thanks for the hit. We have to go."

"Peace."

But Donald didn't budge. "Aren't you going to show them the picture?"

"Haven't we done enough of this?" Sam whined. "I'm so tired."

Donald gave her the stink eye. "Your performance review is going to be rough."

"*Oh, no*," she said, pulling out her phone. "Don't fire me from my fake job that cost all of my cash today." She showed the photo to the stoners. "You haven't seen this guy, have you?"

The black guy just shrugged. "You all look the same to me."

"It's Jack!" the white guy said. "We totally saw him earlier today. Man, did he have a story to tell."

Smiling at Sam, Donald said, "What's a good place to eat around here? I'll buy."

THEY SAT with big beers in front of the German beer bar, facing the evening freak parade on the boardwalk. A heat lamp cooked the tops of their heads, and in between appreciative sips, Jesse and Fuller told Sam and Donald what they knew of Jack's story, adding the pepper-spray incident and the fact that Jack left them to go call someone to pick him up. This did nothing to ease Sam's worry. Even if he'd walked all the way home, her dad should have arrived by now.

Donald insisted that Sam show them the video of Jack's fight. Jesse winced with sympathy a couple of times. Fuller just watched in grim silence.

After this second viewing, Donald was just furious. He stood up. "They're gonna pay for this."

"Who?"

"Whoever!" He headed toward the bathroom.

"My grandpa's sort of pretending he's a private detective," Sam explained.

"He doesn't seem like he's pretending," Fuller said.

"Parkinson's?" Jesse asked.

"I don't think so. But that issue's sort of on the back burner right now. Did my dad say anything about, like, *not* wanting to go home? Maybe he's trying to escape, completely start over?"

Fuller smirked. "Got tired of being rich and white?"

"It's what happened to me," Jesse said, straight-faced.

Donald returned just as the food arrived. No one said anything until they were almost done. Then, Donald, through a full mouth, "What do you guys know about the underground?"

Jesse coughed on his beer. "Like, the London subway? Or the French Resistance?"

"No," Donald said, "like the seedy underbelly of Venice? You know, the gangs? Pushers, pimps, whores? Con men and vixen grifters? Muggers and flashers? Stick-up boys? Pickpockets?"

"Man, we just make stuff and try to sell it. All we know is lately a lot of evil shit is going down, and people are scared."

"The question you gotta ask," Fuller said, "is what's the point of these fight videos? Why do they make them?"

"Besides straight-up sadism?" Sam thought about it for a few seconds. "And money?"

"Yeah. Like, why take people from Venice, torture them, humiliate them, and tell them to never come back? Why would those bikers even care?"

"Someone's paying them to care," Donald said. "*Cui bono*, right? Who benefits from getting rid of the bums?"

"Homeless," Sam corrected.

"Houseless," Jesse corrected.

"Whoever's trying to class the place up, make that paper," Fuller said.

"Developers," Jesse said.

"SBT!" Sam cried.

"I don't know them," Jesse said, "but the tech companies have already taken root. People could make a lot of money turning the whole place into a theme park of itself."

"So it's all a big swindle. But what's it got to do with Jackie?" Donald asked.

"No idea." Sam tried to think, but the old brain was stumped. This was the point at which, in her writing, she might stare at the screen for a week, switching from coffee to wine to whisky before finally giving up.

Donald drained his beer and groaned to his feet.

"Again?"

"I go when I arrive, and I go before I leave." He headed purposefully toward the restrooms.

"Gettin' old is a bitch," Jesse said, looking after him. "My grandfather blew all his money on Russian nesting dolls on eBay before my mom put him in a home."

"Pop's not there yet," Sam said quickly.

"Mm-hm," Fuller said.

"I mean, I know it seems like he thinks he's a private detective, but I think mostly he's just having fun."

"Mm-hm."

Jesse filled the silence that followed her obvious self-delusion, "Are you a lawyer like your dad?"

Sam snorted. "He wishes. I used to be a writer, and kind of a teacher. Now I don't know."

"That's great," Jesse said. "My best work always comes out of not knowing. If I can just relax and embrace it. Hardest part is starting."

"Thanks, Julia Cameron!" Sam said, but she knew he was right. Her biggest fear was that if she did quiet her mind and embrace the fact that she had no idea what to say, she'd find out that she really had *nothing* to say, that her presumption of having a unique perspective on the world was totally unfounded.

It occurred to her that Donald had been gone a long time. Probably hiding in the bathroom to avoid paying for dinner. Down the street an old-timer with a beat-up Telecaster grunted his way through a Bakersfield version of "People Are Strange." He had to compete with sirens wailing from not too far away. Then, for the full Venice Beach experience, a gust of wind carried the sweet funk of premium cannabis.

A bold pigeon hopped onto the edge of the table, swiped a French fry from Donald's plate, and flew away.

"Omen?" Jesse wondered.

"Come here!" Donald called from the doorway, "I think I found our misper!"

They ran inside. On the muted TV above the bar, a young Latina in a pencil skirt and pinstripe blouse was talking to a bruised and blackened man. A building burned behind them.

"Is that . . ." Sam didn't finish because yes, it was.

"Hey, new robe," Jesse said.

This robe might have been white once, but now was smudged with soot, torn and leaking white feathers at the breast. One of Jack's eyes was wide, the other purple and swollen. His cheeks were dirty and dusted with gray stubble, hair powdered with ash, and he spoke distractedly, occasionally scratching at his neck and chest with a bloody-knuckled hand. At the bottom of the screen, the words *Venice Beach: Homeless Hero?* appeared.

Suddenly, handsome Michael Malone stepped in from the side and grabbed the microphone from the reporter. Edging her out of the frame, he wrapped an arm around Jack and held him close as he spoke and stared wet-eyed into the camera. He gesticulated with upraised hand like a prophet. The words at the bottom changed to *Michael Malone – Actor, Activist?* Michael gave the microphone back to Jack, who said something. The picture cut to a wide-eyed, apparently dumbfounded duo in the studio, then to commercial.

"Pay the bill and let's go!" Sam said, rushing out the door with Jesse and Fuller behind her. She glanced back, saw Donald pulling out the thick money clip and peeling off a couple more twenties. They'd definitely be discussing reimbursement later.

The four of them speed-walked south on Ocean Front toward the sirens. In a few blocks, Donald was beginning to fall behind, but Sam could tell they were close. The acrid smell of burning plastics filled the air along with the strong skunky-piney-citrusy smell of cannabis going up by the ounce, or maybe the pound.

They weren't alone. Street people and neighbors all seemed to be heading in the direction of the fire to watch or sniff. Two guys on skateboards pumped past. One shouted, "It's like a volcanic eruption! Of weed!"

28

THE NEWS VAN's floodlights bounced off the glittery eyeshadow and glossed lips of Christine Diaz, weekend metro reporter for KZLA ("The News Monster!"). Touching him as little as possible, she positioned Jack so the smoking building and scrambling fire-fighters would fill the background. She held her finger to her ear, nodded, and began her report.

"So we have no information, as of now, as to how the fire started, but we're just a few doors away from the scene of last week's fire, which is still under investigation. That blaze destroyed Dr. Hoff's Medical Cannabis Consultorium. The building burning behind me is home to," she glanced at her phone, "Kaya Collective, a dispensary specializing in 'top-shelf, high-CBD/high-THC hybrids for surf-and-skate-related injuries.' I can tell you, Bob, that a lot of that marijuana seems to be burning inside that building— and it seems to have drawn some people away from an anti-corruption protest happening a few blocks away on Ocean Front and Windward. Can we get a shot of this crowd?"

The cameraman swiveled the lens away from her across the few dozen people gathered, just in time to catch a beach ball punched skyward.

"But right now," she continued, waving smoke from her face as the wind shifted, "it looks more like Coachella out here, which is adding a crowd control component to the firefighting tasks of emergency personnel."

She yanked Jack close as the camera swung back to her, "With me here is a brave local man who ran into the burning building and rescued the famed Venice Beach Coyote—known to many as Abbot Skinny. The wild," she glanced at her phone, "*canis latrans,* apparently sneaked in through a cracked basement window and became trapped. Sir, if you could, take us through the experience. What did you find when you entered the building?"

Jack had inhaled a lot of smoke while he was inside, and he was having a hard time following her rapid speech. Also, the cameraman's spotlight had burned a huge hole in his vision, so when he looked at her face, he just saw a pulsing green circle.

"Sir?" Christine Diaz said again, in Jack's ear. "What did you see?"

Jack shielded his eyes and squinted. How convey the crackling of the fire, the screaming of what he thought was a baby, the broiling heat that rushed out the door when he flung it open?

When he saw the poisonous blue smoke billowing from piles of burning plastic containers of marijuana and shards of broken glass all over the floor, he would have turned back, but the baby's cry, a desperate wail this time, drew him deeper into the building. Crouching low under the smoke, he rushed down a hallway, saw through a small window a ruined indoor garden, with little pot plants torn out by the roots, crushed into black soil. In the next room, he found smashed computers, two walls completely on fire. The crying came from behind a closed door on the opposite side of the hall. Jack flung it open. It was a dark staircase leading down to the basement.

Jack took a step inside just as a monstrous, grayish, snarling blur exploded out of the darkness. It was all teeth and claws, and it knocked Jack onto his back. The thing tore a chunk of robe from his shoulder and scrambled over him, claws digging into his chest.

Somehow the coyote knew where to go, and Jack followed it, crouching as low as possible back the way he'd come. In the ruined plant nursery, flames were moving across the ceiling, dripping onto floor that wasn't yet burning. The storage room had become an oven, and Jack felt the vinyl floor melting under his hands and feet.

"Sir?" Christine Diaz was saying. "*Sir?*"

Jack had no idea what he'd said, or if he'd said anything at all. "Yes?"

Christine Diaz froze. Her eyes went wide. "I'm sorry, I had a follow-up, but I . . . don't remember it—"

Out of nowhere, Michael Malone appeared between them, wrenching the microphone away from her. Michael hugged Jack with his free hand, said, directly to the camera, "Catherine, Jim, viewers at home, I'd just like to take this opportunity to say that this man right here is a hero. He inspired me tonight! He's taken a stand against the forces of evil, the forces of destruction. He's saved our coyote, and he's also going to save the historically significant 847 Ocean Front—home to poets! And cats!"

Christine Diaz had turned to stone in the face of this sudden celebrity. She didn't even try for the microphone, so Michael went on, "There has been a serious uptick in bad vibes around here, as well as nationally, and internationally, but we can fight it with good vibes. Let's remember the spirit of the people who used to call Venice home, who believed that love is stronger than fear and anger! This is holy ground! Let's honor that, and honor each other. Right, Jack? Lay a quote on 'em!"

The quote bank in Jack's brain bypassed his control center altogether and gave the answer straight to his mouth: "'We must learn to live together as brothers or perish together as fools.' Reverend Dr. Martin Luther King, Jr."

"Nice," Michael said. "I love you, Jack." His eyes passed over the crowd, "And I love all of you people. Especially you, guy in the wacky shirt! And you, lovely MILK. 'Mother I'd Like to *Know*!' (Seriously though, stick around after the show.) I love you all! Your happiness is *my* happiness!"

The applause he seemed to expect didn't come, though there were a couple of woots.

Christine Diaz finally pulled the microphone from his hands and said casually, "Back to you, Bob." Her face froze in a delirious smile until the camera man dropped the lens. Then she gushed, "Wow, Michael Malone. I can't believe this. Can you stick around for another segment? This is going right to the top of my clip reel!"

"Special Ops Pop! What now?" someone shouted from the crowd.

"No, ask the Fat Buddha!" someone else shouted. It was the blond, dreadlocked boy from earlier. "Tell us what to do, Fat Buddha!"

Jack scratched his head. "Didn't Michael just . . . ? Love each other!"

"But, like, right now?" the dreadlocked boy pointed southward. "What should we do?"

That's when Jack noticed, approaching from the south, several policemen. Some of them were in riot gear, and they were stretching, working out arm and leg kinks like football players before kick-off.

"PLEASE DISPERSE!" a deep voice commanded through a loudspeaker mounted atop a midnight-blue MRAP. "CLEAR THE AREA! THIS IS AN UNPERMITTED DEMONSTRATION. YOU ARE IMPEDING THE FIGHTING OF THIS FIRE. START WALKING, PEOPLE!"

But the people booed. Someone screamed, "Down with the pigs! Down with the oligarchs!"

Someone else shouted, "Fuck the police!"

A third person, not far from the second, shrieked, "Earth Shakers! Saboteurs! Get 'em!" It was Phil, unsheathing his rebar.

A flame drew Jack's eyes to another point in the crowd. Standing over it, face lit devilishly from below, Bam-Bam pulled the flaming thing back and threw it high into the air. It arced over the crowd, drawing a blue parabola across Jack's eyes, exploding in a whooshing fireball in front of the line of police.

People gasped. The police scattered, and one cop's uniform caught fire. His colleagues quickly smothered the flames. Meanwhile someone shouted, "Gun!" Jack turned to the noise, saw several hands pry it from the owner's hand, while several other hands and arms clawed at him. Nearby, Phil whacked the biker Clem—or was it Clyde?—in the back with his piece of rebar. The people had superior numbers, and the bikers couldn't escape. But the police had regrouped, and now they began their approach, out for blood.

People tried to reason with them, to explain, but they were beaten back with clubs. Tear gas canisters popped and toxic smoke rose through the crowd. Everyone ran in every direction. The firefighters continued their work on the blaze, somehow ignoring the chaos around them. Three Santa Monica police SUVs arrived from the north. People ran out to the sand. Two LAPD SUVS raced up the beach from the south to close that gap.

Jack watched Michael Malone grab one of the cops guarding the firemen, shout in his ear, gesture to his radio. He saw the cameraman take Christine Diaz by the hand and run with her toward the news van. Someone else bounced off of Jack, knocking him to the ground. People were moving all around him. He cowered, unsure what else to do, when he noticed a pair of shiny black boots that had stopped right in front of him.

He looked up, recognized the young business-casual man from the airplane hangar, the one who'd sat in the shadows with his laptop. Now he wore black pants and a black jacket. Up close, even his hair looked chiseled. He held out his hand, "Come with me if you want to live."

Ignoring Jack's wordless scream, the terminator grabbed him by the lapels of his robe, heaved him to his feet, dragged him through the crowd. Kevlar-covered cops swung at everything that moved in the fog of tear gas and pepper spray, but Jack managed to escape with only a glancing baton blow on his shoulder. The terminator dragged him up Rose toward Pacific. They passed two more police cars heading toward the action with lights flashing and sirens blaring.

"Who are you?" Jack cried.

The man didn't answer. A white sedan shot out of the Speedway alley just behind them, turned onto Rose, then swerved to a stop beside them. A man—Freckles! also dressed in black!—jumped out of the car while the terminator opened the door and nodded toward the empty backseat.

"I don't think so!"

"Get the fuck in the car," Freckles said, narrowing his eyes.

"Help!" Jack cried out. "Help!"

Far down the street, Jack hallucinated Samantha running toward him. And behind her, was that Fuller and Jesse? And behind them, struggling to keep up, *his father*? Couldn't be. Was he dreaming? Had he already died?

The terminator moved faster than Jack could think, and Jack found himself bear-hugged and shoved into—or rather, *at*—the car, head smacking against the frame, and then again against the inside of the far door as the car lurched forward. "Ow! I already had a head injury. Who are you guys? What's going on?"

"Shut the fuck up," Freckles said, back in the driver's seat, rolling right through a stop sign and nearly taking out a kid on a scooter. Next to Freckles sat a woman with a blond ponytail. She didn't look into the backseat, where the terminator sat next to Jack. Freckles sped down Rose, then took a hard right on Lincoln. There was traffic, and the car jerked to a stop inches from the rear bumper of the car ahead of them.

"Just relax, Mr. Waxman," the terminator said. "I'm Chris. Mr. Vigor told us to rescue you. He just wants a word before we take you home."

"Vigor! He can't make an appointment? He employs kidnappers and sadists?" Jack tried to ponder the implications of this Freckles-Vigor connection, but he couldn't take any of it seriously. He knew he should feel anger and confusion, but all he felt was hilarity. His laugh was a bark. "*Twice* abducting me? *Twice* assaulting?"

"I told you," Chris said, "we're rescuing you."

"Great! Take me home!"

"Shut the fuck up!" Freckles said again.

"Could you stop shouting in my ear?" the woman in the front passenger seat said to Freckles. She glanced back at Jack and their eyes met.

Jack gasped. "The jogger!"

She faced forward again, slouched a little in her seat.

"Young lady, you cannot go around pepper-spraying people like that!"

"I thought you were attacking me," she said in a low voice.

"Amy!" Freckles said.

Jack had to warn her: "Listen—Amy—those guys are after you. The members of the community you've been arbitrarily attacking? If you don't stop ... well, they could be dangerous."

Amy thought about that, said curtly, "Thanks for the tip."

"You're welcome." Jack began a new conversational topic. "Do you guys smell marijuana, or is it just me?"

He thought that was hilarious, considering he'd basically been smoke-cured in the stuff, but no one else laughed.

"It's you," Chris muttered.

No one spoke for a while. They were getting on the freeway,

headed north. With nothing else to do and feeling what he could only guess was the sensation of "being stoned," Jack looked out the window. In L.A. you were always behind the wheel, threading the needle between the insane and inattentive. You rarely got the chance to just watch the scenery go by. Now the hills sparkled, and the black silhouettes of thin palms interrupted the purple light-polluted sky quite prettily.

"Palm trees really are strange, aren't they?"

"Shut. The fuck. Up."

"Oh, why don't *you* shut the fuck up," Jack replied. But the cold steel pressed hard against his cheek shut him the fuck up.

29

SAM, Donald, Jesse, and Fuller reached the scene from the north just as the police began to advance on the crowd from the south. Through the smoke and the flashing lights from the ladder truck, two engines, a couple of squad cars, and three vans of local network affiliates, Sam saw her dad in the distance, behind the police keeping the crowd back. He looked so much more fragile than the Jack she'd just seen on TV.

"Phil," Jesse greeted a wide-eyed, bald man holding a white plastic cane. "What happened?"

Phil shrugged. "That guy in the robe over there just saved James Lean."

"Who's James Lean?"

"The coyote," Phil said.

"Oh, I call him Shia LaWolf," Jesse said.

"But he's not a wolf, is he? So that's stupid." Phil scanned the crowd, found what he was looking for. "Got you now, motherfucker," he muttered. With his cane held low, he darted crouching into the crowd as if he were Natty Bumppo stalking a deer.

Beyond him Sam noticed riot police forming a line and stepping forward, swinging their clubs. Behind them an LAPD tank appeared around the corner, a cop barking through the loudspeaker.

"I think maybe we should get out of here," Sam said.

Deep in the crowd, a large man with a shaved head and tattooed neck shouted, "Fuck the police!"

A few feet away from the guy, Phil reappeared and screamed, "Earth Shakers! Saboteurs! Get 'em!" He drew a metal rod from his cane like a sword from its scabbard, and he leaped at the guy.

Deeper in the crowd, another large man had pulled out a gun, but one of the boardwalk's acrobats grabbed his arm and yanked it up high while another jumped onto his back and put him in a sleeper hold. Somebody tore the gun from the guy's hand and enough people had launched themselves at him that the man went down.

Near the cops, there was the bright flash of an explosion. Other fights broke out inside other parts of the crowd, but it seemed the Earth Shakers were badly outnumbered by homeless people, vendors, locals, even a few tourists. They would have quickly subdued the bikers if the police weren't indiscriminately attacking everybody.

A shopping cart, ridden by a motorcycle-helmeted dwarf, pushed by an enormous drag queen, headed like a battering ram into the line of cops. Through the hole they made, Sam spotted Jack. He was getting roughly pulled to his feet by a muscular man with short blond hair: Chris Camfer.

Sam's brain broke. Chris, manhandling her dad? Dressed like some kind of commando? Was he *not* in marketing? Had he been sent to seduce her, for . . . why exactly? She couldn't fathom any reason.

She lost sight of them, caught them again farther away, hugging the storefronts, skirting around the edge of the action.

Sam shouted, "This way!" and pursued, glimpsed the back of Jack's robe before they turned up Rose. She checked to make sure Donald was behind her, was surprised to find Jesse and Fuller still with him.

She rounded the corner in time to see Jack disappear into the white BMW and Chris get in after him. Her car was only half a block up the street. She sprinted to it, had the engine running and was throwing open the passenger door when Fuller and Jesse caught up with her.

Jesse flipped the front seat, looked back at Fuller. "Well?"

"Hell, no. I'm retired."

Jesse dove into the back, but then he leaned his head out. "You sure, Full? These people need you. And you'll just get your ass kicked or thrown in jail if you stay!"

"Shit," Fuller said, and got in.

"OK," Sam said, "where's my—"

"Right here!" Donald gasped in the doorway. He flipped the seat back and fell in. "Go!" he shouted.

"Don't break a hip," Sam sad.

"Don't lose them!"

"Calm down," Sam said. "They're headed toward Lincoln."

Sam spotted the BMW several cars ahead of her, crawling through the Rose traffic. It turned right on Lincoln, a four-lane road. Five cars stood between them, and they lost sight of it for a minute as Sam cut right into the driveway of a shopping center parking lot and then swerved recklessly out of another driveway back into traffic on Lincoln.

Now there were three white cars. "What's with all the assholes with white cars?" she wondered, not for the first time. But only one of the cars was a BMW, so she kept her eye on that one.

She got stuck behind a slow beige Corolla in the left lane. In the right a bus was preparing to make a stop. In front of them the

BMW had pulled into the left-turn lane at the Venice Boulevard intersection, waiting for the green arrow. Unfortunately, so did the slow Corolla. Sam joined the line.

They waited in tense silence for the light to change. When it did, the BMW went, as did the two cars immediately behind it, but the Corolla driver was asleep or texting. Sam pounded on the horn. The driver, a youngish man, started, and began to move forward, but before he passed the crosswalk, the arrow went from green to yellow. "No!" Donald shouted.

"Hang on!" Sam gripped the wheel, wrenched, and stepped on the gas, so they swung across the double yellow lines onto the wrong side of Lincoln. The Mustang roared forward, past the wide-eyed Corolla driver. The tires squealed in protest. Now it was Fuller's turn to shout, "No!"

From the opposite direction, an SUV screeched to a halt in the intersection, its brights flashing at Fuller from ten feet away, but they made it onto Venice and quickly left the honking behind them. Sam was shocked to find all of her mirrors clear of police vehicles. In two minutes, they were only two cars behind the white BMW.

She followed it onto the 405 North, which was crowded but moving at high speed. Sam stayed exactly one car behind it.

"Shit," Fuller sighed. "I knew this morning, soon as that white man hit the ground in front of me, he was gonna be all kinds of trouble."

"Who's kidnapping him this time anyway?" Jesse asked.

"I have an idea," Sam said.

"Sheket!" Donald barked. "We need to concentrate. You know which one they are, kid?"

"Sure."

"So why are you smothering them? Hang back a little."

The 405 was a tightly knit quilt of seventy-mile-per-hour metal, so making a simple lane change was a leap of faith. And

Sam had to do a lot of lane changing, because whoever drove the BMW refused to accept the flow of traffic. Sam weaved in and out at eighty just to keep it in sight. When it exited at Sunset Boulevard, she heaved a sigh of relief and loosened her grip a little.

"Good work, kid."

They followed the BMW east on Sunset around several curves as it snaked through Westwood and into Beverly Hills. Sam had grown up driving this road, and she drove it like a pro. In the backseat, Fuller had his eyes closed, and he seemed to be chanting something to himself.

"Is he OK?" Sam asked Jesse.

"I don't know," Jesse said. "You OK, man?"

Fuller grunted, kept his eyes closed. Just as they got to the flashing yellow light that signaled the last big banked curve before the Beverly Hills flats, he stuck his head out the window. His body heaved. He pulled his head back inside, sheepishly wiping his mouth. "Sorry. Not used to being in a car."

The BMW turned left on Hillcrest, headed predictably up into the hills. Sam followed but tried to hang back so that the brake lights disappeared around each corner for just a moment before reappearing. The houses got even larger and farther from the road the higher up they went. After a few minutes, they passed a private security car, parked on the left facing downhill, overhead light on. The guard inside was doing paperwork. He glanced at them, and Sam waved casually, like, *Hello! Just a girl taking the old muscle car for a ride with my grandfather and two backpackers we picked up!*

The guard waved back.

"The secret Whitey Wave," Fuller said. "I knew it."

Finally, the BMW slowed and disappeared behind a large gate at the end of a cul-de-sac. Sam waited until the gate closed behind the BMW, and then turned the car around, parked out of sight of the gate and shut everything off. The lights of the city spread before them—red and yellow freeway ribbons, airport in the distance, the lights of the port beyond those. In the sky, a string of tiny lights stretched eastward over the desert, airplanes approaching. Listening to the engine click, Sam figured she knew who owned the house, but she had no idea how she, her grandfather, and these two random dudes were going to get her dad out of it.

30

THE HUGE GATE closed behind them. Off to the right, a jowly guard in a golf shirt leaned outside of a little shack and waved before going back inside. The car continued up a curving tree-lined drive for several yards to a broad circle with a stone fountain in its center. Behind the fountain, the house, lit from below, looked like a sixteenth-century castle where Jack and Cynthia had stayed once on a trip to the Lake District.

With Chris in front of him, Freckles and Amy the Pepper-Spray Bandit behind him, Jack climbed marble steps to a massive, leaded-glass front door. They took him through a grand hall lit by a chandelier the size of a tractor tire and edged by a floating stair-case, through a sitting room decorated with cold Cubist paintings. They turned down a hallway lined with professionally taken family photos: Vigor, his generically beautiful wife, and their two children in various awkward poses with variously forced smiles.

Always sad when a daughter looks like her father, Jack thought, as they went through double doors, and into a leather and mahogany library.

Standing up and smiling behind his enormous desk, Vigor

began the long journey around it. "Jack, I'm so glad you're safe and sound."

"Nick! Question! What's with all the kidnapping? And the homeless fights? I guess that's two questions." Jack, failing to put together any kind of strategy, decided to fake bravado. He walked right up to Vigor so it was obvious he was declining to shake his hand. Instead he invaded his personal space and looked him in the eye, which was a mistake. Vigor's head grew two flesh-colored horns. A second set of eyes blinked on his pink cheeks below the original set while his grinning teeth sharpened to points. Jack blinked away the hallucination. What he'd seen wasn't real, he knew, just somehow *true*. When he risked another look, Vigor's face was normal enough, even smiling warmly.

"Jack, this is not a kidnapping. I'm sorry if they were rough with you. I saw you on the news, and I had people in the area, so I made sure they rescued you from talking more nonsense on camera, and also from the riot that seemed—and turned out to be —inevitable. Also, I wanted to talk to you. Please sit down. Are you OK? You don't look OK."

Jack didn't respond. Over the years, he'd developed the habit of checking to see if his books were represented in people's libraries. He spotted none of those familiar spines on Vigor's shelves.

"Tell me the truth," Vigor said, "are you on drugs?"

"Not intentionally." Jack looked at the desk chair, sat instead on the couch. His robe fell open and Vigor politely looked away until he covered himself.

"Seriously, do you have a drug problem? What were you doing on the boardwalk last night? Shoeless, lying in an alley like some kind of junkie? And what's with all the scratching on TV? And the robe?"

"I was mugged," Jack said. "And apparently I'm allergic to coyotes."

Vigor scowled and said to the others, "You guys go sit in the hall." To Freckles, "Barry, you shouldn't even be here." When they were alone in the room, Vigor turned back to Jack. "Now, please explain your comments on the news, expressing what sounded an awful lot like your support for the moocher class. Also, please explain your presence inside a burning cannabis dispensary."

"I don't feel like it. What's the food situation here? Anything to nosh?"

"I can help you, Jack, but I need you to talk to me. You've done quite a job of self-sabotage in the last twenty-four hours, haven't you? Your name is now synonymous with stabbing a man in the eye with a Confederate flag, saving a stoned coyote from a fire, and instigating a riot—"

"So the video did make it onto the internet," Jack said. "And it went viral?"

"It trended for a minute."

"Well, Nick, before I answer any of your questions, why don't you tell me why your employees are wreaking havoc on an entire community?"

"That's a gross mischaracterization," Vigor said. "We're running a multi-pronged campaign to clean up the streets. Some of that work is a little . . . messy, so we outsource it. And the 'community' you refer to? Listen, I've got nothing against them *as people* —I'm sure they're all special in their own way—but they're economic dead weight. They consume valuable city resources, befoul the streets, commit crimes, scare away the economically significant demographic. We're just thinking outside the box, using creative problem-solving to encourage them to relocate. Trust me, Jack, we thought long and hard about each prong in our strategy."

"One of which is to attack innocent pedestrians with pepper spray?"

Vigor clucked, "They're not innocent. They're stealing hard-earned property value. *You* weren't innocent. You accosted Amy, and you were dressed threateningly."

"I didn't even get a word out! I was going to ask her if she knew where I could find a phone. And, what's threatening about a clearly injured man, barefoot, in a bathrobe?"

"Threat is in the eye of the beholder. She *beheld* you as a dangerous lunatic, and I support her one hundred percent. I trust my people, Jack. I tell them the desired outcome, and let them figure out how to achieve it."

"How convenient for you."

Smiling, Vigor sat down in an armchair across from the couch. "Listen, it's not like we can't get past this. My PR team can rehabilitate your brand in an hour, spin the story that you're a brave victim of Venice's sadistic criminal gangs, who fed you powerful drugs to confuse your mind. You were insane when you appeared in those videos and you can't be held responsible. People will eat it up. They're already calling you a hero for saving that mangy coyote, and, after tonight's little riot, they'll demand a full investigation, a law-and-order crackdown. Soon Venice Beach will be like Rodeo Drive with an ocean breeze."

"Ha!"

"So," Vigor ignored him, "all you have to do is tell your story, the *right* story, vote the *right* way on 847, and do your job of making the people—the ones who matter—good, upstanding citizens." He stood up. "Chris will drive you home. Take a couple days to rest, and on Monday morning, get back to work on that Venture Charter School curriculum!"

Jack did not get up. "You think you can tell me what to do?"

"Yes! Because I can put the finishing touches on your destruction by lunchtime on Monday."

"Great! Maybe I'll spend the afternoon at the beach." Jack

thought he heard thunder. It was unsettling, but he knew he couldn't show weakness.

"Man, can't you see you're getting left behind? There's no place on this bus for the 'conscientious centrists.' I'm the only one who's offering you a seat." Vigor leaned forward and sought Jack's eyes. "Because I believe in you. You know, your Nine-Step Process helped get me where I am today."

Jack snorted. "I don't think so. Step Two: Eliminate any options that are illegal. Kidnapping and assault are still crimes. And there's a humane way to deal with homelessness. Show people kindness and understanding, actually try to help them—"

"And they walk all over you! But rough them up a little, threaten to kill them, and they *will* go somewhere else!" Vigor furiously rubbed his hand over his bald head. "Who knows? If we burn down enough buildings, we might even spur those so-called 'street artists' to put down their joints and go find jobs! Maybe they'll earn a place in our society and stop begging for handouts on the street."

The penny finally dropped. "Wait, *you* burned down that building? *And* you burned down that other building!"

Vigor looked at his hands and shrugged. "*I* haven't done anything."

Jack stood up. "I'm going home now, but I'm going to take you down. Freckles," Jack called out, "you can drive me."

"You talkin' to me?" Barry blocked the doorway.

"You see anyone else here with freckles?"

Vigor grabbed Jack's shoulder firmly and turned him around.

"Jack! The drugs are making you very weird. When you sober up you'll see that the end here absolutely justifies the means. We're going to build a huge, beautiful mixed-use complex—high-end retail, celebrity-chef restaurant on the ground floor, luxury condos and five-star hotel above—which will be a huge boon to the community, providing several full-time—"

"Temporary, minimum-wage, non-union jobs."

"Well, with any luck we'll repeal the minimum wage. And one man's 'non-union' is another man's 'right-to-work.' But can't you picture it? A family-friendly, local, commercial-cultural hub! We're investing in the community! Making America great again!"

"No," Jack said. "You're killing it."

Vigor shook his head. "Remember, your reputation is in my hands. Your daughter's sex tape is in my hands."

But Jack found he didn't much care about his reputation right now. And so what if his wife's or his daughter's intimate moments and body parts happened to be made public? From the articles he'd read, it sounded like everyone was videotaping their sexual encounters or photographing their privates and sharing them on their phones and computers.

He'd always thought of Samantha as modest, shy even, but maybe he was wrong. Maybe he didn't really know her at all. Or maybe this was just the era in which, no matter who you were, the internet stole your dignity, permanently. It had already taken Jack's, so why not everyone else's?

This time Jack felt the rumbling of the thunder in his chest. "Does anyone else hear that? That booming?"

Vigor dismissed it with a wave. "My daughter and her friends are watching a movie in the screening room."

"Ah," Jack said. Then, "Home, please!"

"No!" Vigor's jaw tightened. "Jack, I'm not feeling like I can trust you right now, and you know too much for me to not trust you. If I can't trust you, I guess you'll have to be . . . taken care of. Remember? YCBTC?"

For the second—or was it third?—time in twenty-four hours, it occurred to Jack that he might be about to die. He saw his body lying in a shallow grave somewhere in the hills. Or maybe they'd just toss him down a canyon, food for coyotes and crows. Again, his first impulse was to shout, "No! Too young! Too much to do! People won't remember me!" But that was just a momentary backward stumble. One of the mental ruts Michael had been talking about.

He pulled himself out of it. He'd had a good, long run. Sure, all of his relationships were a mess, but when he thought of Immanuel, Harper, Sophia, he gave his parenting a B, maybe even a B+. They were all generally good kids. Even with Samantha, he could probably take a B-. On his marriage, he gave himself a C, but that was a partnership, and Cynthia's D dragged both of them down. Jack couldn't bear to think of his father, gave himself an Incomplete.

"Fix that next time around," he caught himself thinking. Which was odd, since he didn't believe in that.

"Jack, do you realize I work for a *corporation*? I have a fiduciary responsibility to my shareholders." Vigor had begun to pace the floor but he stopped and grinned. "Who knows? Your grisly death might be the catalyst that wins the game for us. Yes . . . your mutilated corpse will be found on Speedway as an extreme example of lawless chaos. The push to crack down and redevelop will be stronger than ever." He tapped his lips with the tip of a forefinger, "Maybe we'll name a little park after you, in honor of your tragic sacrifice."

Jack pictured a patch of pissed-on grass with a stone plaque that forever defined him: *Victim*. Object, not subject. Hilarious, after how hard he'd worked.

Vigor didn't know what to do with Jack's laughter. "You really are high right now, aren't you?"

Jack wiped his eyes. "Maybe I am. Don't let that stop you from doing what you're going to do though. I'm not afraid."

"Wow, Jack. Wow. You're nobler and stupider than I thought. I hope your affairs are in order."

"And I hope you live long enough to understand how foolishly you've behaved."

Vigor punched Jack in the face, but it was Vigor who cried out in pain. Shaking out his hand, he said to Freckles, "Dammit, Barry. Next time, you do it."

31

To be filthy rich is to enjoy nighttime silence. No traffic noise, no pedestrian conversations or domestic confrontations, no planes splitting the air directly overhead. Way up here above the boulevards, there was only the wind in the trees, soft hoot of an owl, and ever so faintly, from deep down in the flats, siren song.

Sam, Jesse, Fuller, and Donald stood behind an old oak in the shadow of the stone wall, contemplating its great height and the likelihood of a top-of-the-line security system behind it.

Fuller pulled at his goatee, "If we had an idea of the layout, we could plan our attack."

Sam took out her phone and switched the map to satellite view. The four of them huddled together to look down at it. The picture wasn't totally clear, but it showed that the house was some distance from the wall, and that it was huge. And it showed a shed or a guard shack near the gate.

"The fact that you can see all that on your phone," Jesse said, "is fucking terrifying."

Sam didn't feel good about this. "Shouldn't we just call the police?"

"You tell police this address, they gonna hurry over here and throw *you* in jail."

"He's right," Donald said. "We don't have any proof Jack's in there, and they aren't going to believe the likes of any of us."

"Gimme a minute," Fuller said. "I went house to house in Baquba. This ain't shit."

"Are you sure?" Sam asked.

Fuller glanced at Jesse, "In for a penny . . ." He cracked his neck, did a couple knee bends.

After a long, long pause Jesse said, "I can come with you."

But Fuller was already running at a section of wall by the oak tree. He leaped toward it, planted a foot against it, and used that foot to launch himself upward to catch a bough of the oak tree. His hands clasped around it, he swung his body over and hooked his leg. With a neat kick, he was straddling the bough twelve feet off the ground and peering over the wall.

"You're a regular Mitch Gaylord," Donald said.

"What the fuck you call me?"

"Relax!" Sam whispered. "He's a gymnast. And everyone be quiet!"

Fuller shushed her and listened. He extended a foot and touched it to the top of the wall. A soft beeping noise came from the other side of the wall, in the direction of the guard shack.

"Motion sensor," Fuller whispered. He disappeared soundlessly over the other side. The beeping continued, but otherwise there was silence. Sam, Donald, and Jesse held their breath and waited. Sam had a small heart attack when headlights appeared behind them. The gate to the property down the street opened, and a car went through it.

On the other side of the wall, someone with a heavy tread walked over gravel. A grunt, a loud crunching of rocks as if by kicks, and then a muted thump, as of a body falling. Quieter crunching, and then the beeping stopped, replaced by the electric hum of the gate opening. Sam, Jesse, and Donald went over and walked through. They found Fuller in the process of duct-taping the wrists of an unconscious man. A pistol and flashlight were on the ground next to him.

"Damn, dude," Jesse whispered.

Sam looked at the limp body. "Is he still alive?"

"Yeah—just knocked him out." Fuller finished wrapping the legs, wrapped a strip around the guy's mouth, and jammed the roll of tape into the back of his pants.

"You wait here, kid," Donald said. "We'll take care of this." Groaning, he bent over at the waist and pulled up his right pant leg. He drew a snub-nosed revolver from an ankle holster that held up a droopy dress sock.

"What the fuck, Pop!" Sam said, forgetting to whisper. "Where did you get that?"

"Gun show," Donald said, checking the load, snapping it shut. "Door prize."

This had gone way, *way* too far. "Can I see it?"

"No!" Donald held it close to his chest.

"Well, I'm not leaving you alone with that thing, and that's my dad in there. Let's do this."

They hustled up the long drive, tastefully lit with very occasional footlights. They found the white BMW parked off to the side of the fountain. All around the car, the air smelled richly of high-quality cannabis.

"Wow," Sam whispered.

"Right?" Jesse said. "Maybe when this is over, we can get into that trunk . . ."

They sneaked around the side of the house, found a flagstone path, and followed it on tiptoe to a side door.

Fuller tried the doorknob. "Unlocked," he whispered. "Sam, you got our six."

"What?"

Fuller sighed again. "It's like a clock face. Twelve is straight ahead, six is behind us. Donald, don't shoot me in the back." He didn't wait for an answer before pushing it open and slipping inside.

Sam swallowed hard. Her mouth was dry, and her muscles felt weak and shaky. She stuck close to Jesse, who went behind Donald, who went behind Fuller.

The door opened into an immaculate hallway, which led to an enormous kitchen. They tiptoed through it, and Fuller cracked open a swinging door that led to a long, dark dining room. Then they found the main hall, where a grand staircase faced the front door, and one side opened up to a darkened living room.

Fuller suddenly dropped to his belly and aimed his pistol into the living room. Sam peered over his shoulder, saw a man in silhouette. She sucked in her breath. The man seemed to be waiting for them. He wore a police uniform and held one hand out in a stop gesture. His other hand rested on a hip-holstered pistol. Sam braced for shooting, her heart hammering in her chest. But there was no shooting. The man didn't move, and neither did Fuller.

Then Fuller whispered, "He ain't breathing." He crept closer, and they followed. The man was a super-realistic sculpture of a policeman, an art piece.

"White people," Fuller whispered, shaking his head.

They passed the sculpture, which even had five-o'clock shadow and hair on its arms. In the light from the hallway, they checked out the white leather couches, overstuffed armchairs and strange art, aggressive charcoal smudges and stabs next to criss-crossed antique swords and daggers.

An odd rumbling noise froze them all. It sounded like an approaching thunderstorm or a subway train running under the next house. It stopped, and they continued their creep.

Sam, shaking with fear and adrenaline, thought a weapon

might make her feel better. She deviated from their path and went to the wall of weapons. The swords all looked too heavy. There was a tomahawk, but it was so old it might crumble in her hands. Next to that, though, she found one that was just right, a polished tree branch with a smooth river stone tied to the end of it. Leather fringe dangled from the handle. She lifted the war club off its hook, hefted it, and took a few silent swings. Jesse followed her lead, but he didn't like the look of anything. Finally, he grabbed a medieval-looking wooden shield with a fleur-de-lis crest.

"Pacifist," he whispered apologetically to Sam. They crept after Donald and Fuller into the next hallway. Here they heard the rumbling again, much louder. It came from behind a closed double-door, under which blue light flickered.

Her father's voice in the next room stopped them all short.

Then they heard a quiet *thock* and a grunt. Then, Vigor saying, "Dammit, Barry. Next time, you do it."

At the doorjamb, Sam tapped Donald on the shoulder and stepped up to get a look. There, on a museum bench, sitting like kids outside the principal's office, were Chris and a blonde woman. It hit Sam all over again: the first time she'd had sex in two years, and it was with a fucking spy, for what purpose? To mess with her dad? She squeezed the club, tested the elasticity of the wood.

In the other room, someone was chuckling, and then that turned into a belly laugh. Sam knew it was her father, but she hadn't heard him laugh like that since she was little.

"Stop laughing," Vigor's voice. "I really hoped to avoid this, but you've twisted my arm here. I mean, if the choice is between this or going to prison, I'm going to do this, every time. Barry, since your people are responsible for this mess, I'll leave cleaning it up to you."

"I'm on it," another voice said from inside the room.

Vigor added, "No more idiot bikers though. Tell Artie I said to help you dispose of the . . . evidence in Venice, and make it look like it was the work of junkies. The four of you should be able to take care of it. I'm going to bed."

"Yes, sir."

In the hallway, Chris took out his cell phone and held it to his ear. "Artie's not picking up," he called into the room.

Vigor shouted, "If that moron fell asleep again, I'm going to put him out on his ass! Go get him."

Fuller and Sam ducked back behind the doorway, listening as Chris's steps came closer. Sam tried to hold Fuller back, but he gave her a look that said, "Bitch, please."

When Chris rounded the corner, Fuller jumped out behind him and stuck the gun in his back.

"*La tataharruk*," he said quietly in his ear.

Chris put his hands in the air. "Who are you?"

"Frisk him," Fuller said.

Sam set down her war club and stepped in front of him, smiling as she slapped his chest.

"Sam?"

"Quiet!" Fuller hissed.

Sam took the gun and holster from his waistband. She handed it to Jesse, who handed it to Donald, who stuck it in his pocket.

Chris snapped an elbow back, knocked Fuller off balance. Twisting, Chris got a hand on Fuller's gun, tried to wrestle it away. Behind him now, Sam kicked Chris's groin like it was a ball crossed into her team's penalty box and she was the only thing between it and the goal. He went down hard.

"*Damn*," said all three of the other males around her.

"What the hell was that?" Vigor said from the library.

Fuller stepped into the hallway and raised his stolen pistol at the woman. "*La tataharruk!*"

The woman held up her hands. Jesse rushed forward,

crouching behind his shield, and relieved her of the pistol holstered under her arm. Donald was right behind him.

Meanwhile, Sam wrapped Chris's wrists and then ankles in tape.

Fuller and Donald had advanced to the doorway of the library. Barry, the third man in the room, had drawn a pistol, and now he grabbed Jack and pulled him up off the couch.

"No last meal?" Jack said.

"Shut the fuck up!" Barry pointed his gun at the doorway with one hand while wrapping the other around Jack's neck so he could use him as a human shield. "You people don't move," he called through the doorway, "or the big man gets one in the head!"

Vigor, unarmed, took a few quick steps to the side of the room, away from Barry.

"Shit," Fuller said, crouching against the wall. "In my experience, this situation doesn't end well."

Donald patted his shoulder. "I'll handle this one." He peered around the doorjamb and shouted, "Give it up, bright boy! You're surrounded."

"Bullshit!" Barry said.

"*Bright boy?*" Jack recognized both the archaism and voice. "Dad?"

Donald dove into the room. Keeping low, he rolled and shot as he came back up, just like the slowed-down climax in the action flicks, except he was an eighty-three-year-old man and so already in slow motion. Barry, like a batter confounded by a change-up, fired too far ahead and missed. He shot again just as Donald's round hit him in the arm—after first grazing Jack's arm. Barry's gun clattered to the floor, Jack and Barry both cried out, and then Fuller was in the room, shouting "*La tataharruk*, motherfuckers!"

Barry raised his bleeding forearm and whimpered.

Vigor remained frozen, seemed to have no intention of putting up a fight. "You people are trespassing on private property," he said.

"Dad!" Jack cried, pressing his hand to his wound. "You shot me!"

"Sorry, Jackie." Donald picked up and pocketed Barry's pistol. "Haven't been to the range in a while. This piece pulls a little."

Jesse came into the room, holding Amy at awkward gunpoint. Sam followed them. Still a little shaky, she gave Jack a hug. "Dad! Are you OK?"

"No! What are you guys doing here?"

"Saving you," Donald said.

"You have a funny way of doing it. I need to sit down." He collapsed onto the couch, feebly grasped a throw pillow and held it against his arm.

"Hey, that's velvet!" Vigor said.

"Can I get one of those?" Barry sat on the floor, clutching his arm. "I'm bleeding everywhere here."

With his good arm, Jack tossed him one from the couch.

Meanwhile, Donald fell onto a chair by the door. Wincing, he looked inside his coat. "Oops," he said quietly.

Sam saw the blood staining his shirt. She rushed to his side. "Is it bad?"

"Just a flesh wound. Here," he took out his handkerchief and pressed it to his side. "Help me put some pressure on it."

Sam did as she was told, feeling hot blood dampen the cloth. With her other hand, she fumbled with her phone and managed to call 911. It rang and rang.

Vigor's laugh was forced, slightly hysterical. "Don't bother! They're already on their way! Breaking and entering. Assault with a deadly weapon. Attempted murder. Destruction of my throw pillows. You're in serious trouble!"

Nobody bothered to answer him.

When someone finally picked up, Sam said, "We've got three

people with gunshot wounds, so we need an ambulance and the police at 36101 Bella Vista Drive, Bel-Air."

"That's right. You're the ones who'll be leaving here in handcuffs. You'll tell your story, and I'll tell mine."

"Sure," Sam said. "But only *our* story ends with the cops finding a car full of stolen weed in your driveway."

Instead of dropping, Vigor's jaw tightened, his cranial muscles visibly flexing. "What's she talking about?" he asked Barry. "Tell me that's not true. Chris swore to me that you wouldn't take any."

"Isn't that the rule?" Barry said. "I swear to Chris that we won't take any, and Chris swears to you, and you look the other way while we supplement the shitty wages you pay us?"

"Why, for Christ's sake, is it in the car?"

"Because we just stole it? During the arson? We were on our way to unload it when you called and said you needed us to turn around and get Waxman ASAP. So that's what we did."

"And thus," Sam said, cringing, silently cursing the lingering influence of her former students' writing, "we connect you to the pot robbery and arson, and previous arson—"

"And the pepper spraying, kidnapping, fighting," Jesse added.

Vigor pinched the bridge of his nose and stood there, eyes covered, for a full five seconds. He lowered his hand and said in a tight voice, "I don't know what you're talking about. I don't know anything about any of this. My people will testify to it." He sneered at Jack. "And don't think for a second you're stopping what's happening at the beach. La Bohème is going up!"

Fuller held out his pistol to Jesse. "Take this before I shoot this motherfucker."

Jesse took it and pointed it at Barry. The pistol in his other hand was still pointing at Amy. He grinned, "Gotta admit, I feel pretty badass right now, so both of you should keep really still."

Vigor kept talking, "You realize you're finished, don't you, Jack? SBT is extremely powerful, and we have extremely powerful friends—*tremendously* powerful, if you get my drift—who are one hundred percent behind us. We'll destroy you."

But Jack didn't hear him. He'd been overcome by a wave of nausea at the sight of Donald's bloody shirt. Now he stared at his wounded, gun-toting father and blood-spattered daughter. "Dad, is it bad?"

"Nah, Jackie. Just down a pint or two . . ."

"Good. Because I really appreciate the effort you put in here. But—"

"Always with the 'but.'"

"—but I think it's time we had a talk about the difference between fantasy and reality. You're *not* a detective. You never were. And you can't go around shooting guns. You could have killed me."

"I don't *go around* shooting guns, and you could've done a lot worse than that scratch."

"He's got a point," Sam said, still pressing her hand to Donald's side. "We saved you."

"And you, daughter," Jack said. "Explain to me why you allowed yourself to be videotaped having sex."

The blood drained from Sam's face. "I did what?"

Jack didn't have time to explain because the French doors burst open in a shower of glass and splintered wood. Black-clad SWAT team members were everywhere, shouting over each other, training laser sights on everyone, but particularly on Fuller.

Fuller's hands were already up in the air.

Jesse had dropped the pistols and stepped in front of Fuller. Holding up his hands, he shouted, "Hands up! Don't shoot! Hands up! Don't shoot!"

Sam held up her own bloody hands.

Jack just sat there, shaking his head.

"Three clear!" one commando shouted.

"Nine clear!" said another.

"Library clear!"

"Hallway clear!"

Earsplitting teenage-girl screams.

"Screening room clear!" crackled over the radios.

"Send in the EMTs," one of the SWAT guys lifted his visor. "So! What's going on here?"

"Ever heard of knocking?" Vigor said, rising unsteadily from the floor. "You just cost the city a few thousand, not counting whatever my chiropractor will charge you for destroying my alignment. And I pressed the panic button at least eight minutes ago. I believe the HOA negotiated a *six*-minute window? But we'll deal with that later. Right now, you need to arrest these people! They've broken and entered, assaulted us, taken us hostage—"

"So fucking typical," Sam said. "Is accusing the other guy of your crimes really the only move you bastards know?" She explained to the captain who had kidnapped whom, and who had set fire to the dispensary and firebombed the doctor's office last week.

Vigor gasped. "What? They did what? This is the first I'm hearing of it! And I don't believe it!"

"Also," Sam added, pointing to Barry. "That guy is a member of a biker gang that does their dirty work down at the beach. They kidnap homeless people and force them to fight each other."

"You have any proof?" The captain asked. "Of any of this?"

"The video's all over the internet!" Sam said.

"Just take a whiff of that car in the driveway," Jesse said. "They totally robbed the dispensary before they set it on fire. That mango-lemon-diesel scent is Kaya's signature Iron Man strain in there."

Vigor did a full-body shrug. "No car of mine is in the driveway. If there's a car with drugs in it, *I* certainly don't know about it."

"Sir, tone it down." The captain stepped away and conferred with his lieutenant, who conferred with his radio. Meanwhile, the

EMTs finally came in and began treating the wounded. Two of them went right to work on Donald.

"Checks out, Captain," The lieutenant reported back. "Intensely cannabinoid aroma surrounding the vehicle."

"Whose car is that?"

"Rental," Barry said, while an EMT in blue gloves wrapped a bandage around his arm.

"You got the keys? Or should we pry her open?"

"Shit." Barry reached with his good hand into his pocket, tossed them to the captain.

"We did it!" Sam said to Donald, giving his good shoulder a squeeze.

He looked at her like she was an idiot. "Of course we did."

32

After two in the morning, Jack woke to find Cynthia standing over his hospital bed with tears in her eyes. She kissed his cheek and stroked his forehead before she began firing questions at him: Was he OK? Did his arm hurt? Why didn't he call? What the hell had happened?

"I'm fine," Jack said, though he hurt pretty much everywhere and had a splitting headache now that the drugs had worn off. He took her hand, made room on the bed for her to sit next to him.

She kept hold of his hand. "I just can't understand why you didn't call at some point."

"I tried. Couldn't remember your cell number."

She laughed and nodded, "I believe it."

"How's my dad?" he asked.

"He's doing OK. The surgery went well. The bullet just nicked his liver."

"Thank God," Jack said. "Though his liver is his favorite organ. What's happened down at the beach? Were people hurt?"

"We were watching the news in the waiting room," she said. "A few injuries and arrests. And they got the fire under control before it spread to any other buildings."

"What are they reporting? Do they know what's really going on?"

"Everyone they interviewed seemed to be saying basically the same thing: some white-supremacist bikers started the trouble. No one knew what they were doing there since they operate out of Long Beach. They arrested a bunch of them. They called you a hero."

"They thought I was homeless. And preaching some kind of beatnik revolution."

"Weren't you?"

"No! I don't know. I *do* know the board isn't going to like any of this. The fight video trended."

"Oh, Jack." She squeezed him tightly and kissed him on the lips. "Don't worry. Whatever happens, we can deal with it."

Jack nodded. Tears welled, because whom did she mean by *we*? Was she going to stick around? Was he? The back of her hand where his thumb touched it was more familiar to him than his own hand, and she was the first good thing he'd smelled since that clementine. He felt giddy just to be this close to her again. Maybe the drugs weren't totally out of his system.

Suddenly their three children were in the room, hugging him all at once.

"Now that you're OK," Immanuel said, "can I just say how cool it is that you got shot? Did you pee yourself? I heard you pee yourself when you get shot."

"No, that's when you die," Harper said.

"No, when you die you pee *and* poop yourself. But when you get shot, you just pee."

Jack smiled. "I didn't."

"Kick-ass."

"Why, thank you," Jack said, not bothering to correct Immanuel's language. He was focused on Sophia. "Listen, Soph, I just want to tell you again that I'm really sorry about writing that

Waxim. It was selfish and thoughtless, and I wish I could undo it."

She patted his less-injured shoulder. "It's not such a big deal. I'll graduate in six months, and then I won't have to see any of those assholes ever again."

The sentiment, and the phrasing, sounded familiar. "Have you been talking to Samantha?"

"In the waiting room."

"She made some good points," Harper said.

"So," Immanuel clapped his hands, "can we wrap this up? I'd like to get *a little* sleep before my frickin' bar mitzvah."

"Pressing your luck, Manny."

"What? I said *frickin'!*"

JACK DREAMED HE WAS A KING, anointed with fragrant oils, wrapped in clean chiton, reclining beside his beloved. After years of strenuous wandering—and a few years of strenuous hero-on-nymph action—he was home with his true love, who'd never given up hope. Together they ate and drank, and went to their marriage bed.

But this was a hospital bed, and Jack had no armor to gird, no suitors nor traitorous servants to murder, thank God. Morning light streamed through the blinds. Cynthia sat on the chair, reading. He raised his head to look at the clock: 9:12, plenty of time before the afternoon service.

The movement caught Cynthia's attention. She got up and leaned over to touch his hand. "Good morning. How are you?"

"Never better." In a way, it was true. His mind was foggy, but he was thrilled to be alive.

"Are you hungry?" Cynthia asked. "I could use a walk to the cafeteria. I'll get you some eggs and bacon."

"Thank you. How about oatmeal?"

She raised her eyebrows. "Do you *like* oatmeal?"

"I do."

"Interesting," she said. "One bowl, coming up."

While she was gone, Jack tried to think about his speech to Immanuel, which he still hadn't written. Shouldn't be too difficult: just start with an early memory, something funny that captures the kid's personality. He tried to remember, but his mind wandered. What to do about the kid's alleged porn addiction? And Harper's alleged pot smoking?

"Hey-hey!" Samantha said from the doorway, moving quickly to the bed for the best hug she'd given him in years. "Are you OK?"

"Sure. How's Papa Donald?"

"Sleeping. The nurse says he'll probably sleep most of the day."

"How about you?" Jack said. "Get any sleep?"

"A few hours. I just called the detectives to see what was up. Chris and that Barry guy aren't cooperating. But I guess they already knew some stuff about Barry: bad-conduct discharge from the Marine Corps, member of an outlaw biker gang—"

"Hold on," Jack said. "*You,* called *them?* You voluntarily placed a phone call?"

"That's funny," she said. "You're funny now?"

Jack shrugged. "I'm trying it out."

"Well, yeah, since it directly concerns a violation of my privacy, I made a phone call. They all still deny any photos or videos exist, but a judge could grant the cops a warrant to search their phones and computers. Even if they don't get that, Chris and his friends are in big trouble, and there's a good chance we can put Vigor in with them."

"I want to believe guys like him aren't above the law," Jack said, "but even if they get him, some other sociopath at SBT is probably already out there bribing city council members."

"Wait—you really care about that building?"

"I care about not letting people like that win," Jack said. After more thought, he added, "And, yes. Michael—who's just a different kind of sociopath—convinced me that 847 is an important symbol of the counterculture. I still don't support all the drug use in that culture, but I'd much rather be on the side of love and community than unrestrained greed. Maybe preservation of that building can remind people that there's more to life than maximizing profit."

Sam hugged him again. "I'm proud of you, Dad. Now that you're an activist, will you come with me to a protest some time?"

"Couldn't be more painful than that Backstreet Boys concert you made me take you to."

"That was 1996, let it go!"

They both laughed, and Jack wiped away a tear before moving on to the next topic. "What about Jesse and Fuller?"

"Back at the beach, invited to the bar mitzvah, as you asked. *Probably* not going to make it, but looking forward to seeing you when we go art shopping."

"Great," Jack looked at her and felt one of those surges of true love, of his happiness being completely dependent on her happiness. "And what about you? How've *you* been? I mean, before yesterday. Did you find another job?"

"Not yet."

Jack noticed that her body had suddenly become tense. He didn't want that at all. He just wanted to know about her life. He missed seeing her every day at the office, realized only now that he'd felt joy every time he saw her stomping down the hallway or muttering obscenities in her cubicle. Instead of launching into his usual advice, peppered with *should* and *need* and *imperative*, he just asked, "Are you writing?"

"Nah."

"That's OK. But don't forget, you're a writer, Samantha."

"Am I? I might just be too lazy, or too afraid of failure."

"Isn't writing mostly about failure?"

"That's pretty much all it is. Maybe that's what attracted me to it in the first place."

"As the Japanese say, 'Fall down seven times, stand up eight.'"

Samantha snorted. "When I don't see you, I have no one to fires at quotations at me."

"It's part of my charm. Remember when you were a kid and we got you a skimboard?"

"No." Samantha said, but Jack knew she was just being stubborn. Once, on a trip to Hawaii, they'd stumbled onto a youth skimboarding competition, and Samantha fell in love, mostly with the beautiful boys and super-cool girls running along the shoreline, dropping their boards and hopping onto them at the perfect moment to meet the wave and ride it for a few seconds. Sometimes they headed straight into the waves, launching themselves off the crests and doing flips and twists before hitting the water.

"We got you that board," Jack reminded her, "and you spent a whole day trying and failing, hitting the sand every which way, sometimes really hard. I was sure we were going to end up in the emergency room, but you kept at it. By the end of that trip, you were pretty good. You were doing it."

"Yeah, and then we came home, and the board went into the garage and was never seen again."

Jack had to admit that was true.

"So, what's the lesson here?" Sam asked. "Besides 'don't spoil your kid'? I should just keep writing until I get bored and stop?"

"Maybe," Jack patted her hand, "but you won't know until you put in the work, see what happens. You used to do it for fun, remember? Find the fun again."

His eyes bugged, and his mouth became a big O.

"Are you OK? Should I get the doctor?"

"No, I found the title of my next book! Find the Fun!"

Samantha groaned, but she was smiling.

33

THE BAR MITZVAH of Immanuel Maimonides Waxman at Temple Shalom Hakol began fifteen minutes behind schedule, due to Rabbi Zimmerman's kibbitzing addiction. Finally, the old man climbed the steps to the bema, where Immanuel waited in black suit, black shirt and tie, standing as tall and tough as his five feet and three inches would allow. God willing there was a growth spurt right around the corner. Behind him, Jack sat next to Cynthia. She squeezed his right hand and smiled at him, her eyes turned into skylights by her blue gown.

Jack had trouble concentrating on the service because his left arm itched terribly in its sling, and his face itched in several places slathered in antiseptic ointment. Despite the physical discomfort, he felt pretty good. He looked out into the crowd, saw Immanuel's friends looking at their phones, texting or playing games, felt only a flash of annoyance. They were just kids acting like kids. He refocused on Immanuel, his only son, his last child, and his heart swelled.

So what if, only an hour ago, he'd received the expected email from Dr. Pinkus, the chairman, that the board had voted to remove him as CEO? The socially conservative members, who held a majority, had determined that his viral infamy was the last straw in a series of leadership errors, including his "vocalization of a pro-abortion stance." Jack managed to find a little humor in that: live by the holier than thou, die by the holier than thou.

Immanuel brusquely led the service, directing people to the right pages of his customized bar mitzvah prayer books. They were glossy and spiral-bound, with incredible illustrations of Immanuel's favorite video-game avatars, elves, wizards, World War II infantrymen, and alien fighters. Jack didn't want to think about the hours Cathy Wong had devoted to making those. Inside were several four-color spreads, all designed and printed at the Waxman Ethics Institute, and collated by an intern named Genevieve, who'd just cut her internship short due to major depression. With a pang of guilt, Jack wondered for the first time whether there might be a connection. He made a mental note to check up on her, send her a gift.

Immanuel's Torah portion was the story of Abraham's near-sacrifice of his son Isaac, and the kid delivered an unconventional but beautiful sermon on the subject.

"God stops Abraham at the last second," Immanuel explained, "and has him sacrifice a ram instead. But what kind of God even pretends he's going to make a guy sacrifice his own son? Even though he didn't make him go through with it, God must have really scared Abraham. That's the kind of thing a bully does, and I have a serious problem believing in a God who's a bully."

"Oh boy," Cynthia whispered to Jack.

Immanuel looked around the room, seemed to appreciate that he'd gotten everyone's attention. "If I've learned anything in school, and in watching the news, it's that bullies are dangerous, and they're way more dangerous when people don't stand up to them. If Abraham would have stood up to God, maybe God wouldn't have done so many other mean things to people later on. Like, he turned Lot's wife into a pillar of salt just for looking behind her? And he killed all the first-born sons in Egypt? Who had nothing to do with the fact that Jews were slaves? And then he drowned Pharaoh's whole army? That's crazy. Think of all those poor Egyptian women, dealing with frogs, and boils, and locusts, and then they lose their children, and then, like, a second later, they lose their husbands? That's psycho! So, today, I'm standing up to God. I don't believe in You."

There were gasps from the more elderly congregants, snickers from the kids. Rabbi Zimmerman pinched the bridge of his nose and muttered, "Oy vey."

"It's OK though," Immanuel said. "I still think of myself as Jewish. I love our food, and our comedians, and that one baseball player we have who's good." He took a deep breath. "The rabbi said it's important to end the sermon on a positive note, so I just want to say I'm really glad to be here with all of you. I'm glad we have these rituals that bring us together. We need to stick together to fight all the bullies. I decided to donate all of my bar mitzvah money to the ACLU and the Southern Poverty Law Center. And I pledge to take Krav Maga classes this year, and this time stick with them, and maybe become an instructor so I can teach other people how to defend themselves. And this is just a suggestion, but maybe we should all start buying guns and training with them? If the bullies try another Holocaust here, we need to be ready—and right now they have all the guns. Oh, and I'd like to finish my sermon by quoting my dad quoting Margaret Mead, who said, quote, 'Never doubt that a small group of thoughtful, committed citizens can change the world; indeed, it's the only thing that ever has.' Unquote."

Jack was crying freely. What an emotional rollercoaster. He went from pride to dismay to total love and appreciation, to laughter, to a much loftier pride. Who knew the kid was so sensitive? Or that he listened?

Cynthia gave her speech, but Jack hardly heard it. He was

trying to figure out what he was going to say. He'd never gotten around to writing anything down, and he just hoped the words would come when he needed them. Cynthia choked up, and Immanuel put his arm around her to comfort her. That started Jack practically weeping, just in time for his turn.

He wiped his eyes, took a deep breath. He mounted the bema and squeezed Immanuel's shoulder. "My only son, becoming a man. It's been a crazy couple of days, so I hope you don't mind if I keep this brief."

"Please!" an anonymous smart-ass said from the back, where Immanuel's friends were clustered.

Jack swallowed the urge to scan the pews for the offender. He just chuckled and went on, "It seems like yesterday that I was changing your diapers for the first time and you peed in my face. That was my first lesson that having a boy was different than having a girl!" Pause for laughter, which was scarce.

Jack felt the temptation to lecture, to speak out against the dangers of porn addiction, about how warped representations of sex and women (and cartoon characters, if Vigor could be believed) could become imprinted on a kid's malleable brain and potentially do long-term damage. But that was best spoken in private, or maybe in a Waxim once Immanuel was in college.

Congratulating himself on his discretion, Jack said, "I was going to talk about adulthood and about all of the new responsibilities awaiting you. I was going to tell you to get ready to work hard, to fight for your beliefs and your ideals, but I can see that you are ready, and I'm so proud of you. But also, I'm a little sad to say goodbye to the boy." Jack swallowed some salt. "Anyway, here's some advice for the man: first, violence only begets more violence. Take your cues from Gandhi, Mother Teresa, Martin Luther King Jr. Nonviolent change is slow and difficult, but it's the only change that's real. You'll get knocked down, but you have to get back on your feet and dust yourself off. You might feel afraid sometimes, and that's OK, as long as you have the courage to persist. As Maya Angelou once said, 'Courage is the most important virtue. Without it, you can't practice any other virtue consistently.'"

Jack paused to marvel at that, the perfect quote popping up in his mind just when he needed it. He continued, "And you might get really angry, because the world seems so unfair, or the bad guys seem to be winning. That's OK too, but you can't let your anger turn into hate. That's how you end up as Darth Vader, right?"

Immanuel nodded, but Jack felt like he was losing the audience. Time to wrap it up: "Finally, Immanuel, my son, remember what you learned about Tikkun Olam. God chose the Jewish people, not just to suffer, but to repair the world. That means we can't stop at protecting ourselves from the bullies. We have to protect everyone else from them too."

Immanuel nodded at him like he knew exactly what he meant, and then he initiated the hug. Jack sobbed. He couldn't help it.

The rabbi stepped to the microphone, held out sheltering arms, and asked the Lord to bless the Waxman family and the whole congregation, to keep them, and to grant them peace.

There were a few sniffles in the audience. Jack noticed that some of them came from Samantha, sitting next to her sisters in the front row.

DURING COCKTAIL HOUR, Jack ran into Michael Malone, drinking water near the bar. He wore a slim gray suit and looked as relaxed and well rested as if he'd just returned from a spa vacation. "Hey!" he pumped Jack's hand, "lots of naches!"

But Jack felt a surge of anger. "What are you doing here? You're lucky I don't call the cops on you."

"Are you kidding? You invited me yesterday! After you forgave

me for drugging you and told me you'd found peace and understanding."

"I don't remember that." Mostly he just remembered flashes of
indescribable awe at the beauty of life alternating with waves of
abject terror.

"You have an OK morning?" Michael asked. "Sometimes the
day after can be pretty rough. But man, I woke up energized and
purposeful for the first time since my retreat. And I owe it all to
you."

Jack didn't follow. "How's that?"

"You're right, we need to do more. Vigils are well and good, but
we need decisive action."

"We who?"

"We me and you, dummy! I made some calls this morning,
spoke with a few of my more philanthropically inclined friends.
So far I've got solid promises for around two million."

"*Dollars*? You raised two million dollars this morning? For
what?"

"For fixing the underlying problem."

"Fracking?" Samantha said, butting in between them with a
full glass of red wine. "Because that is literally undermining this
whole country."

"I'm talking about what's below that," Michael said, adding,
before Sam could interject, "not literally. What causes companies
to frack? What causes them to push a pipeline through sacred
Native American land? To risk their only water supply? To declare
that the real America belongs only to white men of European
descent? To criminalize being homeless instead of helping people
find homes?"

"You mean, what causes man's inhumanity to man?" Jack said.
"Easy: lack of empathy, the Fourth Key to GRREATness."

"Bingo," Michael said. "We need a radical program of reeducation. I'm thinking community service, meditation, the study and practice of creative arts. Why arts, you ask?"

"I didn't."

"Because it's the artists who'll create the new myths and rituals that will resonate with people, that will help them find meaning and understanding and not be so freaked out all the time. The old gods are dead, just like Immanuel said in that awesome sermon, but we need new ones to replace, you know, mammon."

"I'm with you so far," Jack said, "though STEM is all the rage—"

"This is the soil below the stem. We need to connect people to each other. That's how we turn scared, suspicious people into open, compassionate people. That's how we wipe out homelessness, hunger, and violence, not just at the beach, but everywhere."

"I think," Sam butted in again, her wine glass now empty, "you might have to kill the internet."

"That's just a symptom," Michael said. "If the people on the internet were happier, they'd be nicer to each other."

Jack scratched his bruised cheek. "Sounds great. But Michael, you're not even an organization, let alone one with 501(c)(3) status."

"See? That's the kind of thing I need you for. Let's get on that right away. What should we call ourselves?"

Jack didn't know. He was flattered by the attention, by the fact that Michael thought he needed him, for whatever madness this was. But he couldn't accept. "Listen, I'm tainted goods now. The fighting video . . ."

"Forget about that. The collective memory of our society is, like, twenty-one hours. And you didn't really do anything wrong. I actually was totally inspired by your moves in that fight. I'm thinking we should write a musical around your whole experience. I know a guy who knows Bill T. Jones, and I bet he'd come up with some sweet choreography." When neither Jack nor Sam replied, "See, Jack? I'm firing on all cylinders!"

Jack still didn't know what to say, and Michael kept selling: "Remember yesterday? Before we lost each other? That feeling of touching the key, having your finger on the pulse of the whole universe? Like you could identify with every creature in the whole world, even, like, resentful, racist xenophobes whose parents didn't give them love, who were abused, who were neglected? We just loved them all. That was real, Jack."

Despite his doubts, Jack was moved. "All right. I've got nothing else going on."

"Yes!" Michael slapped him too hard on the back.

Sam snorted and went back to the bar.

"Maybe this could work," Jack mused, eyes roaming the room, passing over the sweet faces of family and friends. "Start with a Housing First model, attached to a school with an academic and community service program, a sort of interdisciplinary study of . . . connection? Connectivity? We can sort out the language later, but it does sound interesting." Jack looked back at Michael, but Michael was gone. He'd used his weird celebrity powers to slip away just before Jack's relatives approached.

"Aw, nuts," ancient Aunt Lillian said, looking after Michael. In her advanced age, she'd shrunk in height as much as she'd expanded in width so that she was almost perfectly spherical. "I wanted to get his autograph. Who put your makeup on, Jackie? You look like a zombie."

"Oh," Jack kissed his elderly aunt's powdery cheek, "I could say the same to you!"

He spotted his daughter Harper lingering near the bar, and he put his good arm around her. "How are you?"

"Bored," she said. Then, "Fine."

"Are you stoned?" He looked right into her eyes, but they just looked right back at him, clear and judgmental.

"No! I'm not stoned at my brother's bar mitzvah. I wouldn't mind a drink, but I can't even get Samantha to order me one."

Jack was glad to hear that. "Just know that I'm watching you, and after yesterday, I'm familiar with all the signs and symbols, all the vocabulary, of the nugheads."

"What? You don't have to worry," she said, "I don't smoke pot. It makes me paranoid."

"I believe you," Jack kissed her cheek, "but just know that I'll know. I'll always know!"

"Ugh," she pulled away from him and said to Sophia, just walking up to them, "he's totally lost it."

"Time to go in," Sophia pulled his arm. Earlier she'd asked him to forgive her for praying to God to do something nasty to him. He was taken aback, but he assured her she wasn't to blame for his Venice misfortune. An old quote, attributed to Voltaire, even popped into his mind, though it hadn't done much for him until that moment: "To understand all is to forgive all."

In the ballroom, the tables were named after Immanuel's favorite video games, and various unlicensed logos were mounted above sprays of flowers in the center of each table. After a deafening call to party backed by a song with exactly one lyric—the word "party"—the shaven-headed, gold-chained DJ Bernstizzle grunted into his microphone, "All right, all right! Welcome to Immanuel's Cy-*Bar* Mitzvah World! Let's all get to our feet and make some noise for the man of the hour! That's right, he woke up a boy, but he's going to bed a man . . . Mister! Eeeeeeeemmanuel! *Mai*monides! Waxman-axman-axman-axman-n-n-n!"

Letting the echo die down and the applause build, Immanuel stepped into the room as if he'd just won the heavyweight title. Then came the obligatory dancing of the Hora, the lifting up and parading of the bar mitzvah boy on a chair. Tthey lowered him and a second chair appeared. People grabbed at Jack's arms, pulling him into the middle. They were laughing and dancing, but he had a terrifying flashback to the gladiator circle. He backed up, made Cynthia go up alone.

When the lengthy song and dance was finally over, the DJ told Immanuel to dance with his mother, and Jack with his daughters. Jack danced with Sophia, and then Harper, and even Samantha, who mostly just hugged him and swayed, her head on his shoulder.

"OK, now the proud parents dance with each otha'!" the DJ shouted.

Cynthia smiled as she walked toward him. He looked into her eyes, studied them for some hint of the future, but they told him nothing.

They danced to their song, Louis Armstrong's "A Kiss to Build a Dream On," as they had at their wedding, and at Harper and Sophia's bat mitzvahs. Louis just wants one kiss before you leave him, and Jack noticed, not for the first time, that the lyrics didn't exactly describe a lifelong partnership. But maybe that's why he'd always loved this song. Leave-taking was inevitable, so you just had to appreciate the togetherness while you had it. He nuzzled his wife's hair, inhaling her clean sweet scent. He pressed his lips against her neck.

Then, over the speakers, the DJ shouted, "Find your seats now, yo, 'cause the salad is bein' *served*!"

34

SAM WENT BACK to the hospital the next morning, as soon as her hangover permitted driving. She got to Donald's room just as the hospitalist was closing the door behind her. The doctor was a little shorter and barely older than Sam, and she told her that Donald was awake and lucid. They would keep him for a few days to make sure no infection set in, and to pull his tooth.

"It's refreshing to see an elderly person who's been shot by someone else," the doctor added. "Usually we just get botched suicides. As for the dementia—"

"What?" Sam's stomach dropped.

"The dementia? He kept telling us that his name is Donald West, and he's a private detective."

"Oh, that?" Sam tried to play it cool. "That's just, like, a running joke. He was kidding around."

The doctor's perfectly plucked eyebrows went up in sympathy. "Maybe the trauma confused him," she allowed, "but he *was* carrying a concealed handgun. Before the trauma occurred."

Sam had no defense for that. "What are you going to do to him?"

"*I'm* not going to do anything—except make sure the wound

heals. But he needs tests to determine what's causing the delusions. He's not presenting other symptoms of Parkinson's, so it's probably something else. I don't want to alarm you, but it could be a tumor."

The doctor looked at the folder in her hands and took a long breath. "But the good news is, his medical issues will help keep the district attorney off his back. The DA's office will just want assurance that he won't be a danger to himself or anyone else. My guess is they'll demand that he enter a long-term care facility."

Sam couldn't picture Donald agreeing to that. She felt tears welling, and she looked away, embarrassed.

"Which, he should do anyway," the doctor added, awkwardly patting Sam's shoulder. "I'm sorry," she said. "You can go in and see him now."

DONALD WAS SITTING up in bed with his eyes closed. He opened them and greeted Sam with a weak but cheerful "Hail the conquering hero!"

"I've watched that movie with you, so I get the irony." Sam kissed his waxy cheek and took the chair by the bed. "How are you feeling?"

"Pretty good. Morphine! Which finally took care of my toothache. Also, I got to skip the bar mitzvah."

"Yeah?" Sam said. "Wait—did you get shot just to get out of going to temple?"

"Lucky coincidence. But what a scrape, huh?"

"It was a close one," Sam agreed.

His head dropped back onto the pillow. "Tell me the story."

"What?"

"Tell it to me." He closed his eyes and folded his hands over his stomach.

He made Sam tell it all. He savored each detail and added his own, especially regarding his heroic charge into the room, his focus on making his shot no matter what harm came to him.

"Though I didn't *quite* make that shot," he allowed. "I was aiming for right between that punk's eyes."

Sam tried to laugh, but it was horrifying to think what more damage Donald might have done. He pressed the morphine button, and she decided to get him while he was doped. "Listen, Pop, they say you have dementia, maybe a brain tumor. They're going to put you in a long-term care place."

Donald's eyes went wide. "You gotta help me, kid!" He picked at the IV tape on the back of his hand. "We'll go on the lam! Drive into the desert, ditch the ride, hoof it into old Mexico. Call me Cesar, and I'll call you Magdalena—"

"What? Hey, stop that!" Sam leaned over and steadied his frantic hands. "Pop," she looked into his eyes, forced them to make contact, "Pop! You can't run from this. I think we just need to face it."

Donald saw the tears falling down her cheeks, and he gave up. He sat back in the bed and took a long, heavy breath. "Aw, don't cry, kid." He patted her hands. "Sure, it's all right. Bound to happen, really, if I kept on not-dying. I'm surprised my brain got me as far as it did, the way I treated it. Now . . . I'm a danger to myself and others."

Sam sat back down in the chair by the bed, still holding his hand. An unhappy silence settled over the room. Then Donald said, with a quiet chuckle, "Your grandmother said that to me once: 'You're a danger to yourself and everyone around you!' That, I remember like it was yesterday. But my address? I got nothing. I think there's a six."

Sam laughed as she cried. "Two sixes."

"Also," Donald said, "it's not like I'm dead yet. You know, lots of those retirement homes have a real seedy underbelly. Rampant drug use, gambling, casual sex."

"Really."

"Yes. Let's make sure I get into one of those, OK?"

"OK," Sam caught a sob before it escaped. "I'll start doing some research."

SAM TOOK the freeway and promptly got stuck in hellish beach-going traffic. How had she ended up back in this doomed city? The cars in all five lanes had come to a complete stop.

In her impatience, she'd pulled too close to the big ass of a maroon minivan, so she was blind to whatever had happened up ahead. Accident, probably. She wished quickly that any people involved were OK, even if it was the prick in the Charger who'd passed her on the right and then cut her off a few miles back. Just because people were reckless didn't mean they deserved to die. She was proud of herself for not wanting them to die.

The minivan did not move. Sam fought the urge to pick up her phone, then picked up her phone. Her inbox was full of petitions to sign, supporting: the elimination of the electoral college, a livable minimum wage, the designation of monument status to all Native American lands to save them from oil and gas pipelines. Also, there was an invitation for a "peaceful public gathering" to demand government action on the climate emergency, scheduled in Santa Monica for tomorrow. Sam decided she would go.

Below all these emails, there was still the one from Lisa. Sam needed to write back. She *would* write back, but only after she did some other writing, which, she suddenly realized, was all she wanted to do right now.

The minivan in front of her inched forward, and Sam tried to leave some space between them. No point in cursing the traffic. She knew she was going to stay in L.A. this time. Someone had to look out for those other fucked-up Waxman kids. And her dad obviously needed constant supervision, needed someone around to tell him when he was full of shit. Her mother was fine without her, but Sam had grown attached to their Sunday brunches and Wednesday phone calls. And of course, she had to stick around for Papa Donald, to make him feel loved so he would know it even when he forgot everything else.

The minivan suddenly accelerated. All the cars in all the lanes accelerated. No accident at all. Maybe something had fallen into the road and the highway patrol had run a break.

It was smooth sailing all the way to Lincoln. Sam exulted in speed and space. She was glad that Donald had Friday's adventure to remember, and that he'd enjoyed her telling of the tale. She'd enjoyed telling it too.

As soon as she got back to her apartment, Sam opened her laptop, dusted off the old word-processing icon, and started making notes for a new project. She didn't know what it was, but there seemed to be more than a short story here. A novel? About a quixotic old detective and his young, street-smart-but-world-weary female apprentice? A couple of misfits themselves, they'd be go-to private investigators for all the other misfits out there. They'd take the cases no one else would touch, fighting for the downtrodden, the destitute, the defenseless. They'd never forget their humanity (despite the old man's enjoyment of outdated stereotypes), and they'd never let the heaviness get to them. They'd take their licks, to be sure, and there would never be a final victory. There never is. But together, working one case at a time with integrity if not professionalism, the funny old man and the angry young woman would tip the scales a little in favor of justice, goodness, and love.

ACKNOWLEDGMENTS

Mom and Dad, thank you for giving me unfailing love, support, an education, and a sense of humor. And thank you for helping me pay rent while gently suggesting several fallback plans.

My sisters Jennifer and Rebecca, my brother Michael, thank you for confidently assuring me that fallback plans are bullshit.

Neil, Bess, Anne, and Michael, thank you for cheering me on and tolerating my inability to hold up my end of a conversation until I was thirty-two.

Karen Callahan, thank you for saying, "Take a year off, write your book!" and not leaving when that year turned into seven. Also, thank you for constantly reading, listening, laughing, and questioning.

Melissa Tapper, I'll never be able to repay you for your advice, encouragement, and consolation. But here's a free copy.

Elise Choi, thank you for your brilliant copy editing. (I'm sorry for any typos I added after you finished.) I hope this is just our first collaboration, as there are still some Yiddish words you don't know.

Friends who read and commented on drafts: Tawnya Baer, Jadzia DeForest, Sean Gallagher, Jackie Kraut, Nora Lehmann, Tom McConnell, Amanda Nowlin-O'Banion, Margaret Park Bridges, Michael Resnick, Brad Siskin, David Andrew Stoler (Next year in Winnipeg?), Jessica Taylor, Nick Taylor, Cathryn Tusow, Janis Williams, and Jonathan Zimmerman, thanks to all of you. If you ever need help moving heavy furniture, I will jump to find you a reliable service.

Rachel DiPaola and Maureen Luna-Long, thank you for allowing me to quote your parents' poetry. Jack Waxman may not appreciate their work, but I certainly do.

John Arthur Maynard, thank you for writing the definitive

history of Beat Venice in *Venice West: The Beat Generation in Southern California*.

James Heffernan, thank you for for your insightful, funny, and moving lectures on James Joyce's *Ulysses*. You helped me see not just the genius in that book but also its huge, loving heart. I'm only sorry you haven't done more voice-over work.

Bob Thurman, thank you for your podcasts and books, which have pried open my third eye and given me great joy.

To all of my English teachers and writing professors, thank you for your patient instruction. I'm sorry for all those years I spent blaming you for making me want to write.

People of the Venice Beach boardwalk, thank you for being kind and answering my questions when I wandered around awkwardly chatting you up. There will be no royalties.

Finally, reader, thank you for reading. Be ~~GRREAT!~~ good to yourselves and each other.